NEVER ANY END TO PARIS

Enrique Vila-Matas

NEVER ANY END TO PARIS

*Translated from the Spanish by Anne McLean*

A NEW DIRECTIONS PAPERBOOK ORIGINAL

This work has been published with a subsidy from the Directorate-General of Books,
Archive and Libraries of the Spanish Ministry of Culture.

The translator gratefully acknowledges the use of quotations from the following works:
Anthony Burgess, *Ernest Hemingway and His World* (Thames & Hudson, 1978); Mar-
guerite Duras, *The Afternoon of Monsieur Andesmas* (John Calder, 1964) and *No More*
(Seven Stories, 1998); Graham Greene, *Travels With My Aunt* (Penguin, 2004); Ernest
Hemingway, *Complete Stories of Ernest Hemingway* (Scribner's, 1987) and *A Moveable
Feast* (Scribner's, 1964); and Georges Perec, *Species of Spaces* (Penguin, 1995).

The translator would like to thank Rosalind Harvey for her invaluable help with this
translation, as well as Miguel-Martínez-Lage, Daniel Gascón, and Enrique Vila-Matas
for hints and clues and patient clarifications.

Manufactured in the United States of America
First published as a New Directions Paperbook (NDP1202) in 2011.
Published simultaneously in Canada by Penguin Books Canada Limited
New Directions Books are printed on acid-free paper.

*Library of Congress Cataloging-in-Publication Data*
Vila-Matas, Enrique, 1948-
[París no se acaba nunca. English]
Never any end to Paris / Enrique Vila-Matas ; translated from the Spanish by Anne
McLean.
p. cm.
ISBN 978-0-8112-1813-9 (pbk. : alk. paper)
1. Paris (France)—Fiction. I. Title.
PQ6672.137P3713 2011
863'.64—dc22

2011002601

10 9 8 7 6 5 4 3 2 1

New Directions Books are published for James Laughlin
by New Directions Publishing Corporation,
80 Eighth Avenue, New York 10011

*For Paula de Parma*

NEVER ANY END TO PARIS

I

I went to Key West in Florida this year to enter the annual Ernest Hemingway look-alike contest. The competition took place at Sloppy Joe's, the writer's favorite bar when he lived in Cayo Hueso, at the southern tip of Florida. It goes without saying that entering this contest—full of sturdy, middle-aged men with full gray beards, all identical to Hemingway, identical right down to the stupidest detail—is a unique experience.

I don't know how many years I spent drinking and fattening myself up believing—contrary to the opinions of my wife and friends—that I was getting to look more and more like Hemingway, the idol of my youth. Since no one ever agreed with me about this and since I am rather stubborn, I wanted to teach them all a lesson, and, having procured a false beard—which I thought would increase my resemblance to Hemingway—I entered the contest this summer.

I should say that I made a ridiculous fool of myself. I went to Key West, entered the contest and came last, or rather, I was disqualified; worst of all, they didn't throw me out of the competition because they discovered the false beard—which they did not—but because of my "absolute lack of physical resemblance to Hemingway."

I would have been satisfied with just being admitted to the contest; it would have been enough to prove to my wife and friends that I have a perfect right to believe I'm looking more like the idol of my youth every day, or, to put it a better way, it would have been the last thing left that allowed me to still feel in any way sentimentally linked to the days of my youth. But they practically kicked me out.

After this humiliation, I traveled to Paris and met up with my wife and in that city we spent the whole of this past August, which she devoted to museum visits and excessive shopping and I, for my part, devoted to taking notes towards an ironic revision of the two years of my youth I spent in that city where, unlike Hemingway, who was "very poor and very happy" there, I was very poor and very unhappy.

So we spent this August in Paris and on September 1, as I boarded the plane that would take us back to Barcelona, on my seat, row 7 seat B, I found a couple of pages of notes for a lecture entitled "Never Any End to Paris" that someone had forgotten, and I was extremely surprised. It was a lecture to be delivered at a symposium in Barcelona on the general theme of irony, in three two-hour sessions over the course of three days. I was very surprised because in Paris I had just written a bunch of notes for a lecture with the same title that was to be delivered at the same symposium and was also planned to last three days. So I felt like a real idiot when I realized that I was the one who had just dropped those notes on my seat, the same way others throw down the morning paper to take possession of their assigned places in the plane. How could I have forgotten so quickly that I was the one who'd just thrown those notes down? All I can tell you now is that they were destined to become "Never Any End to Paris," the lecture I have the honor of delivering to all of you over the next three days.

2

You'll see me improvise on occasion. Like right now when, before going on to read my ironic revision of the two years of my youth in Paris, I feel compelled to tell you that I do know that irony plays with fire and, while mocking others, sometimes ends up mocking itself.

You all know full well what I'm talking about. When you pretend to be in love you run the risk of feeling it, he who parodies without proper precautions ends up the victim of his own cunning. And even if he takes them, he ends up a victim just the same. As Pascal said: "It is almost impossible to feign love without turning into a lover." Anyway, I propose to ironically review my past in Paris without ever losing sight of the dangers of falling into the chattiness that every lecture entails and, most of all, without forgetting at any moment that a chatterbox showing off is precisely the sort of thing that constitutes an excellent target for the irony of his listeners. That said, I must also warn you that when you hear me say, for example, that there was never any end to Paris, I will most likely be saying it ironically. But, anyway, I hope not to overwhelm you with too much irony. The kind that I practice has nothing to do with that which arises from desperation—I was stupidly desperate enough when I was young. I like a kind of irony I call benevolent, compassionate, like what we find, for example, in the best of Cervantes. I don't like ferocious irony but rather the kind that vacillates between disappointment and hope. Okay?

3

I went to Paris in the mid-seventies and there I was very poor and very unhappy. I would like to be able to say that I was happy like Hemingway, but then I would go back to being the poor, young man, handsome and stupid, who fooled himself on a daily basis and believed he'd been very lucky to be able to live in that filthy garret that Marguerite Duras rented him for the symbolic sum of a hundred francs a month, and I say symbolic because that's how I understood it or how I wanted to understand it, since I never paid any rent despite the logical, though luckily only sporadic, protests of my strange landlady, and I say strange because I presumed to understand everything anyone said to me in French, except when I was with her. Not always, but often, when Marguerite spoke to me—I remember having mentioned it with much concern to Raúl Escari, who was to become my best friend in Paris—I didn't understand a word, not a single word she said to me, not even her demands for the rent. "It's because she, great writer that she is, speaks a *superior* French," Raúl said, though his explanation didn't strike me as terribly convincing at the time.

And what was I doing in Duras's garret? Well, basically trying to live a writer's life like the one Hemingway recounts in *A Moveable Feast*. And where had the idea that Hemingway should be my virtually supreme reference come from? Well, when I was fifteen years old I read his book of Paris reminiscences in one sitting and decided I'd be a hunter, fisherman, war reporter, drinker, great lover, and boxer, that is, I would be like Hemingway.

A few months later, when I had to decide what I was going to study at university, I told my father that I wanted to "study to be a Hemingway" and I still remember his grimace of shock and incredulity. "You can't study that anywhere, there's no such university degree," he told me, and a couple of days later enrolled me in Law School. I spent three years studying to be a lawyer. One day, with the money he'd given me to spend over the Easter vacation, I decided to travel to a foreign country for the first time in my life and went directly to Paris. I went there entirely on my own and I'll never forget the first of the five mornings I spent in Paris, on that first trip to the city where a few years later—something I couldn't have known at the time—I would end up living.

It was cold and raining that morning and, having to take refuge in a bar on the Boulevard Saint-Michel, it didn't take me long to realize that by a strange twist of fate I was going to repeat, to *protagonize* the situation at the beginning of the first chapter of *A Moveable Feast*, when the narrator, on a cold and rainy day, goes into "a pleasant café, warm and clean and friendly," on the Place Saint-Michel and hangs up his old waterproof on the coat rack to dry, puts his hat on the rack above the bench, orders a *café au lait*, begins to write a story and gets excited by a girl who comes into the café and sits by herself at a table near the window.

Though I went in without a waterproof or a hat, I ordered a *café au lait*, a little wink to my revered Hemingway. Then, I took out a notebook and a pencil from the pocket of my jacket and started to write a story set in Badalona. And since the day in Paris was rainy and very windy, I began to make the day like that in my story. All of a sudden, in a new and fantastic coincidence, a girl came into the café and sat by herself at a table next to a window near mine and started to read a book.

The girl was good-looking, "with a face as fresh as a newly minted coin if they minted coins in smooth flesh with rain-freshened skin." I looked at her with startled eyes. In the prudish, Franco-ruled Barcelona I came from, the very thought of seeing a woman alone in a bar was inconceivable, let alone reading a book. I looked at her again and this time she disturbed me and made me excited. And I thought I'd put her in my story too, just as I'd done with the miserable weather, I'd have her walking in Badalona. I left that café converted into a new Hemingway.

But a few years later, in February 1974 to be precise, when I returned to Paris—that time, though I didn't know it, not to stay for five days but for two years—I was no longer the vain young man of that rainy and cold morning. I was still quite an idiot but maybe not so vain; in any case, I had learned by then to be somewhat shrewd and prudent. And that I was one afternoon, on Rue Saint-Benoît, when my friend Javier Grandes, whom I had gone to visit—or rather to spy on—in Paris, introduced me to Marguerite Duras in the middle of the street and she, surprisingly, after a few minutes—guided perhaps by her trust in Javier—had already offered me the garret room, which had sheltered before me a string of more or less illustrious bohemian tenants and even the odd, also illustrious, politician. Because many other friends of Duras had lived in that garret, among them, Javier Grandes himself, the writer and cartoonist Copi, the wild transvestite Amapola, a friend of the magus

Jodorowsky, a Bulgarian theater actress, the underground Yugoslav
filmmaker Milosevic, and even future president Mitterrand, who in
1943, at the height of the Resistance, had hidden there for two days.
I was, in fact, shrewd and prudent when Duras, in the final question of the coquettish, intellectual interrogation to which she submitted me, pretending she wanted to find out if I deserved to be
the new tenant of her garret, asked who my favorite writers were
and I listed her along with García Lorca and Luis Cernuda. And
although Hemingway's name was on the tip of my tongue, I was
very, very careful not to mention him. And I think I was quite right,
because even though she was only flirting and toying with her questions, surely an author not much to her taste—and it seemed unlikely that Hemingway would be—could have ruined that game.
And I don't even want to think what would have become of my
brilliant biography without that garret.

4

I went to Paris this August and, walking with my wife past the corner
of Rue Jacob and Saints-Pères, I suddenly remembered the episode
when Hemingway, in *le water* of Michaud's restaurant, approves the
size of F. Scott Fitzgerald's dick. I remembered the scene from *A
Moveable Feast* with such precision that I went through it in my head
at great speed and even felt the temptation to look at my own dick,
anyway, I recalled it so quickly that in a few seconds I was left without it, without the scene, that is, my dick remained in place. Then, I
wandered for some stray seconds, with nothing to think about until
I bought *Le Monde*, took a taxi and went with my wife to the terrace
of the Café Select, on the Boulevard Montparnasse, and there, while
she was in the washroom, I unfolded the newspaper and entered fully
into the first sentences of an article by Claudio Magris in which he
spoke of a giant plot to assassinate summer: "Summer mine, do not
draw to a close, sang Gabriele D'Annunzio, who loved it for being

the season of plenitude and abandon and would have liked it never to end ..."

Everything ends, I thought.

Everything except Paris, I say now. Everything ends except Paris, for there is never any end to Paris, it is always with me, it chases me, it is my youth. Wherever I go, it travels with me, it's a feast that follows me. There can be an end to this summer, it will end. The world can go to ruin, it will be ruined. But to my youth, to Paris, there is never any end. How terrible.

5

In the novel *Travels With My Aunt*, by Graham Greene, there is a brief dialogue that was going to be the general epigraph of this three-day lecture. I didn't read it at the very beginning, when I should have, but in any case I'll read it now. It is, ladies and gentlemen, a rather unorthodox epigraph, for it doesn't illuminate the text that follows, in this case my lecture. Generally epigraphs are like a résumé of what awaits, they help us to better understand what's coming next. My epigraph, however, does not illuminate the text that follows at all. Or to put it another way, it illuminates, but it does so absurdly. It illuminates my lecture, because I doubt anyone'll ever figure out exactly what it was I was trying to say about irony, in the same way we don't know what Graham Greene meant to say with his dialogue. He probably didn't mean anything. Do you understand me when I say one says the most by *not saying anything?* Here's the dialogue, my epigraph for this talk:

"Now you're being ironical again. I mean I wanted to tell you my great trouble, but how can I do it if you're ironical."

"You said just now that irony was a valuable literary quality."

"But you aren't a novel."

6

Am I a lecture or a novel? God, what a question. I'm sorry, ladies and gentlemen. It's as if I were going back to the days when I was young, desperate, living in Paris, and never stopped asking myself questions. Horizons of hope usually open up before young people, but there are some who choose despair, and I was one of those, since I didn't know very well which way to go through life and, what's more, I had the impression that despair was more elegant, it *looked* better than being a pathetic, young man filled with hope. The fact is today I have the impression I'm turning back into that young man who used to ask himself so many questions. Am I a lecture or a novel? Am I? Suddenly, everything is a question. Am I someone? What am I? Do I look like Hemingway, or am I nothing like him? From the looks on your faces, esteemed audience, it seems you share the opinion of my wife and friends. You're of that same tendency, just like the organizers in Key West. I don't know why, but it feels as though you're disqualifying me too. Doubtless you're doing so guided by good sense. I, however, need to believe that every day I look more like the idol of my Parisian years, since this is now the only link I have back to the days of my youth. Besides, I think I have a right to be able to see myself differently from how others see me, to see myself however I want, not to be forced *to be* this person other people have decided I am. We are how others see us, granted. But I resist accepting such an injustice. I have spent years trying to be as mysterious, as unpredictable, as reserved as possible. I have spent years trying to be *an enigma to everyone*. To this end, I adopt a different attitude with every single person, striving so that no two people see me in the same way. However, this difficult task is proving futile. I continue to be as others wish to see me. And from the looks of things everyone sees me the same way, however they want to. If at least someone—I'm no longer saying everyone—but just someone, could see my likeness to Hemingway ...

7

Jeanne Hébuterne killed herself.

On this most recent visit to Paris I walked around chasing her shadow, reading other people's ideas about her, interested in the youth of this unhappy artist, Modigliani's lover, mother of his child—a little girl—and expecting another when the painter died of alcohol and various illnesses.

Jeanne had lots of problems with the bourgeoisie, with her family. The day after Modigliani's death, nine months pregnant, she opened the fifth-floor window in her parents' apartment at number 8, Rue Amyot, Paris, and let herself fall backwards. I read the story of her suicide thirty years ago, when I was young and living in Paris, I read it and I remember imagining the street and the fall, I imagined the whole scene, and then forgot it. But Jeanne came back to me this August in Paris, when I happened to read an article about her love affair with Modigliani and her desperate death. And that suicide at the age of nineteen again made a deep impression on me, except this time I intended not to forget. I read her story again while in Paris and I realized I could look for number 8, Rue Amyot and, if the building and the street still existed, examine the place where Jeanne bid farewell to life.

Not only did the street and the house still exist but they were near my hotel. After walking through narrow alleyways, aided by a map of the city, I ended up on that short street with its solid, old buildings, which can't have changed much in the last eighty-two years. From the street I looked up at Jeanne's window on the fifth floor, I looked at it from the place, possibly the exact place, where her suicidal body landed, and I felt as if my entire youth and my entire summer were encapsulated in that moment of life and death, encapsulated in Rue Amyot, Paris, a city teeming with commemorative plaques, but without a single one here at the site where Jeanne took her own life. Today, nothing in Rue Amyot recalls the tragedy that took place eighty-two years ago. Not even a bouquet of flowers from someone secretly cultivating her legend, not one sad piece of graffiti on the wall. Nothing. It seemed clear she wasn't considered an important enough artist, even though her death was possibly more artistic than Modigliani's entire oeuvre. However, she committed suicide, and suicides, as we know, do not get plaques, aren't celebrated or commemorated.

Directly across the street from number 8, Rue Amyot, where Jeanne, drawing a tragic and gymnastic line in the air, threw herself into space, a clean, bright gym has been set up for the bourgeois residents of the neighborhood, who are bound to be advocates of exercise and family values and not too fond of art, bohemianism or pirouetting oneself to death. Perhaps the people working out installed themselves there on purpose. Like those enemies of tobacco who plant themselves with a morally reproachful look in front of the first poor suicide case they see smoking.*

---

\* Once I had written this passage for my lecture, I found out by chance—to my great surprise—that "La cena," a marvelous story by Augusto Monterroso that I had read many times, takes place in an apartment at number 8, Rue Amyot, Paris: an address that, despite having read the story many times, I'd never really noticed, probably paying more attention to what went on in the story. It seems that the second-floor left-hand apartment was occupied for quite a while by the writer Alfredo Bryce Echenique, who held a dinner party one day—the dinner that gives the story its title—and invited Monterroso, but also Kafka, whom they awaited unsuccessfully in Rue Amyot.

Although, many years later, I found that street with a certain amount of difficulty "after walking through narrow alleyways, aided by a map of the city," for Monterroso it proved rather simple: "Just as in every big city, in Paris, there are streets that are hard to find; but Rue Amyot is easy to find if one gets off the Metro at the Monge stop and then asks for Rue Amyot."

8

The past, said Proust, is not only not fleeting, it doesn't move at all. It's the same with Paris, it has never gone on a journey. And on top of that it's interminable, there is never any end to it.

9

This summer, while in Paris reviewing my past, I went to Nantes one day with my wife, on the TGV, invited to give a lecture on irony, that is, on the same theme that I am speaking of today, except in Nantes. Since I only had a few notes destined to become what is now *Never Any End to Paris*, I gave the lecture a different focus.

"Ladies and gentlemen," I said, "as you can see, I bear a certain resemblance to Hemingway and I like to think I look more like him every day, which doesn't mean that, like him, I lack a sense of irony, on the contrary, irony is my forte."

I looked around to see how the audience would react and the first thing I saw was my furious wife, she's never been able to tolerate my insistence—pathetic, she calls it—on believing I look more like the idol of my youth every day.

As for the audience, I saw that some were taking my resemblance to Hemingway as a joke I was playing on them, while others were looking as if they hadn't even heard me correctly. The smiles and absent gazes of the people in the audience—I didn't know which were worse—contrasted with my wife's rage.

"Irony is my forte," I continued, "irony and the ability to predict what is going to happen. I have come to Nantes to tell you all that it is going to rain."

There was absolutely no threat of rain, but I said that so the audience would begin to sense the rainy ambience of the story I planned to read them. "First and foremost," I said, "I'd like to tell you that I have come to Nantes so that you can all help me comprehend 'Cat in the Rain,' a story by Hemingway that I have never really understood. And I'd also like to tell you that my ability to foretell what is going to happen enables me to reveal that tomorrow, back in Paris, I plan to write a story called 'What They Said About the Cat,' a story about what takes place here, about the interpretations you give me of the story I will now read to you."

When they found out that they were about to become literary material, the members of the audience glared at me defiantly (to reproach my audacity), or in anguish at the uncomfortable prospect of seeing themselves turned into characters in a story.

"Hemingway's story," I said, "according to Gabriel García Márquez, is the best story in the world. I read it and didn't understand a word, not a single word, of what happens in it, and what I understood least was how it could be the best story in the world. I am going to read it to you. In order to interpret it, keep in mind that Hemingway was a master of the art of the ellipsis and in all his stories, his trick was that the most important part of what he was telling does not appear in the text: the secret story of the tale is constructed out of the unsaid, out of implication and allusion. This would explain why the story might seem very trivial to you if you aren't aware that Hemingway uses these techniques of implication and allusion."

I read them the story where a young American couple, probably newlyweds, on a trip to Italy after the Second World War, are in a hotel room feeling bored. Outside it is raining; they have a room on the second floor, overlooking the sea and a plaza with a war monument in the middle of a garden with large palm trees and green benches. While the husband reads calmly on the bed, she seems nervous, worrying about a cat outside, under one of the green benches, that is trying to avoid the drops of water falling on all sides of its hiding place. "I'm going to go down and get that kitty," she says. "I'll do it," offers the husband from the bed. "No, I'll get it," she says. A banal, though sparkling, conversation is struck up, constructed with Hemingway's celebrated talent for writing dialogue.

In the end, she goes outside with a maid and doesn't find what she was looking for. "There was a cat," she says. "A cat in the rain?" asks the maid, and laughs. When she returns to the room, she tells her husband that the cat was gone and then studies her profile in the mirror, first one side and then the other, and she looks at her throat and the nape of her neck and asks her husband if he doesn't think it would be a good idea if she grew her hair out. "I like it the way it is," the husband says, and carries on reading. Someone knocks at the door and it's the maid who is holding a cat struggling to free itself from her arms. It is a gift from the owner of the hotel.

I invited the audience to interpret the story and their interpretations were quite varied; I retained the following: 1) The story recalls another also by Hemingway concerning white elephants and the secret story is really about a woman's pregnancy and her unspoken wish to have an abortion. 2) The story seems to be talking about the young woman's sexual frustration, which leads her to want a cat. 3) The story actually just portrays the sordid atmosphere of Italy recently emerged from a war in which it had required American help. 4) The story describes post-coital tedium. 5) The newlywed woman is tired of cutting her hair short *à la garçon* in order to satisfy her husband's homosexual desires. 6) The woman is in love with the owner of the hotel. 7) The story demonstrates that men are incapable of reading a book and listening to their wives at the same time, and all this dates back to the Stone Age, when men went out to hunt and women stayed at home cooking in the cave: men learned to think in silence and women to speak about things that affected them and to develop relationships based on feelings.

Finally, a woman of a certain age said: "And what if the story is what it is and nothing more? What if there is nothing to interpret? Maybe the story is totally incomprehensible and that is where its charm lies."

I had never thought of this, and it gave me a good idea for how to end the story I planned to write in Paris the next day.

"Tomorrow," I said to the audience," I will write my story about what has happened here today and I will end it with what this woman has said, her words have reminded me that I always feel very happy when I don't understand something and it works the other way around: when I read something that I understand perfectly, I put it aside in disappointment. I don't like stories with understandable plot lines. Because understanding can be a sentence. And not understanding, a door swinging open."

I felt these words had come out just right. But then a young woman raised her hand, smiling with a strange happiness. "It's all very well," she said, "that you have found the ending to your story, but since your lecture was going to be on irony allow me now, Mr. Hemingway, to be ironic and request, for the good of all your readers, that this story you plan on writing tomorrow be comprehensible, please, so that we can all understand it."

10

The next day, on my way back on the TGV, as the train rushed through the Loire valley, I read, almost in homage, the first volume of a collection of essays by Julien Gracq, a writer born in this part of France, in the village of Saint-Florent-le-Vieil, in the very center of the region of Mauges. The speed of the train made the marvelous landscape impossible to see, though luckily I already know it quite well. Between the Loire and the Sèvre, between the Layon vineyards and those of Muscadet, the plain, where one can get lost, is characterized by dense woodland, ash woods, grasslands, deep valleys, hamlets nestled together, and the slopes flanking the longest river in France. I was reading the first volume of *Lettrines*, and suddenly, not long after the train had sped past Gracq's own village, I discovered, not without some surprise, that this writer, whom I had imagined would only be concerned with authors of serious artistic stature, was talking about Hemingway.

His not at all condescending comments on the writer led me to think that if one day I happened to visit Monsieur Gracq, I would try to ensure that he wasn't the first person ever to notice that I bear or might bear a certain resemblance to Hemingway. I wouldn't want him to throw me out of his house in a rage.

Julien Gracq writes: "If I had to write a study on Hemingway, I would entitle it *On Talent Considered as a Limit*. He sets up dialogue with the same certainty with which Sacha Guitry takes the stage: he knows he will never bore us; he puts marks on paper as naturally as others walk down stairs. His mere presence bewitches us; then we go outside to smoke and stop thinking about him. This sort of talent, repeated in book after book, does not allow for incubation or maturation, for risk or defeat: it is nothing more than an interlude."

And he adds: "In the hunt for the exact word, there are two breeds: the trappers and the stalkers: Rimbaud and Mallarmé. The second group invariably has a higher percentage of successes, their yield might not bear comparison ... *but they never come back with live specimens*."

(Rimbaud and Mallarmé. For a moment I recalled a terrifying question that Marguerite Duras had asked me about them one day when my guard was down ...)

11

In Key West, once disqualified and expelled from the Hemingway look-alike contest, I started to think, quite intensely, about Marguerite Duras and above all about the evening in the house at Neauphle-le-Château where, as she explained the pallid but intense plot of her novel *The Afternoon of Monsieur Andesmas*, she actually became that book. If it's true we become the stories we tell about ourselves, this is exactly what happened to Marguerite that evening, she turned into that story which takes place on a plateau halfway up a hill where, aging and immobile, M. Andesmas, able to see only the edge of a ravine filled with light and crisscrossed by birds, resting in a wicker armchair, waits for Michel Arc. It is a story of waiting, waiting for death, perhaps. It's hot. Rising from the chasm, the bottom of which M. Andesmas cannot see, comes music from a record player. It's the summer's hit song: "When the lilacs will bloom, my love, / when the lilacs will bloom forever." The record player is in the village square. People are dancing. A reddish-brown dog walks past and disappears into the forest. Michel Arc keeps him waiting, he takes a long, long time, too long. M. Andesmas falls asleep and the shadow of a nearby beech tree moves toward him. There is a gust of wind. The beech tree trembles ...

There are no half-measures in the literature of Marguerite Duras. You either love it or hate it profoundly. Her writing is no interlude, this seems clear to me. That day, in Key West, I remember that I suddenly began to think first about Marguerite Duras and then—I suppose in order to stop agonizing over being disqualified—I began to think of the many writers who were better than Hemingway. For years I'd known deep down that there were many better writers. In fact, within a few months of moving to Paris, I'd stopped reading Hemingway in order to devote my time to other writers, some of whom immediately seemed better; though he has always been like a great father to me, *Papa* Hemingway, whom I've never wished to entirely dethrone, and the proof is in my insistence on believing I look like him. After all, he influenced my vocation with these lines that drove me to be unhappy in Paris: "There is never any ending to Paris and the memory of each person who has lived in it differs from that of any other ... Paris was always worth it and you received return for whatever you brought to it. But this is how Paris was in the early days when we were very poor and very happy."

There is never any end to Paris.

I remember the days when I started to plan the first book of my life, that novel I was going to write in the sixth-floor garret of number 5, Rue Saint-Benoît and which would be called, from the moment I discovered the plot in a book by Unamuno, *The Lettered Assassin*. Even though I had the most idiotic relationship with death in those days, or precisely because of that, the novel proposed to kill anyone who read it, killing the reader seconds after he or she finished it. It was an idea inspired by reading Unamuno's *How to Make a Novel*, which I discovered in one of the book stalls on the banks of the Seine; the title caught my attention, since I thought it would be about the very thing I didn't know how to do. But it wasn't, it was about everything except how to write a novel. However, in a paragraph where Unamuno speculates about books that provoke the death of their readers, I found a good idea for a story.

One day, I bumped into Marguerite Duras on the stairs—I was on my way up to my *chambre* and she was on her way down to the street—and she suddenly showed great interest in what I was up to. And I, trying to sound important, explained that I intended to write a book that would cause the death of all who read it. Marguerite looked stunned, sublimely astonished. When she was able to react, she said to me—or at least I understood her to say, because she was speaking her *superior* French again—that killing the reader, apart from absurd, was quite impossible, unless, for example, a swift and sharp poisoned arrow were to fly out of the book directly into the heart of the unsuspecting reader. I was very annoyed and even began to worry I'd be out of the garret, fearing her discovery that I was a dreary novice would lead her to evict me. But no, Marguerite simply detected in me a colossal mental confusion and wanted to help. She lit a cigarette slowly, looked at me almost with compassion and eventually said, if I wanted to murder whoever read the book, I would have to do it using a *textual effect*. She said this and carried on down the stairs leaving me more worried than before. Had I understood correctly or had I misunderstood her *superior* French? What was this about a *textual effect*? Perhaps she had been referring to a *literary effect* that I would have to construct within the text to give readers the impression that the book's very letters had killed them. Perhaps that was it. But then, how could I achieve a literary effect that would pulverize the reader in a purely textual way?

After a week of tough questions and black shadows that, to my despair, hovered over my literary endeavors, I bumped into Marguerite on the stairs again. This time, she was on her way up—like so many buildings in Paris, this one had no elevator—to the third floor, where her apartment was. And I was heading down from the sixth floor, from my modest *chambre*, on my way out. Employing her *superior* French once more, Marguerite asked me, or I seemed to understand her to be asking me, if I had managed to kill off my readers yet. In contrast to our previous exchange, this time I decided not to give myself airs, that is, not to make a fool of myself, to try not only to be humble, but also to take advantage of whatever lesson I might learn from her. I told her, with difficulty, in my *inferior* or, if you will, muddled French, the trouble I was having getting my novel started. I tried to explain to her that, following her advice, I now wished only to cause the death of the reader by carrying out the crime within the strict confines of the writing. "It's very hard to do, though, but I'm on the case," I added.

I saw then that if I didn't really understand Marguerite, she didn't understand me either. A serious silence fell. "But I'm on the case," I said again. Silence again. Then, trying to ease the tension, I attempted to sum up what I was going through, and stammered out the following: "Advice, that's what I need, some help with the novel." This time Marguerite understood perfectly. "Ah, some advice," she said, and invited me to sit down right there in the lobby (as if I looked very tired); slowly she put out her cigarette and left it in the ashtray at the entrance, and went, a little mysteriously, to her office, returning after a minute with a piece of paper that looked like a doctor's prescription containing some instructions that might— she said, or I thought I understood her to say—be useful to me for writing novels. I took the paper and went straight out. I read those instructions not long after, still on Rue Saint-Benoît, and felt as if the whole weight of the world had landed on my shoulders, I still recall the immense panic—the shudder of fear, to be more exact—I felt as I read them:

1. Structural problems. 2. Unity and harmony. 3. Plot and story. 4.

Time. 5. Textual effects. 6. Verisimilitude. 7. Narrative technique. 8. Characters. 9. Dialogue. 10. Setting(s). 11. Style. 12. Experience. 13. Linguistic register.

### 12

And why was I so taken with the idea of killing my readers when I didn't yet have even one? Today I tell myself that perhaps I chose this idea out of the suspicion that there couldn't be anybody anywhere who, when they read me, wouldn't easily be able to tell that I was a novice writer. That's why I wanted to kill the reader. I did, however, look for various arguments to justify to myself this violent, textual crime. I remember, when people asked back then (and they asked me quite often) what I had against readers of my *text*, concealing the real reason for my murderous instincts, I would pompously reply: "I want to write like Miles Davis, who always plays the trumpet with his back to the audience." People would then ask me, "So you like Miles Davis?" And then I went quiet. I went quiet because I didn't actually know whether I liked Miles Davis or not. I'd seen him play in Barcelona, that much was true, in the Palau de la Música Catalana and what had impressed me, more than the jazz, was that his performance had caused a scandal among the bourgeoisie of my city because, unlike all the other American musicians who had passed through that musical sanctuary, he had played with his back to the audience. The fact was he only did it so he could concentrate better, and not to show disdain for his public (which would have been stupid), but the sensitive, bourgeois Barcelona audience took it as an insult.

In those days, I think I turned my back on the world, on everybody in it. Readerless, with no concrete ideas about love or death, and, to top it all off, a pretentious writer hiding his beginner's fragility, I was a walking nightmare. I identified youth with despair and despair with the color black. I dressed in black from head to toe.

I bought myself two pairs of glasses, two identical pairs, which I didn't need at all, I bought them to look more intellectual. And I began smoking a pipe, which I judged (perhaps influenced by photos of Jean-Paul Sartre in the Café de Flore) to look more interesting than taking drags on mere cigarettes. But I only smoked the pipe in public, as I couldn't afford to spend much money on aromatic tobacco. Sometimes, sitting on the terrace of some café, as I pretended to read some *maudit* French poet, I played the intellectual, leaving my pipe in the ashtray (sometimes the pipe wasn't even lit) and taking out what were apparently my reading glasses and taking off the other pair, identical to the first and with which I couldn't read a thing either. But this didn't cause me too much grief, since I wasn't trying to read the wretched French poets in public, but rather to *feign* being a profound Parisian café terrace intellectual. I was, ladies and gentlemen, a walking nightmare. It wasn't entirely my fault, this is also true. We all encounter a small world at birth, a world that is generally the same wherever we are born. Mine, though, seemed to have been smaller than most. I soon saw that my minimal world required urgent expansion, and had traveled to Paris for no other reason and managed to stay and live there. I was partly right to be desperate, as I didn't know where to go, or what to be in this life. It occurred to me to solve this awkward problem by becoming the first thing that made sense, and that had been—after I happened to read *A Moveable Feast*—to be a writer, something which actually increased my desperation even more, since, don't ask me why, I spent a long time convinced that in order to be a good writer you had to be completely desperate.

Anyway, in those days, ladies and gentlemen, I was, I insist, a walking nightmare. There were people in my neighborhood who, quite rightly, crossed the street when they saw me coming. Raúl Escari, for example ("an intelligent and refined being, a true writer who refused to write, the most brilliant of Marguerite Duras's circle of young friends in the 1970s," the poet José Miguel Ullán wrote), the great Raúl Escari, who avoided me at first when he saw me in the street, and later ended up being my best friend in Paris. Today Raúl lives in Montevideo, near his native Buenos Aires, and occasionally he calls me up and, across the distance, from a phone booth near where Lautréamont was born, sends me phrases that spring spontaneously from his unsurpassable intellect.

13

Reading the words the poet Ullán wrote about Marguerite Duras, it's as if I were seeing her now: "Marguerite was always asking questions. They were echoes, a filtering of what she wondered herself. She brought discord and persuasion, melodrama and comedy. She demanded to be told she was right when that was not really what she wanted at all. Glass in hand, smoking constantly, she went from coughing fits to interminable pauses. She twisted her ring-laden hands, played with her glasses, or improvised some gentle flirting with the aid of her silk *foulard*. She laughed and cried often. Easily? Who knows! In fact, less was known there all the time. Less, in any case, than she wanted to know."

I will always remember her as a violently free and audacious woman, who wholeheartedly and openly embodied—with her intelligent use of verbal license, for example, which in her case consisted of sitting in an armchair in her house and, with real ferocity, speaking her mind—I remember she embodied all the monstrous contradictions to be found in human beings, all those doubts, that fragility and helplessness, fierce individuality, and a search for shared grief, in short, all the great anguish we're capable of when faced with the reality of the world, that desolation the least exemplary writers have in them, the least academic and edifying ones, those who aren't concerned with projecting a right and proper image of themselves, the only ones from whom we learn nothing, but also those who have the rare courage to literally *expose* themselves in their writing—where they speak their minds—and whom I admire deeply because only they lay it on the line, only they seem to me to be true writers.

14

I used to read a lot of Perec, though I barely took it in. It would have done me a lot of good to pay more attention to this writer, as I would have discovered back then the charm and joyful irony of, for example, *Species of Spaces*, the book Perec published in Paris in February of that year, 1974, the very month I arrived in the city and bought the book at the Gare d'Austerlitz, and, while I did like it— the alternative the book offered of living in a single place or many stuck in my mind—I thought this Perec was nowhere near as good as, for example, Lautréamont, or all the French *poètes maudits*.

Yesterday I thought again of the alternatives Perec's book offers of living in a single place or many, of being sedentary or a traveler, of being a rank nationalist or a spiritual nomad:

"To put down roots, to rediscover or fashion your roots, to carve the place that will be yours out of space, and build, plant, appropriate, millimeter by millimeter, your 'home': to belong completely in your village, knowing you're a true inhabitant of the Cévennes, or of Poitou.

Or else to own only the clothes you stand up in, to keep nothing, to live in hotels and change them frequently, and change towns, and change countries; to speak and read any one of four or five languages; to feel at home nowhere, but at ease almost everywhere."

I enjoyed myself hugely yesterday when I again met those lines of Perec's, which I summarized on a sheet of paper like this: "In short, going out with one's grandchildren to pick blackberries along the narrow paths of the nationalists, or traveling and losing countries, losing them all traveling in the lit-up trains of the nocturnal world, being forever a foreigner."

## 15

I do think irony is a powerful device for de-activating reality. But what happens when we see something we've seen, for example, in a photograph, and suddenly we see it *in real life*? Is it possible to be ironic about reality, to disbelieve it, when we are seeing something that's *real*?

Perec in *Species of Spaces*: "Seeing something in real life that for a long time was just an image in an old dictionary: a geyser, a waterfall, the bay of Naples, the place where Gavrilo Princip was standing when he shot Archduke Franz Ferdinand of Austria and his wife Sofia, the Duchess of Hohenberg, on the corner of Franz Josef Street and Appel Quay, in Sarajevo, across from the Simie Brothers' Tavern, on June 28, 1914, at a quarter past eleven."

Ironic or not, the questions I now ask myself are these: Does reality really exist? Can you really see something *in real life*? In terms of reality, I share Proust's opinion, who said that unfortunately our sad, fragmented, far-sighted eyes can perhaps allow us to measure distances, but they don't give us directions: the infinite *field of possibilities* stretches out, and if by chance reality appeared before us it would be so far removed from possibility that, in a sudden faint, we would collide with this wall that suddenly appeared and fall down stunned.

What do we see, then, when we think we are seeing something *in real life*? I would say that, when this happens, when it looks like we are faced with reality, we are more than permitted to be ironic about it, even if only to ward off the possible chance appearance of what is really real and the wall that would leave us knocked out, without any irony at all.

I can think of lots of occasions when it could be said that I *saw* something *in real life*, visions I later wondered whether I should treat ironically—in essence a way of admitting I believed in this truth—commenting, for example, on the luck I'd had in not really having seen this reality, since I would have been knocked unconscious; or else I could do without irony entirely and take very seriously what I'd just *seen in real life*, then try and move towards an irony without words, that is, make use of a silence of profound stupor, *reinvent* irony.

One night I dreamed I went down in history as the man who reinvented irony. I lived in a book that was a huge cemetery where, on most of the tombstones, the names of the different kinds of irony had worn away.

### 16

"I saw eternity the other night," wrote Henry Vaughan in a daring line. Whether he saw it or not, I hereby send the poet my utmost respect. This line of his appears indisputable, mainly because, as Celan would say, nobody bears witness for the witness. The syntactic crack of the whip recalls the unforgettable ending of the movie *Blade Runner* when the character who's about to die begins his poetic sermon with the tremulous, moving and very true *"I've seen…"*

I've seen *in real life* the study in the house in Coyoacán, Mexico, where Trotsky was killed. I'd seen it before in the cinema. The movie Joseph Losey made about Trotsky's assassination was filmed on location, as the scene was still intact thirty years after the crime. Trotsky's family continued to live in the house for a while after the assassination, and after them, there was no one else. Identical to the day of the assassination, Trotsky's study was kept in very good shape with, for example, the entire library complete. The only thing missing from the crime scene was the ice pick the Stalinist Ramón Mercader had used to kill him. I'd seen the film and visualized, memorized the murder scene, but I never imagined, as I was watching the film, that one day I would be there in person, at the very scene of the crime, I never imagined I would see Trotsky's study *in real life*, that room where something happened that changed the course of history.

I went to see the study with my friend Christopher, a Mexican writer who lived in Coyoacán, a few steps away from the crime scene. There was nobody else in the house, so, at a certain moment, we found ourselves alone in front of Trotsky's desk, not knowing what to do or say. You could hear the buzzing of a mosquito. I found it hard to disassociate that study from the one that appeared in the fiction of Losey's movie. Even so, I tried not to forget that this was the *real* place where Trotsky had been assassinated. So—I thought—this is a historic place. I couldn't think of anything else. I just kept repeating obtusely to myself, this is a historic place. I looked down at the floor, just for something to do, I looked at the carpet and then, in the middle of the silence and overcome by a strange sensation that fluctuated between anodyne and transcendental (what we feel when faced with any supposedly important historic event), I saw, or thought I saw, one of Trotsky's bloodstains on the carpet, not completely cleaned up, or else not darkened enough by the passing of time.

I focused on the bloodstain, felt a grotesque temptation—in order to do something—to cross myself. I realized I was silently practicing a new form of irony. "I saw the stain the other day," I imagined saying when I returned to Barcelona and people asked me how things had gone in Mexico. "What stain?" they would ask me, and then, instead of keeping quiet and sinking completely into my new re-invented irony, that is, into the silence of a wordless irony, I would return to classic irony. "Oh nothing," I would reply, "I was just saying that I saw Trotsky's blood *in real life*."

17

I've also seen Paris *in real life*. Although I haven't lived in the city for years, I always have the feeling that I'm still there. Remember the slogan of the idol of my youth, the writer Hemingway: "If you are lucky enough to have lived in Paris as a young man, then wherever you go for the rest of your life, it stays with you."

Naturally, I don't know every single street in Paris, but I've at least heard them all mentioned or read their names somewhere. Even if I wanted to, I would find it very hard to get lost in Paris. I have lots of reference points. I almost always know which direction to take in the Metro. In Barcelona, since the dizzying changes leading up to the Olympic Games and afterwards that have transformed this once elegant and secretive city into an overwhelming touristy place, I'm much more likely to get lost. If I were dropped, for example, in an empty street in the Olympic Village, it would take me a long time to get my bearings, let alone find a bus or a subway station.

In Paris I know the bus timetables very well and I know how to explain my desired route to a taxi driver. Paris is fantastic among other reasons because, unlike, say, German or Spanish cities, it has retained the names of many of its streets for centuries. Aside from this, I'm familiar with the characteristics of the neighborhoods in Paris, I can easily identify churches and other monuments, and I know where the stations are. Many places are linked to precise memories: there are houses where friends I haven't seen for ages used to live—the old Hotel des Pyrénées on Rue de l'Ancienne Comedie, for instance, where Adolfo Arrieta and Javier Grandes lived, and which today is divided into modern apartments—or cafés where strange things happened to me: Café de la Paix, for example, next to L'Ópera, where one day a strange man at the next table tried to convince me that with my figure I would really suit a jacket identical to the one worn by Yves Montand in his latest movie; Café de Flore, where I struck up a brief conversation with Roland Barthes, who told me that, after thirty years of being a customer at the bar, the cashier had seen him on television and found out he was a writer and asked him for a signed copy of one of his books and he'd decided—since she'd seen him on television, a visual medium—to give her *Empire of Signs*, his only book that was lavishly illustrated; Café Blaise, where under the effects of a remarkably potent tab of LSD I was very nearly murdered by a very evil girlfriend; Café Les Deux Magots, where the architect Ricardo Bofill inexplicably told me, I don't know how many times, that it was very easy to stand out in Barcelona but very difficult—"as I am doing at the moment," he repeated over and over again—to triumph in Paris; La Closerie des Lilas, where I got into the habit of sitting at what had once been Hemingway's regular table and of slipping out without paying every time; Café Bonaparte, where, in the company of Marie-France (a transvestite who dressed like Marilyn Monroe and with whom I was filming *Tam Tam*, an underground movie by Adolfo Arrieta), I watched in astonishment as an enraged madman came into the place with a hammer, picked one of the customers at random and gave him a resounding blow to the head that left him stone dead; the café near the crossroads of Rue du Bac and Boulevard Saint-Germain, where Perec recommended sitting and watching the street with rather systematic attention and writing down what one saw, what caught one's attention, forcing oneself to write down even "what is of no interest, what is most obvious, most common, most colorless."

I like to sit on the terraces of Paris cafés, and I also like to walk through the city, sometimes for a whole afternoon, with no fixed destination, although not exactly at random or aimlessly, trying instead to let myself be carried along. Sometimes I take the first bus that stops in front of me (as Perec pointed out, you can no longer hop on a bus while it's moving). Or else I walk deliberately down the Rue de Seine and come out under the arch that leads to the Quai de Conti, where I might discover the silhouette of my friend La Maga leaning against the iron parapet of the Pont des Arts.

I like Paris—the Place de Furstenberg, number 27, Rue Fleurus, the Moreau Museum, Tristan Tzara's tomb, the pink arcades on Rue Nadja, the bar Au Chien qui Fume, the blue façade of the Hotel Vaché, the bookstalls on the riverbank. And above all I like a back street, near the Château de Vincennes, where there is a modest ancient signpost informing you, as if you were just approaching a village, that you're about to enter Paris. I like walking through a part of the city I haven't seen for a while. But I also like doing the opposite: walking through a place I've just walked through. I like Paris so much that there is never any end to the city for me. I like Paris very much, because it doesn't have any Gaudí houses or cathedrals.

### 18

I also saw Perec himself *in real life*. It was halfway through 1974, the year he published *Species of Spaces*. I'd seen lots of photographs of him, but that day, in a bookshop on Boulevard Saint-Germain, I saw him arrive for the launch of a book by Philippe Sollers and do some very strange things I won't go into now. What is certain is that for quite a while, so impressed to be *seeing him in real life*, I watched him intently, so intently that, at one moment, his face was a hair's breadth from mine. Perec noticed this anomaly—a stranger was a whisker away from his goatee—and reacted by commenting out loud, as if trying to let me know I should take my face elsewhere: "The world's a big place, young man."

### 19

There was no table in my garret. Only a wardrobe, a big old mirror, and a mattress on the floor. One Sunday morning two weeks after renting this *chambre*, I went with Javier Grandes to the Marché aux Puces and bought a dilapidated, woodworm-ridden table for eighty francs and, with Javier's help, took it on the metro back to my *chambre*. That day I stopped being a writer without a desk. When I think of this today, I find it hard to even imagine myself without a table to write at. But I shouldn't feel too surprised. After all, there is always a first desk, there is always a first time for everything.

The concierge didn't like the table, she had no time for the inhabitants of the sixth floor, the garret *locateurs*. She had to clean the communal washroom every week and nobody paid her, and this drove her literally out of her mind. Apart from this, she hated Marguerite Duras. The concierge was from Valencia, in exile since the Spanish Civil War. But she didn't want anything to do with me, no matter how Catalan I declared myself to be, compatriots though we may have been. She had become very French and, what's more, thought there were considerable differences between Catalans and Valencians. In honor of all the concierges of Paris, she was in a permanently bad mood. When she saw my table, she made a huge effort not to fly into a rage, saying something I've found difficult to forget: "The French don't want to work any more, they all want to *write*. Now all we need is for the Catalans to start imitating them."

The old wooden table, together with the typewriter that had traveled with me from Barcelona, lent a distinctive air to my garret, which began to look more like a writer's *chambre*. And it looked even more like one when I bought a few notebooks, two pencils and a pencil sharpener. Now I had everything I needed to write. "The blue-backed notebooks, the two pencils and the pencil sharpener …, the marble-topped tables, the smell of early morning, sweeping out and mopping, and luck were all you needed," I'd read in *A Moveable Feast*. So now, according to Hemingway, I had everything necessary for writing and, what's more, a desk (which he perhaps took for granted) and a typewriter (something he didn't mention because he wrote in longhand), a little Olivetti that came from my father's office. I had a table and a typewriter and pencils and a pencil sharpener and also—the luck Hemingway mentioned came in here—money that my father had said he would wire me for a few months, just a few months, "so you won't starve to death," and in the hope that I would change my mind and decide to return to Barcelona and my Law studies.

Thanks to Unamuno, it hadn't taken me long to find the plot of my novel (the story of a manuscript that was passed around and caused the death of whoever read it), but, as Duras had indicated in her list of instructions, I lacked all sorts of details: knowing, for example, what kind of *structure* to give my story. I soon found it, I found it the day I realized I could just copy the structure of an already existing book, one I liked, if possible. It was that simple, or so it seemed to me. I couldn't spend too much time worrying about *structural problems* when there were still other issues to resolve that seemed even more complicated, such as *unity and harmony* or *narrative technique*, not to mention *linguistic register*, which seemed to me the most enigmatic of all. So, as far as structure was concerned, it was better not to have too many scruples. After all, I told myself, young writers copy models, they imitate the writers they like, and it's not worth the risk of complicating things even further, otherwise I might never write anything at all.

And which book did I like? I decided to choose one that wasn't exactly to my taste (and this was because I didn't understand it at all), but that had a structure that seemed to be of a high intellectual standard, of this I was sure. And I chose Vladimir Nabokov, who had used a voluminous *corpus* of notes on a mediocre poem as a clever and complex way to construct his novel *Pale Fire*. I didn't think twice about it and set to work. I decided my novel would be organized in the form of a prologue and commentaries on a manuscript of poetic prose that would appear in the middle of the book. I wrote the prologue, and then, one after another, with exasperating slowness due to my being a novice writer, came the diabolical notes or commentaries, behind which crouched the Death of the unsuspecting reader who, towards the middle of the book, would unknowingly read the manuscript that, as my malevolent narrator would reveal at the end of the book, caused the death of all who read it.

Once *The Lettered Assassin* was finished—no easy task, it took me two years to write fifty pages: the two years that are the subject of this ironic lecture on my years of literary apprenticeship—I submitted it, feeling terrified (terrified of publishing, above all), in Barcelona to the editor Beatriz de Moura, who was a friend of mine. She took the manuscript, gazed at it with astonishment for a few seconds, looked at me and said: "What have you done?" I didn't know if she was telling me off for something. Now I was twice as terrified as before. "Pale Fire," I said in a choked voice, as if revealing my own "pale fire" as a novice writer rather than the title of a book. "So you're going to be a writer," she said. "Well, yes," I replied. She stared at me, I didn't know whether furiously or pitying me in some way. I felt I had to add something. A humorous note, for example, that would ease the tension hanging in the air. "A writer like Hemingway, after all I'm five foot ten like he was," I said. She went on staring at me, I didn't know where to hide. I swallowed and added: "Though my shoulders aren't as broad."

20

When I went to Paris this past August, I went out one afternoon with my wife to Rue Delambre, in Montparnasse, to see if the Dingo Bar was still there, the place where, in April, 1925, Scott Fitzgerald and Hemingway first met.

Rue Delambre is quite short, full of bars and hotels, behind the legendary Le Dôme Café. We walked the length of it in five short minutes and verified that no trace remains of the Dingo Bar, which is not really too surprising, given that seventy-seven years have gone by since Hemingway was sitting there one day "with some completely worthless characters" when suddenly Scott Fitzgerald practically fell on top of him, saying he'd heard of him and liked his stories and introducing the tall, pleasant man with him as Dunc Chaplin, the famous baseball pitcher, a man Hemingway, not really a fan of that sport, had never heard of.

It was the start of a friendship, one that began well and ended very badly. In *A Moveable Feast,* it says that a few days after this first encounter the two men took a train trip to Lyon, going to this city to pick up a convertible the successful writer had left there and off they went, the rich, brilliant and already very famous writer

(Scott Fitzgerald) and one who was a bit younger and still a novice (Hemingway), a writer without money and anxious for success and happy to have met this big literary star. And we also hear how the train journey was a huge disaster and the drive back in the convertible even worse and we learn the young writer had to nurse the older man, taking care of him in a hotel room in a little village called Châlon-sur-Saône: where the acclaimed writer, reeling from the alcohol he had drunk, said he was dying, but that he was dying from a cold, and the ambitious, novice writer had to take care of everything, try to keep the acclaimed writer calm, mix him lemonade and whisky and give it to him with a couple of aspirins, then sit down and read the newspaper and wait for the successful author to sober up.

While poor Hemingway was reading the paper, he heard Fitzgerald say to him: "You're a cold one, aren't you?" Looking at him, Hemingway understood that, if not in his diagnosis, at least in his prescription he had been wrong, and the whisky was going to work against them. "How do you mean, Scott?" "You can sit there and read that dirty French rag of a paper and it doesn't mean a thing to you that I am dying."

Fitzgerald was not dying. All that had happened was that he'd got drunk and very wet because of the rain that had fallen relentlessly on his infamous convertible, the top of which—due to the express wishes of his wife Zelda—had been removed. It's curious to note that the dialogue that took place in this hotel room in Châlon-sur-Saône, and that Hemingway recounts in *A Moveable Feast*, recalls the scene and dialogue in "Cat in the Rain." Fitzgerald seems to take on the female role while Hemingway attempts to read quietly in the hotel room and wait for the downpour to pass. In the story of the cat in the rain the wife wants to have longer hair so she can put it up in a bun, and she also wants a kitty to sit on her lap, and moreover, wants to eat at a table with candles and her own silver and she wants it to be spring; in the hotel in Châlon-sur-Saône, a demanding Scott Fitzgerald, through the mists of alcohol, speaks in a tone identical to that of the little woman in "Cat in the Rain": "I want my temperature taken," Fitzgerald says, "then I want my clothes dried and for us to get an express train to Paris, and to go to the American Hospital at Neuilly." Hemingway tries not to get worked up and tells him their clothes aren't dry yet. And Fitzgerald interrupts him: "I want my temperature taken." The only thing missing now is for him to add: "And I want a kitty to sit on my lap and purr when I stroke her. And I want to grow my hair long and eat at a table with my own silver and candles. And most of all I want a cat, I want a cat, I want a cat now. And to go as quickly as possible to the American Hospital."

Back in Paris, Hemingway would confess to his wife that he hadn't learned anything from the famous writer on the trip. And if there was one thing he'd learned, it was never to go on a trip with anyone you do not love.

The Hemingway-Fitzgerald episode is one of the most outlandish in the history of meetings and misunderstandings between two talented writers. In general, one writer can learn very little from another. And then there is the matter of rivalry and inflated egos and the envy a poorer writer feels towards a richer one, and so on. The relationship between the episode in the hotel in Châlon-sur-Saône and the story "Cat in the Rain" is demonstrated to a certain extent by the soft sound ("like a cat") Hemingway's wife makes when, in *A Moveable Feast*, he tells her he plans never again to travel with anyone he doesn't love and proposes they should go to Spain. "Poor Scott," Hemingway finally says to his wife. "Poor everybody. Rich feathercats with no money," she adds.

"Poor Scott," I also said to my wife in Paris in the middle of August this year, back in our hotel again without having found any trace of the Dingo Bar on Rue Delambre. "Poor, poor Scott," said my wife then, "you know what? I'll be back in a minute, I'm going to look up the Dingo on the internet, I'll go to that internet café on the corner, I'm sure I can find out the bar's address."

I was stretched out on the bed, half absorbed in reading a news-paper. "Don't get wet," I told her, without noticing I sounded just like the character from "Cat in the Rain." She came back a little while later, with all the information. The Dingo Bar used to be at 10, Rue Delambre, the address of the Italian restaurant we'd seen earlier and had thought, in all fairness, that it looked dreadful.

"L'Auberge de Venise, remember?" I remembered perfectly. On the sidewalk across the street from the restaurant we had seen a *clochard* who looked a lot like Hemingway, and she'd said: "He really does look like him, unlike you, who look nothing like him."

She also brought another interesting piece of information from the internet café: at number 15 on the same street, where the Hotel Lennox is now, there is a studio, which was rented by my esteemed Marcel Duchamp, after he gave up his New York life forever. Duchamp, the last remaining artistic legend of my youth that hasn't been completely shattered.

"Rue Delambre might be small, but it certainly has more charm and class than we suspected, don't you think?" said my wife. I didn't reply. Outside it was still raining. There was undoubtedly a cat in the rain out there. I was still half absorbed in my newspaper. Like in a Hemingway story.

21

A quote from Rilke: "Scale the depths of things; irony will never descend there." And one from Jules Renard: "Irony is humanity's sense of propriety." I'm going to be honest: I think both quotes, debatable though they might seem, are perfect. But the one I like best is my own: "Irony is the highest form of sincerity."

22

Occasionally my sense of irony reaches Paris itself, and then I like New York. I would go further: every time someone mentions Duchamp, I think my life has been a mistake from the start and, instead of living in Barcelona and being in love with Paris, I should have quit bothering about such nonsense and lived in New York from day one, in Duchamp's apartment, for example. And I should have read Hemingway there, sitting in a comfortable armchair reading about his exploits as a hunter, fisherman, lover, boxer, war reporter, and drinker. And thinking the whole time: What a brute!

23

Each paragraph of *The Lettered Assassin* was a struggle for me to write. However, when my father sent a letter from Barcelona to tell me he wasn't going to wait any longer for me to finish my damned novel and had decided to shut off forever the merry flow of money, I wrote a letter of such literary agility, in sharp contrast to the agonizing stiffness when writing my novel. Whenever I re-read that letter, I am surprised how it's written: my style is far superior to that of the dubious *Lettered Assassin.* This letter proves the old Spanish expression that says hunger sharpens the wit.

   "Dear Father: I have reached the age at which one is in full command of one's own qualities, and the intellect reaches its maximum strength and capacity. It is therefore the time to carry out my literary work. To do so, I need peace and quiet and freedom from distractions, not to have to ask Marguerite Duras for money, or to spend all my time worrying about how to convince you of the value of financing the writing of this novel, which eventually, when it is finished and published and receiving acclaim, will fill you with paternal pride and great satisfaction for your generosity to me. With love from your son ..."

With this letter I managed to delay the definitive end of the money orders for a while. My father, equipped with an undeniable sense of humor and a very restrained and sparse style, replied:

Dear son: I have reached the age at which one finds oneself obliged to admit that one's son has turned out to be an imbecile. I am giving you three months to finish your masterpiece. By the way, who is Marguerite Duras?"

24

Without Javier Grandes's joie de vivre, my two years in Paris would have been an even bigger disaster. I'd met Javier at a party thrown by Lucía Bosé in Puerta de Hierro, Madrid, where Michi Panero introduced us. Javier was a very cheerful person, but at the same time he had a very scandalous view of life. He starred in the underground films his friend Arrieta made and he was also a painter and a bullfighter and the very incarnation of bohemia. I'd gone to Paris just to see him, with no other aim than to spy, as much as possible, on his bohemian life. Without this modest intention of observing Javier's Parisian world I don't think I'd ever have met Duras and so my garret would not have existed and the novel of my life would have taken a different path, perhaps a bullfighting or political path, why not? I was so open to life that any mad idea could infiltrate and change mine.

Speaking of politics, I should say that a month after taking possession of my *chambre*, my anti-Francoist Spanish student stance had changed and I became a firm radical leftist, of the *situationist* line, with Guy Debord as my master. I began to think that being anti-Franco was of very little consequence indeed and, under the influence of situationist ideas, with my pipe and my two pairs of fake glasses, I began to walk around the neighborhood converted into the prototype of the secretly revolutionary, poetic intellectual. But in fact, being a situationist without having read a single line of Guy Debord, I was on the most radical extreme left, but only through hearsay. And, as I've said, I didn't practice, I devoted myself to *feeling* extremely left-wing and that was it. What really interested me was the noble idea of forgetting the stifling atmosphere of Barcelona and being able to enjoy, in self-imposed exile, the free French air. But I soon gathered it was reactionary to consider yourself an exile instead of being a real exile, that is, a political exile from Franco's Spain. There was, it seemed, a subtle difference, or at least this was what my terrifying compatriots started pointing out to me when I went to see them in the bars where they met up and plotted. The atmosphere I'd left behind in Barcelona was stifling, but that of my exiled compatriots in Paris (none of whom, moreover, were situationists) seemed just as bad, if not worse, and so finally I stopped going to see them, and avoided those bars that left me feeling bitter and depressed by their obsessive, unbending conversations about what would happen when Franco died, worn out by their leaden political analyses, and, above all, disheartened at how ground down many of them were by heroin or dire Spanish wine.

I concentrated on making foreign friends and gradually cut myself off from the awful world of my exiled compatriots, a world revolving exclusively around the anti-Franco movement, which didn't attract me in the slightest. I found politics unattractive, and saw it as a pastime or activity ultimately demanding you choose between idealism and pragmatism, something that seemed not only rather dull but also repugnant. I only ever went to one anti-Franco event, an homage to Rafael Alberti, and was paralyzed when I found myself in a corridor face to face with María Teresa León, who was on her own and asked me suddenly—I was very shy and also on my own and, moreover, a situationist—if I had seen her husband. "Rafael Alberti," she added solemnly, pronouncing her *R*s in a spectacular, unforgettable way. She stood there waiting for my reply. "Over there," I said, pointing to a spot as far away I could see.

Everything about Spain began to feel very far away to me, but so did Guy Debord, who soon seemed not very near at all, although I was still a situationist and felt I was his disciple, but a disappointed disciple, since I had gone to see his movie *La société du spectacle*, a cinematic version of his books, and had been profoundly bored, as it was a film to be *read*. The only thing that appeared on the screen were texts, very occasionally punctuated by the fleeting vision of a few images intended to illustrate the horror of the world of show business but which came from movies I really liked, such as *Johnny Guitar*; it was only at these moments, when the fleeting images of great fictional films appeared, that I enjoyed myself; which led me to feel somewhat disconcerted and to distance myself from Debord, at least as a filmmaker, although I didn't renounce his religion and remained his follower, I didn't want to be just a vulgar anti-Francoist. Everything about Spain began to feel very far away, apart from my friends Javier Grandes and Adolfo Arrieta, who I saw as two *pure* artists and, moreover, they seemed brilliant to me—and I don't think I was wrong. Everything Spanish was gradually fading away, but to be honest I have to admit there were nights when this disciple of Guy Debord returned to his garret alone and sad and somewhat drunk and started reading Luis Cernuda aloud and suddenly felt very Republican and emotional and ending up crying at the lines: "*soy español sin ganas / que vive como puede bien lejos de su tierra / sin pesar ni nostalgia*."

That was how I lived in those days and perhaps that's why I cried: I lived as best I could, far away from my country, and I didn't know—how could I?—that I was protagonizing my novel about the years of my literary apprenticeship; I didn't know much, at times I knew only that I was a Spaniard with two pairs of fake glasses and a pipe, a young Catalan who didn't really know what to do with his life, a writer who turned into a young Republican if he read Cernuda, an unenthusiastic young Spaniard who lived as well as he could, far from his country, in a Paris that was not exactly a moveable feast.

25

Anyone who wants the island of Key West—coastal and tropical, a little decrepit, hot and humid—can have it as far as I'm concerned. It's just as horrible today as when Hemingway set himself up in that old stone house, a belated wedding present from his second wife Pauline's uncle. Although not an ideal spot, it didn't totally disappoint Hemingway, it was a good place to come home to after tarpon fishing in the Tortugas waters or bear hunting in Wyoming. Even so, no matter how you look at it, Key West has little going for it; if anything, it might be that, as in Hemingway's day, sailors still fight bare-knuckled in rumba bars.

Apart from these bars, I was so bored in Key West (I guess being disqualified didn't help), I spent many hours imagining in great detail the story of my friendship with a "thingamajig" called Scott, who in a previous life had been a Parisian demon, the demon Vauvert.

I say thingamajig and, maybe to be more precise, I should say *odradek*, that Kafkaesque creature in the shape of a spool with old, broken-off bits of thread of various sorts and colors wound around it. No more than a wooden object, but also an animate creature, with a real and eternal life, who, in the case at hand, will outlive all the customers of his place of residence, La Closerie des Lilas, Paris: that's where he resides, unobserved by everyone except me. I've talked to him whenever I've been to this café over the last thirty years.

"So, what's your name? I asked the first time I saw him. "It used to be Vauvert, now it's Scott," he said in a voice that sounded like the rustling of fallen leaves. "And where do you live?" I asked. "Always here, on this site, which is called La Closerie these days, always between the door and the bar; a while ago I was in the cellar of an abandoned house here." He laughed a strange laugh, the laugh of someone with no lungs.

I did some investigating, asked who the devil Vauvert had been.

"What ever happened to the *Monstre Vert*, to the devil Vauvert? No one ever found out and now no one ever will," the lunatic Gérard de Nerval wrote at the end of an intense, romantic text dedicated to the legend of this ancient Parisian monster and devil. Today it's taken for granted that no one ever knew and no one ever will find out what became of the devil Vauvert since the moment, sometime back in the 1820s, when a police sergeant saw him for the last time. Nevertheless, as you see, I've heard from him, I've actually known him for thirty years; I know he scarcely moves from that spot where one day, almost two centuries ago, he was seen to disappear, only now he looks different, he's no longer a demon, now he's an *odradek*. The fact is he's still in the same place where he disappeared. As Kafka would have said, *he went far away to stay right here.*

In days gone by, the *Monstre Vert* lived in his own castle, the Castle Vauvert, in the center of Paris, but his luxurious abode was destroyed by fire, and then he hid, according to Nerval, "in the cellar of a vacant house, at one end of the Jardin du Luxembourg, on Boulevard de Montparnasse, by Avenue de l'Observatoire," in other words—though Nerval never knew it—exactly where La Closerie des Lilas was built years later, a bar where Fitzgerald and Hemingway, sometime back in the 1920s, often met, first as colleagues and friends and later as rivals and enemies.

We know that in Nerval's time the devil Vauvert caused a lot of trouble, a specialist in orgies and in bewitching the bottles of wine till they danced, wine from the cellar of that vacant house demolished years later to make way for—perhaps not by chance—the bar where Fitzgerald and Hemingway resolved their differences so many times and which, today, is the perfect hiding place for the old devil, bewitcher of bottles, Vauvert, an ideal spot for our *odradek*, the secret ghost of La Closerie des Lilas.

Scott the *odradek* (that's what I call him, and I'm the only person in the world who has anything to do with him) is the living memory of the relationship between Fitzgerald and Hemingway. He's nothing more than this, which, when you think about it, is quite a lot. Isn't it a lot *to be* the memory of the friendship between those two writers? I suspect his old, broken-off threads must belong to a magnetic strip on which he has, to his despair, recorded every one of the pair's meetings and misunderstandings. He knows everything that passed between them. He calls himself Scott and identifies with the author of *The Great Gatsby,* arguing so that Hemingway (who, for him, is me) will never forget what happened.

Walter Benjamin said that an angel reminds us of everything we have forgotten. Scott, *odradek* that he is, always to be found between the door and the bar of La Closerie, reminds me, when I go to this café, of every last detail of what went on between the two friends. He is the soul, he is the devil, he is the *odradek,* he is the memory of this relationship between Hemingway and Fitzgerald. When I was young and went often to La Closerie, he, thinking I was Hemingway, would always remind me, as Fitzgerald, of the most forgotten anecdotes in our history of confrontation. And there were nights when he tragically took on *in person*—or would it make more sense to say *in object?*—the whole sad saga of the enmity between the two writers, and then he would become impossible, sinking into a foul mood, and repeating the most ironic phrases Hemingway had used about his old friend in that bar, and then he would imitate the other's equally ironic answers. And he would end up embittered by so much irony, in such a terrible state between the door and the bar, diabolically inciting me to leave the premises without paying, something I started to do almost as a matter of course on my last visits to this place where, convinced that after such a long time no one would remember me, I dared to return in the middle of August this year, understandably nervous, mainly because—though I knew perfectly well I'd see him—I wondered, after such a long time, if Scott would still be there.

I went to La Closerie this August and at first I didn't see him. I went without my wife, to avoid her reproaching me yet again for going on believing I looked like Hemingway, and above all so that she wouldn't find out that my imagination had created an *odradek* in La Closerie that speaks to me as if I were Hemingway. I sat down at the bar, waiting for a table. I looked around several times and saw nothing, perhaps he wasn't there anymore. Until suddenly, when I least expected it, I heard someone behind me say with a laugh: "You owe a lot of money." I thought immediately of all the times I had left that place without paying. Terrified, I turned around but couldn't see him, it seemed as if he wasn't there. I looked everywhere, but he had to be between the bar and the entrance. But he wasn't there, or else I couldn't see him. The voice, in any case, was his, unmistakable, like the rustling of fallen leaves. And his laugh was the same, the laugh of someone with no lungs. "Remember I was your supporter, remember I introduced you to Max Perkins," I heard him say all of a sudden. And then I saw him. He was in the darkest corner of the bar. He looked like he'd drunk every single bottle in the cellar of the old vacant house. "What are you doing here, Scott?" I asked him, perhaps using too thuggish a tone of voice. He was silent for a long time, holding out against time just as the wood he's made of also resisted. I was already seated and talking to the waiter when, coming out of the very wood of my table, I heard his unsettling voice again. "You owe me lots of money, Hemingway. I helped you succeed," he said, and laughed somewhat bitterly. I could have sworn that for a fraction of a second, under the direction of the *Monstre Vert*, all the bottles in La Closerie des Lilas did a little dance.

Though I could see he was drunker than ever, essentially he was still the same as always, still laughing without lungs, but laughing like the immortal being he was, and the old broken threads of this beautiful and damned thingamajig hadn't aged at all, the old threads of my beloved, secret Scott.

26

One evening, I went to Raúl Escari's apartment planning to get him to give me some guidance on the meaning of the expression *linguistic register*, the greatest enigma as far as I was concerned on the sheet Marguerite Duras had given me with instructions on how to write a novel. "You really want to know that?" Raúl responded when I asked him about it. "So you know what it is?" I said hopefully. "I know, but I can't be bothered to tell you," he replied. And he added: "Act instead of asking." This last clearly disconcerted me, I wanted to know what he'd meant. "I mean you ask too many questions when really you should be doing something, in this case just start writing. Once you do that without asking yourself so many questions you'll come face to face with *linguistic register*."

We were back where we'd been at the beginning of the conversation. "Couldn't you tell me what a *linguistic register* is like, what sort of characteristics it has?" With great annoyance at having to explain this to me, Raúl said at last: "You don't speak the same way in the living room as you do in the barracks, with your family as you do with students, in a political meeting, in church, or the bar on the corner. You get the picture now? By the way, why don't we go to the bar on the corner?"

Once we were at the bar, he deigned to say: "We change the language we use when our surroundings change. Get it?" "But," I said, "you talk the same way in this bar as you do at home." "Well, if, for example, your mother came and sat down with us now, I would speak in a different *register*." "I get it," I said. Then, as if annoyed that I got it so quickly, he added: "We shouldn't really be talking about *linguistic registers* in this bar so much as *diaphasic varieties*, which are the various idiomatic styles individuals adopt according to the communicative situation they find themselves in."

"And isn't a *linguistic register* the same thing as a *diaphasic variety*?" I asked. "Of course it is," he replied, "see, now you know what a *register* is!" Indeed, now I knew, though I had found out by a tortuous, though actually very subtle, intelligent route. I changed the subject. I decided to investigate why he, so obviously a writer, hadn't written for years. Out of the blue, I asked him which register he'd write in if he did write. He didn't reply. I insisted and he kept quiet, I got no reply. Just a smile, a perfect smile. His register, the most elegant I have ever known, was a close relation to laughter and silence.

27

Nothing in life is immutable, everything can be modified. I, for example, could go and live in New York, which is what, deep down, I really want. I could set myself up in an apartment in New York instead of being in Barcelona talking about how there is never any end to Paris. Nothing is immutable, everything can be modified. Think of the works of Flaubert. We can easily transform them with our imagination. It's enough to entertain the suspicion that had Flaubert had a little more time and sufficient money to put his literary legacy in order, it would be quite a different oeuvre today, as he certainly would have finished *Bouvard et Pécuchet*, suppressed *Madame Bovary* (the annoyance the book's tyrannical fame caused its author should be taken seriously), and changed the ending of *A Sentimental Education*.

Admitting the unmissable disparity between our work, but with the understanding that everything can change, I tell myself now that, before it's too late, I should, for instance, change the ending to my seventh novel, improve the ninth (I didn't take advantage of the many possibilities of the plot), suppress the third, and so on. But, above all, the most urgent thing would be to revise *The Lettered Assassin*, a poisonous and criminal book, my funereal literary debut. Perhaps I would change only the title, and call the book ironically *Pipe-smoking and Despair: The Errors of Youth*. I don't know. I think it might be good to put a bit of a spring in my first literary steps, to beautify something that was a rather sinister coming-out. Since it's so like a funereal monument—like Tutankhamun's tomb: whoever opens it dies—I should do to that book what the surrealists proposed to cheer up the sinister and solemn Pantheon of Paris a little: slice it down the middle and pull the two halves fifty centimeters apart.

### 28

Speaking of pantheons, the most ironic phrase I know—perhaps *the* ironic phrase *par excellence*—is the epitaph Marcel Duchamp wrote for his own tombstone:

*D'ailleurs, c'est toujours les autres qui meurent.*
(After all, it's always other people who die.)

### 29

Is the person who just asked me to speak up deaf or an excessive admirer or trying to sabotage this lecture?

Anyway, whatever the reason, I'll speak louder.

I live in Barcelona, I'm attracted and fascinated by this neverending Paris, but I don't kid myself, I'd like to spend more time in New York, where, by the way, I've spent only one night in my life.

New York is a desire that comes from far away. For many years I had a recurring dream in which I saw myself as a child in the fifties standing in the large patio of the building where I lived with my parents in a mezzanine flat on Calle Rosellón in Barcelona, opposite the Cinema Chile. In this dream I saw myself playing soccer on my own (as I used to do as a child), in the shadow of the eight- or ten-story buildings that surrounded the patio. But there was something different from the past: these apartment buildings had been transformed into the skyscrapers of a city with something undeniably magical about it, New York City. And having skyscrapers,

instead of the normal houses of my neighborhood, gave me a powerful feeling of complete fulfillment and happiness, the feeling that
comes from living not in a backwater, but in the capital of the world,
New York. I had this dream of grandness so many times I figured
I must want to get to know this big city, to exchange the modest
splendor of my provincial childhood world of post-war Spain for
the center of the world.

One day, out of the blue, I was invited to spend a night in New
York.

I was asked to take part in a conference in a library in Manhattan.
Though a single night wasn't much—the following days I had to be
in Providence and Boston for two other conferences—I accepted
the invitation and traveled to New York, above all I traveled to find
out what happened when one finds oneself in real life inside one's
most recurring and happiest dream.

Shortly after arriving in New York, at night in the solitude of
my hotel room with my suitcase not yet unpacked, I looked out the
window and contemplated the skyscrapers surrounding me. Visu-
ally it was like in my patio dream, but nothing special happened. I
was inside my dream and at the same time everything was real. But,
as was to be expected, my sense of fulfillment or happiness hadn't
increased because I was there. I was in New York, and that was all.
I got into bed, fell asleep, and then dreamed I was playing in a patio
in New York, surrounded by houses from Barcelona. And suddenly
I discovered that the *duende* of the dream was never New York City,
but rather the child playing in the dream. The child I had been was
what had caused that particular dream to be my dream of dreams.
The next morning, despite the fact that I was in New York, I was
hugely upset when I found myself awake. New York was the least
of it, with its skyscrapers and undeniable allure. What mattered
least was confirming that, actually, I did like New York better than
Paris. And what mattered most was that on waking up, the child
had disappeared, I had lost the true *duende* of the dream. I walked
around like a sleepwalker the whole day, the only day of my life that
I spent in New York.

30

*The Lettered Assassin* (a book written by the assassin herself, though the reader shouldn't know it until the end) opens with an almost perfect first sentence that speaks of how occasions for laughter and tears are intertwined in the narrator's life (a sentence that's actually the last one I wrote in the whole book and of that more later). Then it goes on: "It was last year, in an old hotel in Bremen, I was in search of Vidal Escabia. Through a labyrinth of corridors I had arrived at his room, number 666, and since the door was ajar ..."

The murderess tells the reader that in room 666, in the old hotel in Bremen, she discovers the lifeless body of Vidal Escabia, and next to the corpse she finds, dropped on the floor, as if death had struck as he read it, the original manuscript of *The Lettered Assassin*. And a little further on the murderess reveals that in May 1975 she sent the victim a personal letter from Worpswede, near Bremen, along with the manuscript of *The Lettered Assassin* and some notes on the text.

The reason I chose Bremen and Worpswede—a city and village I knew nothing about, only that they were German—was really very simple. Due to the demands of the plot, I needed the name of a city that wasn't too far from Paris. At that moment, the book I had closest at hand in the garret was *Letters to a Young Poet,* by Rainer Maria Rilke. I opened the book with my eyes closed and there was the fourth letter, dated July, 1903, in *Worpswede, near Bremen.* I realized straightaway that I had found the city I was looking for, but also a village with a strange name it would be a shame not to use. And that's how it happened that these two places, the strange-named village, Worpswede, and the city of Bremen, appeared on the first page of my first book and as time went by—there are few pages I have visited more frequently than the first page of *The Lettered Assassin*—they ended up becoming mythical names for me, two names that became *part of me.*

Allow me to leave aside irony for a few moments and to recall tenderly what I was reading in those long-ago days. I think I saw Rilke and Unamuno as if they were writers of self-help books. It seems, just as with Unamuno's *How to Make a Novel*, I had Rilke's book there in my garret with the basic idea that, just as the title hinted, it would show me how to write. I'd bought it in La Hune bookshop like a man who acquires a pearl, thinking it will solve all his problems. I can only see this purchase as touching and it makes me think that possibly here today, in this room, there might be a young poet in the audience listening to this lecture thinking he can learn something from this ironic account of my years of apprenticeship.

If this is the case, I would recommend this young poet not make such a lamentable mistake. If we come into this world in order to learn, and yet, learn nothing—we leave it knowing less than ever— the young poet is even less likely to learn anything from a lecture where the only certainty the lecturer has—well, maybe this young man will learn something, maybe he'll learn what I'm about to tell him, which is no small thing—the only certainty I have is that per- severance in the habit of writing is usually in direct relation to its absurdity, while we usually do brilliant things quite spontaneously.

I don't think there's any harm in saying that if I learned noth- ing from the book by Rilke, it's also true, and odd, that this book *in its own way* did help me with something, it helped me not only to find the names of a German city and village, but also to write the first sentences of the letter written by my assassin, sentences exactly the same as those of the fourth letter from Rilke to the young poet, a letter sent from *Worpswede, near Bremen*, July 16, 1903, which begins like this: "*About ten days ago I left Paris and traveled to this great northern plain, where the vastness and silence and sky ought to help me rest.*"

And if these two places have indeed been accompanying me over the years, it never occurred to me that one day I might travel to them, as in fact happened a few months ago when I was invited by some professors to give a reading of my work in Bremen; inadver- tently, they were offering me the chance to go to the first city and the first village I named in my whole body of work. I accepted the invitation immediately but it didn't take me long to start wondering whether they would put me up *in an old hotel in Bremen* and above all to speculate about the possibility, as literary as it was terrifying, that, whether the hotel was old or not, the number of my room might be 666.

If 666 was the number of my room—something I believed or wanted to believe was highly unlikely—I would have to accept from that moment that I was a dead man. Perhaps my entire oeuvre—I said to myself—had consisted of this, writing for thirty years just to end up returning to its origins, to finally return, in a diabolical closed circle—let's not forget that 666 is the number of the Beast—to the first sentences I wrote in my first book, returning and becoming a fatal victim of those sentences, just as my manuscript had made a victim of Vidal Escabia, the first character I ever killed.

I went to Bremen and the hotel was modern and the room number (as was only to be expected after all) was very far from being 666. Relaxed, that very night I liberated myself at once from my ghosts and, when I'd finished my reading in the city, over dinner, I joked rashly about my now dispelled fears. "And what if 666, where the Beast really is waiting for you is in Worpswede?" I will never know who asked this question. The fact is that the following day I decided to go to Worpswede, partly because I wanted to defy the Beast, but also because I was curious to see this village with the strange name that had infiltrated the first pages of my first book. On the bus, on my way to the village, I had the strange feeling that I was entering, thirty years after having written it, the first page of *The Lettered Assassin*. Once in Worpswede, where I discovered that Rilke had traveled to this tranquil village in 1903 because he was friends with Paula Modersohn-Becker, I visited the museum-house of this interesting but ill-fated painter. And I bought several books about the artistic history of the place and also a German edition of *Letters to a Young Poet*, Rilke's book I'd had in my garret in Paris and that I'd lost a long time ago and where the writer speaks of *the vastness, silence and sky* of that *great northern plain* where oddly (or not) I found myself at that moment.

Modersohn-Becker painted people as if they were still lifes. When she died, Rilke dedicated a poem to her, "Requiem for a Friend." She had a spark of genius that death snatched away at the age of thirty-one, leaving Rilke devastated: "Somewhere there is an ancient enmity between our daily life and the great work ..." I spent a long time in the museum and then walked through the village and, with the help of the landscape paintings I had seen in the museum, began to imagine I was walking through Worpswede in the early twentieth century, walking through the *great northern plain*, as dusk fell, pushed on by a light wind. Under an immense sky the fields spread out in dark tones; rolling heather-covered hills stirred in the distance, bordered by fields of stubble and newly harvested buckwheat. And all this gradually appeared to me so forcefully and so realistically, that I actually felt scared. Then I remembered the number 666 and also the fact that I had come to this village knowing I risked finding myself face to face with this number and that the diabolical circle of my work could suddenly close at any moment. But the number 666 was nowhere to be found. I had some trivial strawberry ice cream on the terrace of a roadside café, next to the stop for the bus that took me back to Bremen.

My fear of the Beast ended there, ended in that strawberry ice cream.

31

Strawberry ice cream?

Two weeks went by and Bremen and Worpswede had been left behind when I had to travel from Barcelona to Malaga: this involved a couple of busy hours of work, then a night in the Hotel Larios and returning home the next day. It's common knowledge that things happen, end up happening, or sometimes happen when you least expect them to. On the return leg of this short trip, I had to fly from Malaga to Barcelona on Spanair flight JKK666. I could hardly believe it. How dare they give the number of the Beast to an airplane? For a long while, waiting for the diabolical flight to be called, I worried that what I'd presumed could happen to me in Bremen might happen on this very plane. Because it's also common knowledge that, as both God and the Devil have recently demonstrated far too well, they are anything but perfect and instead, very clumsy, and are often known to arrive late to their operating theatre. But then I thought the opposite, I told myself it was absurd to fall into the trap of believing in things with such a pronounced literary charge and there was absolutely no reason anything should happen to me. So I boarded the plane.

The young man in the seat next to mine was one of those nervous youths we've all come across at one time or another on planes, one of those who don't stop moving, as if they've just drunk an awful lot or taken a strong hit of cocaine. The stewardess tells us to fasten our seatbelts, and we think we're going to get a break. But this isn't what happens at all, because they carry on fidgeting restlessly and nervously with that seatbelt fastened, they even start to make us feel as upset as they do. He managed to affect me so much I couldn't help giving him an angry glance, while also trying to repress my most primal instinct, which was to slap him across the face and put a triple safety belt on him. The guy was still uncontrollable and fidgeting in his seat, picking up the airline magazine, for example, then putting it back, doing this I don't know how many times. Not to mention the absurd questions he kept asking the stewardesses, the nervous glances towards the little window and other charming touches. I took a good look at him; he was dressed all in black, from head to toe. I looked carefully at his head, examined his face in detail, and shuddered: this young man with a diabolical air and somewhat murderous aspect looked a lot like me at the time when I wrote *The Lettered Assassin*.

At that moment, the plane took off.

Was he an imposter, or someone completely unrelated to me, or was he me myself, quite a few years younger? Doubtless the second, and apart from the fact of traveling on flight JKK666 and his looking rather demonic, there wasn't too much to get alarmed about. But just in case, I tried to keep him in line. I shot him another defiant glance. I gave him—as far as possible—the same icy and terrifying look I'd imagined my lettered assassin to have when I was writing the book. I thought I had stunned and confused him, but that was only wishful thinking. I was planning on not looking at him or worrying about him anymore, when he resumed his nervous habit, picking up the airline magazine and giving it a compulsive glance before putting it back in its place again. More irritated than ever, I was about to give him one last very serious and threatening reproachful glance when the thought came to me clearly that if in the 1970s, following Hemingway's example or letting the despair of youth take him over, if this man had committed suicide, I would not be alive. I realized I had always depended on this young assassin and if he forgot about me, I would die. And vice versa, of course.

I made a note in my diary about this and tried to get him to read it. I wrote: "Sensation of being in two times and two places at once." The diabolical youth was too nervous to read what I was writing. I wondered what would happen if, for example, I said to him: "When you get to my age, you will want at any cost for someone to recognize that you look like Hemingway." He would certainly take me for a madman or think I wanted to strike up an amorous relationship with him, anything but guess he was the same as me when I was young. I traveled beside him in a rigorous and repressed silence until we got to Barcelona. And when we landed in that city I let him go ahead of me in the aisle so he could get off first. "Youth first," I said to him, venting my frustration, trying to make up with these words for what I'd suffered throughout the interminable flight. "And the devil is everywhere," he replied insolently, almost pushing me over. I've never seen anyone in such an immense hurry to get off a plane, and I've seen some pretty nervous people.

32

Hemingway said that when spring arrives in Paris, even if it's a false spring, the only problem is to find the place where you can be happiest. I well remember the first day of the spring of 1974, not the first official day of spring, but a splendid April day. I even remember the date, April 9, a day when the rain stopped completely and everyone left their winter clothes at home and the terraces of the cafés filled up. Everything invited happiness, a grave setback for my habitual state of youthful despair. Paris is a gray and rainy city, but when spring arrives and the terraces fill and street singers seem to emerge from every corner singing *La Vie en Rose*, the city turns into the best place in the world to be happy (even if a person might not want it to be and prefers *la vie en noir*).

On that April 9, I was about to cross Boulevard Saint-Germain with Marguerite Duras and Raúl Escari when suddenly a large black car, almost funereal and not at all spring-like, braked hard and stopped in front of us. I looked inside and saw Julia Kristeva, Philippe Sollers, Marcelin Pleynet, and a fourth person I wasn't able to identify. Sollers rolled the car window down and spoke with Marguerite for a few seconds. I didn't understand a word of what they said. Then, the car pulled off and disappeared into the distance, finally vanishing at the other end of the boulevard. Then suddenly Marguerite said: "They're going to China."

Once again, I thought, she's speaking in her *superior* French. They're going to China, repeated Raúl in a very solemn and ironic tone, and couldn't hold back a cheerful giggle. And I laughed so as not to contradict him. The strange thing is it was true. In April and May of 1974, a French delegation made up of three members of the magazine *Tel Quel* (Sollers, Kristeva, and Pleynet), together with François Wahl and Roland Barthes, visited China. They went from Peking to Shanghai and from Nanking to Sian. On his return, Barthes published a famous article in *Le Monde*, where he revealed his disappointment with what he had seen and heard. He thought Chinese tea was as bland as the landscape. This and certain reflections on Maoism are what I remember most about this article, which I read on the day it appeared—May 24, 1974, another extraordinary spring day—in my garret, secretly astonished at what it said there. The article was called "Alors la Chine," and there are some who swear it has passed into the history of twentieth-century French literature.

33

Think of what the fundamental reasons for despair might be. Each of you will have your own. I propose mine: the fickleness of love, the fragility of our bodies, the overwhelming meanness that dominates our social lives, the tragic loneliness in which, deep down, we all live, the ups and downs of friendship, the monotony and insensitivity the habit of living brings along with it.

On the other side of the scales, we find Paris. This city, perhaps because there is never any end to it and because it is wonderful as well, can take anything, it can counter any of the causes a man can come up with to be unhappy. If one is young in Paris, as I was in those days, and still hasn't really discovered the true and essential causes for despair, it is incomprehensible that I felt so unhappy in Paris. My God, what was I doing in despair in Paris? I couldn't have been stupider.

I reflect on this and remember this *pensée* of Cioran's: "Paris: city in which there may be certain interesting people to see, but where you see anyone but them. You're crucified by the annoying ones."

And I think when I lived in Paris I never learned to distinguish between interesting and annoying people, very probably because, weighed down by my stupid despair, I belonged to the large group of those annoying ones.

## 34

I believed that living in despair was very elegant. I believed it for the entire two years I spent in Paris, and in fact have believed it nearly all my life. I've been mistaken until August of this year, which is when this cherished belief in the elegance of despair teetered and came crashing down for good. When it fell like a house of cards, other no less picturesque beliefs began to collapse as well. Such as, for example, the belief that it is essential to be thin in order to be an intellectual and that fat people—as I was growing fatter, with a huge guilt complex, I thought this more and more every day—are not poetic, nor can they be intelligent.

I went to Paris this August and, while waiting for my wife, who was going to join me there the following day, I left the hotel at dusk and walked down Rue de Rennes until I got to the Café de Flore, blending in with the crowds in the streets, walked towards number 5, Rue Saint-Benoît. I acted as if I still lived there and I was just coming home like on any other evening. But I suddenly realized there was something ghostly about me, something a little like a corpse who'd been granted permission to rise from the tomb for a few hours and return to the abandoned streets of his youth and discover none of them were as they had been, that everything was very different.

I walked through the streets of my neighborhood like a sad ghost and soon discovered how inelegant despair could be, especially if the one in despair was a ghost. Lost in the crowds, I walked through those so familiar streets of old, lost and not recognizing anybody in the neighborhood and not even able to go into my building and up to the garret, since I didn't live there any more; I felt like a dead man on leave, a ghost, and this was a devastating feeling, because I saw the deep and insurmountable gap that separated my youth from my adulthood, and verifying this was very painful; I realized the incessant and vast universe of Paris had been moving away from me for a very long time.

I walked around like a ghost at dusk and never have I comprehended so fully the notion we all have of the tragic loneliness of the dead. In the past, walking about like a ghost would have seemed very elegant to me. But that August evening, seeing I was no longer anybody in my neighborhood in Paris, I discovered just what kind of great disaster was hidden inside an "elegant" despair. It was not at all pleasant to walk in despair through the streets of my old neighborhood. If it wasn't elegant to want to die, it was even less so to be dead and walking through the places where you had once been alive.

I recalled a British film in which Napoleon was put off a ship at Paris while a double took his place on Saint Helena. Bonaparte's problem was that nobody in Paris recognized him and he soon realized if he insisted too much on his identity, he ran the risk of ending up like the dozens of lunatics who filled the asylums of Paris each claiming to be the one and only real Napoleon.

And I thought too of a strange friend from those days, a young Parisian who lived on Rue Jacob, near my garret, I thought a lot about this friend who would walk through the neighborhood believing he was Napoleon when he fell into the black pit of dementia. I'd sometimes find him sitting *à la* Bonaparte in the small, comfortable garden of the Delacroix Museum in Place de Furstenberg, and occasionally I talked to him. "You see," I remember he said to me one day, "yesterday I was a pataphysicist while today I'm only Napoleon."

What was this about being a pataphysicist? I was a *situationist*, but I'd never heard of the pataphysicists. Were they related to the situationists? When I found out something about the pataphysicists a few days later, I decided to remain a mere situationist to avoid excessive confusion in my literary and political personality.

I began to take the route of madness of my strange friend from Rue Jacob, the neighborhood Napoleon, and I started to dress as a young man with the air of a lettered assassin, with intellectual glasses and a ridiculous Sartresque pipe (I didn't realize the pipe made me look even more bourgeois, instead of giving me the image of a *poète maudit*), rigorously black shirt and trousers, black glasses, too, my face inscrutable, absent, terribly modern: all black, even my future. I only wanted to be a *maudit* writer, the most elegant of those in despair. I shoved Hemingway brusquely aside and started to read, on the one hand, Hölderlin, Nietzsche and Mallarmé, and on the other what could be called the *noir pantheon of literature:* Lautréamont, de Sade, Rimbaud, Jarry, Artaud, Roussel.

In those days, I started walking around the neighborhood streets believing myself to be an *interesting* person. Sometimes I sat on the terrace of the Café Flore or Chez Tonton and tried to get passersby to notice me, to observe me, with my Sartresque pipe, reading with the air of a young, dangerous French poet. Sometimes—I was well practiced—I looked up from the book I was pretending to read and at that moment my penetrating *maudit* writer look was at its most piercing.

In those days, I would often say I couldn't bear life and that, more than anything, I wanted to die. "Basically, a trick to avoid the humiliation of accepting that, after the death of God, you're no longer anybody," commented my intelligent friend, Raúl Escari, years later from Montevideo (birthplace of Lautréamont). But now, for the first time, I realized that perhaps elegance could be something different from what I had always thought, perhaps elegance was living in the happiness of the present, which is a way of feeling immortal.

No one is asking us to live *life in the pink*, but they're not asking for black despair either. As the Chinese proverb says, you cannot prevent the dark birds of sorrow from passing over your head, but you can keep them from nesting in your hair. "I do nothing without happiness," Montaigne said. At the beginning of *Anti-Oedipus* we find this great sentence by Foucault: "Do not believe that because you are a revolutionary you must feel sad."

But in my youth in Paris in those days I believed that happiness was stupid and vulgar and, with notable falsity, I pretended to read Lautréamont and kept on irritating my friends by forever implying that the world was sad and it wouldn't be long before I killed myself, since all I thought about was being dead. Until one day I met Severo Sarduy in La Closerie des Lilas and he asked me what I was going to do on Saturday night. "Kill myself," I replied. "Well, let's meet up on Friday then," said Sarduy. (Years later I heard Woody Allen say the same thing and I was flabbergasted, Sarduy had beat him to it.) From that day on, I annoyed my friends less with this idea of dying by my own hand, but for a long time I maintained my belief— which wasn't completely destroyed until August of this year—in the intrinsic elegance of despair. Until I discovered how inelegant it is to walk, sad, in despair, dead, through the streets of your neighborhood in Paris. I realized it this August. And ever since I've been finding elegance in happiness. "I have embarked on the study of metaphysics several times, but happiness always interrupted," said Macedonio Fernández. Now, I think going through the world without experiencing the joy of living, rather than elegant, is just so humdrum. Fernando Savater said that the Castilian saying *to take things philosophically* does not mean to be resigned to things, or to take things seriously, but rather to take them happily. Of course. After all, we have all eternity in which to despair.

## 35

One June evening in 1974, in a restaurant on Rue Saint-Benoît (Barthes had returned from China and the days in Paris were starting to get hot), Marguerite Duras asked me which literary destiny I preferred.

"Mallarmé or Rimbaud?" she asked.

I choked on my coffee.

I had no idea what she was talking about. I'd read both poets quite carefully and been dazzled, but I was far from understanding that each represented a literary alternative, one sedentary and one nomadic: Mallarmé not moving from his home in Paris his whole life, never once leaving his desk, conceiving of language as a creative and transformative force born to craft enigmas rather than explain them; Rimbaud, leaving Paris and writing behind at a very young age to lose himself in an African life of adventure, becoming a businessman who liked "above all to smoke and drink liquor as strong as molten metal."

Adolfo Arrieta, who was dining with us, saw my anxious face and quickly came to my aid, explaining in a few seconds exactly what sort of dilemma Marguerite had just presented. This dilemma has accompanied me my whole life. On that day, my first impulse was to choose the Rimbaud option, close to Hemingway's apologia of ways of life based on risk and the mythification of *virile* conceptions of existence, to let myself be seduced by adventure, put myself on Rimbaud's side, a poet who "wrote silences, nights, noted the inexpressible, nailed vertigo." But straightaway I thought, dull and boring as it might seem, I should choose Mallarmé, since an enthusiastic declaration of nomadic principles could lead Marguerite to ask teasingly why the hell, if I liked Abyssinia and Rimbaud so much, did I not leave Paris and free up the garret. Additionally, it wouldn't do to forget that the man who had written that he liked smoking and strong liquor had become a sober, stingy hypocrite in Africa: "I drink only water, fifteen francs a month, everything is so expensive. I never smoke."

I was about to choose the Mallarmé option when I started to doubt dangerously, and I've been doubting to this day, which is really more like Mallarmé than Rimbaud, since home and one's desk are ideal places for doubting, and have the added advantage of keeping one from going mad, which, when you look at it, is not a bad thing at all, above all if you believe, as I do, that what makes us mad can never be doubt, but rather certainty, any certainty, even if it's as simple as the one I have now that this first of three sessions comprising this three-day lecture is but a fragment away from reaching its end. I will now read you my fragment on the order and disorder of desks, and finish for the day.

36

I think I unconsciously reflected this dichotomy between Rimbaud and Mallarmé in *The Lettered Assassin*, where I invented two diametrically opposed writers. The first, Juan Herrera, was a writer of a certain category who had distinguished himself throughout his whole life for being fanatical about order, bourgeois order to be more precise. He had written many pages on the attacks of disorder (the totalitarianisms of the 1930s) on order. The other was called Vidal Escabia and was a dreadful writer and the living image of disorder. The first was rather sedentary and the other a recalcitrant nomad. They had, obviously, very different desks.

Herrera arranged his (the same one he'd had for his whole life, in Paris, Sète, and Trouville) according to an unchanging scheme: pens, pencils, ashtray, magnifying glass, letter opener, dictionaries, paper, glass of mineral water, and a little box of aspirin, sleeping pills, and appetite suppressants. Herrera—fictional counterpoint of Thomas Mann, a bourgeois writer who I, as a situationist, despised—was superstitious and tended to attribute his moments of scant literary inspiration to the inexact placement of one of the objects on his work table. Vidal Escabia, on the other hand, had never had a desk (nor did he need one, because other people wrote most of his novels for him), and was tremendously absent-minded, and would forget the manuscripts of his books, written by others, in taxis; he wrote (or, rather, pretended to write) at the busiest beaches or bars, a pen never lasted him three days, the only dictionary he'd ever owned was one of synonyms he'd been given in Lima and lost in a brothel (nobody ever knew why he'd taken it there), he was a passionate promoter of any idea of chaos and an enthusiast of his own disorder.

I think Vidal Escabia was a lot like me, since I'd never had a desk until I got to Paris and, what's more, I'd spent my life paying homage to disorder and writing nonsense at busy bars and beaches, never at a desk. I loved chaos and detested *bourgeois* stability and

I think I identified with Escabia, and felt very fond of him, even though he was a bad writer, I wouldn't say he was my model writer, but I would always prefer him, if pressed, to Thomas Mann, that is, to Juan Herrera, the unbearably serious, sedentary writer, always checking to make sure everything was precisely in order.

The irony of fate. When I described in *The Lettered Assassin* the orderly arrangement of objects on Juan Herrera's desk, I could hardly have imagined, as time went by, I would end up having the same desk in Barcelona for more than a quarter of a century, and would go to pathological extremes, following all kinds of superstitions, to keep the objects on my desk arranged just so, that is, I would turn into a sedentary writer, into any old Thomas Mann.

So, am I a lecture or a novel? Am I Thomas Mann or Hemingway?

## 37

Irony undoubtedly already existed in Ancient Greece. We find it in Socrates, Plato's *Symposium* actually being the first modern novel. In the Middle Ages, however, irony was seen as dangerous, inconceivable, inappropriate, you could be burned at the stake if you chose to practice it. We find it again in Cervantes, Renaissance man. He introduces irony into the heart of the novel, into its very structure. And then, it's there right on up to our own time. "If reality is a plot," says Ricardo Piglia, "irony is a private plot, a conspiracy against that plot." Irony isn't an addition, it's part of the mechanisms of representation of the world, offering a shadow angled over that world. In any case, irony is a rhetorical figure, it belies language. And yet, I don't want to belie anything I've just said about it. Everything I've said about irony is not at all ironic. The fact is, after all, art is the only method we have of pronouncing certain truths. And I can't think of a greater way of stating truth than being ironic about our own identity, which is what I've been doing in this lecture since yesterday, always with the best of intentions.

38

One day, I was sitting with Martine Simonet (*la plus belle pour aller danser*, the most beautiful woman in the neighborhood, my platonic love), Javier Grandes, and Jeanne Boutade on the terrace of the Café de Flore (Sarduy called it the Flora) and none of us had said anything for quite a while, seriously absorbed in observing and studying the people around us and those who walked by. on the street, when it suddenly occurred to me to ask Martine what was guaranteed to make her roar with laughter.

"Banana peels," she said, "when people slip and fall flat on their faces. I'm very traditional."

In those days I divided the customers in Café de Flore into three groups: the exiled writers, the French writers, and the mixed and rather extravagant clientele who were extraneous to literature, but not to quirkiness. It's possible that since then I've never seen so many eccentrics gathered together anywhere else in the world.

"The facile trope applies: the Flora has its fauna: regular, almost immovable, cloying and sure," wrote Sarduy around that time. I well remember some of those who made up that extravagant and sickening fauna: the young blond man, for example, who could only sit where Jean-Paul Sartre had written *Nausea*; the Zsa Zsa Gabor impersonator, who arrived, every day at dusk, with her seven little white dogs; the young Mallorcan millionaire Tomás Moll and his eternal secretary, working on a book that became infinite; the American painter Ruth Stevens, haggard and scurvy-ridden; Roland Barthes hiding behind *Le Monde* so no one would bother him; the fat transvestite there every night, obvious and black; David Hockney, with a falsely absent look in his eye; the unbearable Muscovite grandmother, disheveled and diabolical; Paloma Picasso and her Argentinian boyfriend, and so on.

I spent hours there in the Flore with my friends laughing at the customers and especially at the people we saw walking past on the street, in front of the café. Of course, depending on where my table was, there were some days, when I decided to leave and go back to the garret (just a few steps away), that I was quite capable of walking around the whole block just so I wouldn't have to pass the terrace and become the latest victim of the commentaries and jokes.

Of course, it wasn't always like this, for it actually took me a long time to get up the nerve to go into the Flore, and even longer to learn how to laugh at the people in the street and inside the café. In fact, the day I asked Martine that question, in a way, I'd really been finally, fully integrated into the fauna of the Flore for just a few hours. That day I was aware, just as I'd suspected the first time I walked into the Flore, that I hadn't really been exiled to France or to Paris, but to one area of Paris, the Latin Quarter, and very specifically to one of its cafés, the Flore.

The first time I went to the Flore I already suspected that going there meant asking for literary asylum in the café, forming part of a long line of generations of writers who had gone into exile *right there*, in that exact place. I felt on that first day that entering the Flore meant embracing an order of *displaced* writers, accepting membership of something resembling a continuous delegation. The Flore seemed to contain every language, to be every literary café in the world. "To be exiled in the Latin Quarter," I had heard Sarduy say, "is like belonging to a clan, to be included in a coat of arms, to be marked by this heraldry of alcohol, absence, and silence in which generations of writers and poets have followed each other." I was excited by this responsibility of embracing the order of those who are forever foreign, but at the same time I worried I wasn't up to the task, that I wouldn't be worthy of the writers who'd preceded me, as I was already aware that to write as well as them, or even better, my writing would have to start acquiring consistency and texture. How would I do it? With difficulty, I thought. I had a long way to go. Would I ever be worthy of this tradition of café writing and exile? Perturbed by all this, the following days I ended up imagining that the stateless tradition of the Flore was speaking to me, and even thought I heard some of the lucid and also tragic voices of those who had gone before, voices that seemed to make up a chorus named Exile. It's your turn, I heard them say.

My turn? For a long time, I used to wake up in a cold sweat in the middle of the night, lying there on the horrible mattress in the garret, still seeing the walls and tables of the Flore that had shown up in my dream. And I remember perfectly that many times, although I'd already woken up, I could still hear the voices of the chorus. The chorus of the displaced, of exile.

Now it's your turn, Exile said. And, drying my sweat, I thought that Marguerite should have added an item called *Responsibility* to her list.


### 39


Is it advisable to leave Paris? No, I don't really think it is. For the woman who accompanies the intrepid Harry in "The Snows of Kilimanjaro" it's not advisable at all. Deep in dangerous Africa, she says to Harry at one point in Hemingway's story: "I wish we'd never come. You never would have gotten anything like this in Paris. You always said you loved Paris. We could have stayed in Paris." This woman, if only because she is fickle, and slight, and didn't like leaving Paris at all, reminds me at times of Kikí, the only person in the world who I know for certain wanted to murder me.

"The Snows of Kilimanjaro" is a story in which Hemingway relates, in an elliptical way, that he'd already had a narrow escape, that he sees a portent of death in the snowy peaks of this proud mountain, whose "western summit is called the Masai *Ngaji Ngai*, the House of God." Hemingway was convinced that the snows of Kilimanjaro, which he identified with death, were definitive, perpetual. We too were convinced of this until very recently. In an accelerated world with everything changing, it was comforting to know that death, like the snow on Kilimanjaro's summit, would always be there, untouchable, deliciously cold and stable. Nevertheless, all our calm certainty of the eternity of the snow on that African peak collapsed not long ago when we learned that within twenty years not a trace will be left there. This piece of twenty-first century news is comparable to one from the nineteenth, similar to news of the death of God that Nietzsche then divulged.

Within twenty years the eternal snows of Kilimanjaro will die. I wonder what Hemingway would have said if he'd known what we now know, that is, if he'd found out that after God it would be Death that dies. I remember a photograph of Hemingway with his wife in Africa, with the majestic Kilimanjaro in the background, his wife Mary looking at the camera holding a shotgun. And I also remember him in another African photograph, next to the great adventurer Philip Percival, whose bravery he admired so much.

Harry looked, and "all he could see, as wide as all the world, great, high and unbelievably white in the sun, was the square top of Kilimanjaro. And then he knew that there was where he was going." Hemingway had a very brave and dignified way of heading toward death, toward the snowcapped peaks. But it's clear that, if it were possible for him to come back to this world in twenty years' time, it would be impossible for him to write that line: "then he knew that there was where he was going." By that time, the place that gave his story its title, that space of silence and its imposing, high-altitude climate (there where he was going), having lost its perpetual snows, won't be the same, it won't be Death.

In twenty years, it will be necessary to go back to Paris to look for something more eternal, admit that the woman in Hemingway's story was right, that it wasn't advisable to leave that city. It seems to me that she, despite her fickle nature and slightness, was able to sense that Paris, unlike the condemned snows of Kilimanjaro, will always be immortal, will never end. Because, isn't it true, ladies and gentlemen, that there is never any end to Paris?

40

It must have been September 1974, we were in the Café Blaise, at the top of the Eiffel Tower, and suddenly reality for me stopped being what it was, and as I looked at the city I saw only an intersection of four roads, one of which clearly led to the summit of Kiliman-jaro. My absolute astonishment at this sight and my sudden and devastating farewell to a reality that until then had seemed unique and immutable are among the most enduring memories of that day when, accompanied and guided by Kikí, I took my first tab of acid.

Shortly after noticing its first effects, I began to feel—still doubt-ful, but growing less so by the second—that perhaps I was immor-tal, and finally I felt this with full force. I suddenly had the nearly unequivocal impression that I was *something more than alive* and if it occurred to somebody at that moment to shoot me in the heart, for example, it wouldn't kill me, at least not at that moment, since I felt in my body an infinite surge of uncontrollable power.

With doubts about my immortality diminishing by the second, I started to wonder what would happen if I leapt into space from the Café Blaise. I was so far gone I was quite capable of doing it. I looked at Kikí and she seemed distracted, observing the movements of some children as they played with balloons on the terrace. "Right now what I'd like," I told her, "is to throw myself into space and land on my feet, safe and sound, on the asphalt. Do you think with the strength of the acid I could manage a miracle like that? What do you think would happen if I did that, you think I'd kill myself?"

Kikí loved Indian philosophy and adored the musician Ravi Shankar; Katmandu was the center of her tormented hippy world and she often talked to me about certain crossroads with snow-covered mountains in the background, crossroads of different *spir-itual pathways of life* in which Buddhist wisdom would help you choose the one true way. Kikí was a fickle, slight and frivolous young woman I was hopelessly in love with until that day at the Eiffel Tower when I luckily started to get my first intimations of the existence of irony, an activity I believe sometimes endows us with a selfish prudence, fortunately inoculating us against sentimental exaltation. Thanks to irony—which allows us to avoid disappointment for the simple reason that it refuses to entertain any hopes—after that, I'd never get my hopes up about any Kikí—who today, incidentally, is a mother in Reims, as well as obese, alcoholic, and not at all Buddhist—thanks to irony I no longer get my hopes up. For a long time, my slogan has been a phrase from Cervantes which when applied, for example, to the now fat Kikí, leaves one in love with irony: "There is no heavier burden than a slight and fickle woman."

"You wouldn't kill yourself, you wouldn't die, you'd just go far away from Paris, but you wouldn't kill yourself," Kikí replied that day in a hypnotic and very persuasive tone. "Oh, really?" I said, somewhat puzzled. And she said: "You won't croak if you focus properly on the fall with the right karma, understand? You have to brake mentally in the air as you fall. If you do that, you might even land on your feet, you'll see." "But I wouldn't land on my feet on the ground in Paris?" I asked. "You'll land on your feet, but it won't be in Paris," she replied.

I was in love with her. I'd listened so closely to all the instructions she'd given me about how to act under the effects of LSD that I nearly threw myself confidently into space from the top of the Eiffel Tower. But at the last minute something stopped me believing I could mentally slow down my body as I fell. And that something—not just a timely intervention on the part of my natural intelligence—was the discovery that Kikí was monstrous, since she, knowing as she did that acid opens up dangerous breaches in the mind, was openly trying to get me to kill myself. I saw that not only did she not love me at all, but what she said was an attempt to get rid of me, perhaps because she wanted to make off with what little money I had in the garret, or perhaps simply, just as I'd suspected, because she found me odious. Luckily, irony came to my rescue at the last minute and endowed me with a selfish prudence, immunizing me against the murderous and persuasive voice of the terrible Kikí.

"I don't understand why you think leaving Paris would be advisable," I told her. "What?" she asked somewhat surprised, as if she hadn't expected me to still be there, perhaps she thought I was already dead. "Nothing," I said, "I just want you to know that eternity isn't that much longer than life." I spun on my heels and left, walked out of the Blaise and left her, left her forever, which is just a manner of speaking, because actually the callous Kikí had already left me months before. I went down in the elevator of the Eiffel Tower and shortly afterwards, in the street, at the crossroads, I went down a road that went beyond even the reality that had replaced the previous reality; I went, to the rhythm of acid, toward a different reality where time and space didn't exist: I went, in a manner of speaking, beyond the perpetual snows of Kilimanjaro; I went to the country where things have no name and there are no gods, no men, no world, where in the background there's only the abyss.

Many hours later, back in the garret, the drug's effect had almost worn off; I was looking distractedly at the ceiling when suddenly I shuddered in terror, as if at that precise instant I'd returned to normality, to reality. And I realized the seriousness of what had happened.

"Damn," I said in fright, "it's not every day someone tries to murder you."

41

Even though I'd come across a real assassin while writing about a lettered one, I rejected the idea of giving the narrator of my novel the look of the malicious Kikí. Oddly, a few days later, almost by pure chance, at a party at Marguerite's, I encountered the extremely perturbing look of a girl that seemed to me ideal for my femme fatale, my murderess.

We've all fallen prey to uttering hackneyed and schmaltzy phrases, referring to the previous night as "an unforgettable evening." But, at the end of life, only those who really haven't experienced unforgettable evenings are ridiculous, as Pessoa would say. I think I'll be spared from being ridiculous because I remember at least one evening that was truly unforgettable. A night in Marguerite Duras's house. A lively get-together, with many guests; I felt like I was in a film, as if I were in the reception room of the French vice-consul's house in Calcutta, since the music playing on the record player was the soundtrack to *India Song* composed by Carlos d'Alessio.

Among the guests, there was a young actress, with a face of absolute beauty, an actress not yet famous but who would be before long, a girl named Isabelle Adjani. She had just filmed *L'Histoire d'Adèle H* with Truffaut, but the film hadn't been released yet and on that day she wasn't yet a famous actress. I thought I could grow to like her more than my platonic love, more than Martine Simonet herself. But I didn't dare say a word to her the whole of that long evening. In fact, I barely spoke during the entire party, which was carried along, very animatedly, by Dyonis Mascolo, Edgar Morin (who sang several songs by Joan Manuel Serrat), and Duras. I spent the whole night naively waiting for Adjani to fall in love with me. And only at the end of the party, since this hadn't happened, did I resort to alcohol so I could dare say something; I drank three glasses of cognac in a row and finally, taking advantage of a brief lull in the general conversation, I said that if I were a film director I'd immediately hire Isabelle. I said it like someone writing a love letter, a ridiculous love letter. Then, after the huge effort this took for me, I sank back deep into the sofa. The ceiling fan spun, but as slowly as in a nightmare. Everyone looked at me and laughed thinking I'd spoken ironically, as everyone, except me, knew that she'd just finished filming with Truffaut. I didn't get it, I thought my brief intervention had gone down rather well, and then, with the help of the fourth cognac, I dared to look Adjani straight in the eye, trying to look at her as steadily and profoundly as possible.

At that moment, an ill-timed fly landed on my left eye and, having to swat it away, I looked away from her. Annoyed, I thought flies were always sticking their noses in where they weren't wanted. When I resumed my steady and profound gaze, I discovered at that precise instant Adjani was giving me a look as icy as it was terrifying. I was disabled for the rest of that unforgettable evening, as I saw with total clarity and horror that if those eyes could kill, not a soul would be left alive. But every cloud has a silver lining. I realized that, as compensation, I'd found the femme fatale for my book. Now I knew exactly what sort of look my *lettered assassin* would have.

"Thanks for being so gallant," Adjani said sarcastically. And everyone laughed a lot, as if they found it funny that the nightmarish ceiling fan was turning even more slowly.

42

Among the contributions drugs made to the construction of *The Lettered Assassin*, three stand out above the rest: 1) Grand questions about whether the visual reality accepted by common sense has anything to do with true reality. 2) The discovery of my taste for simulation and transvestism. That unforgettable, dangerous day in the Café Blaise, after the incident with Kikí, I walked home to my *chambre*, and once I was in it, many hours before I returned to normality and to reality, I realized I felt very bad about my body and also my bourgeois, corseted way of dressing and began to change my clothes frenetically, searching the mirror for a different presence from the usual one; I ended up dressed as Hemingway in his female version, that is, I dressed up as a little boy with a girl's blonde ringlets, just as Hemingway's mother dressed him when he was little, in pink gingham with a flowery hat, a look, by the way, that has always made me think that Ernest's entire virile-literary career can be read as an extreme reaction to the image of the effeminate mommy's boy. 3) The discovery of the fragility of my incipient writing, mainly attributable to my scant experience as a reader, which led me to decide, given that I could barely subsist on literary material (I had little reading experience), that I would draw sustenance from the visual, cinematographic lessons the drug had provided me.

Okay! Since this three-day lecture is an ironic review of the years of my youth in Paris, I can now find it very easy to laugh about the *non*-literary material that began to nourish *The Lettered Assassin* from that day on. Certainly an author who has come to the experience of writing after having imbibed the contents of the family library seems much more respectable than one who has begun to construct his literary edifice after an acid trip. The quality of my early poetics seems scant if, as I'm saying, it was basically sustained by a drug that simply widened my visual field of perception. And yet, I'm not sure now that I should reproach myself at all, rather quite the reverse. Because while it's true that later on I read quite a lot and my literary knowledge was strengthened, it's also true that LSD, by opening up my visual field, was not at the time by any means an insignificant source of inspiration. Besides, some of those perceptions of a distinct reality have lasted firmly and still today carry a highly remarkable energy, and are the reason I can laugh at realist writers, for example, who duplicate reality and so impoverish it.

43

A few days after the party with Isabelle Adjani at Duras's house, I was sitting calmly in the Flore waiting for Jeanne Boutade when the person at the next table, a young man who said he was called Yves, began talking to me just like that, in somewhat accelerated speech at first, but soon acquiring a slow and lucid rhythm. He went from asking me if I liked *croques-monsieur*—he scarcely heard my courteous reply—to talking about the neighborhood, Saint-Germain-des-Prés. He'd spent his whole life there, he told me. He was very fond of Rue Mazarine, where he'd been born. When he was a very young boy, Saint-Germain was still a provincial neighborhood. I looked at him quite carefully: I saw a sweet smile beneath curly hair and two myopic or worried eyes behind a pair of round glasses. He liked me, that seemed totally obvious. I entrusted my fate to Jeanne Boutade and hoped she'd be on time and help me escape, without offending Yves, from that small misunderstanding.

In two minutes we'd covered seven or eight different topics and I don't know how we settled on the subject of May '68. Just a few years had passed since those events, he said, but it felt like an eternity. I thought he was right about this. Since I'd arrived in Paris I'd barely thought, nor had it occurred to me to think, that I was in the city where, just a few years before, events had taken place, according to what I'd been able to read, that had convulsed the Western world. If I really thought about it, none of the people I spent time with talked about May '68. And besides, that student revolution mattered very little to me; I felt only a certain curiosity to know what had happened.

"Nothing happened," Yves told me. "Nothing?" I asked. "That's right, nothing. All I remember from it all is a feeling of great emotion as dawn broke, that day we thought the world was going to change," he said. "What sort of emotion?" I asked, sincerely interested. "We were on the barricades and no one was tired and it seemed like Paris was waking up from years of a dull and cretinous life. We had a very exciting moment of collective inspiration, started to sing Jacques Dutronc and that really seemed like the Revolution: *Il est cinq heures, Paris s'éveille ...*"

"And that was it?" I asked him. He became thoughtful, concentrating very hard. At that moment, as on so many other evenings at that hour, Roland Barthes walked into the Flore and quickly glanced around at the café fauna. Two steps behind him, and it even looked as if she was with him, came Jeanne Boutade, who quickly noticed my awkward situation with the man at the next table and, to give me a hand, she said that we had to get going if we didn't want to be late for the party Copi was having over in la Bastille. I stood up and gave a sign to the thoughtful and concentrating Yves to let him know I was leaving.

"The Revolution," he said then, with melancholy, "reminds me of the definition of life a family friend, Dr. Gottfried Benn, always used to give. Life, the doctor told us, lasts twenty-four hours and at most is just congestion."

44

It was raining and the wind was very strong, and in this violent mixture the New York air seemed like a shattered mirror. I was walking with Sonia Orwell down Park Avenue, near the building where Khrushchev used to stay when he went to the UN and in the middle of a general assembly, possibly loaded with vodka and humor, thumped his desk with his own shoe. Sonia Orwell and I walked slowly, as if it were a warm, calm day under a turquoise sky and the hard, slippery streets were long Caribbean beaches with pearly reflections.

I had seen Sonia Orwell, outside of that dream, only once in real life, one morning in Paris when, as I passed the third floor on my way down from the garret, I saw that Duras's door was ajar and thought my landlady must be lurking behind it, poised to ask for the rent I owed her for the umpteenth time.

Somewhat terrified, I tiptoed past the crack in the door, but it opened suddenly and I saw a strikingly beautiful older woman who was sweeping the hallway very happily and who looked at me. "Is Marguerite home?" I asked, flustered; I asked this because I thought I should say something. "No, she's gone out," the woman answered. "Will she be back soon?" She thought for a minute, smiling, she seemed to know me well, to know exactly who I was and even to know—as Big Brother would have—the precise amount of money

I owed to Marguerite. "Listen," she told me as she began sweeping the landing and the stairs, "no one goes very far when they know the joy of coming home again." Logically confused, wondering if this lady was suggesting I return to the garret, I decided to resume as soon as possible my habitual headlong rush down the stairs. Later, that night, Adolfo Arrieta told me the woman was Sonia Orwell, who was staying with Duras for a few days. I thought that one day I'd be able to tell my grandchildren that I saw George Orwell's wife sweeping a staircase.

But I don't have children, I won't have grandchildren. Instead of grandchildren, ladies and gentlemen, I have you. But I don't want you to think I'm just a man who saw Orwell's wife sweeping a staircase. You should stick with the dream about New York, it's more poetic.

45

A few days before I was born, in March 1948, Hemingway, who was approaching his fiftieth birthday and deep in a creative crisis, fell in love in Venice with an eighteen-year-old girl named Adriana Ivancich. "That merely imaginary love," she told me when I interviewed her at her home last year.

Fifty years is nothing, thought Hemingway, as the disconcerting birthday grew nearer. In those days, he had the impression he was washed up as a writer, but at the same time he resisted accepting this. Perhaps the fault lay with Cuba, living on that island. Needing to stimulate his creative imagination, put it into action, he left his fighting cocks and his daiquiris in the Floridita bar in Havana and returned to Europe, the center of the art world.

Venice became Hemingway's new mistress. He and his fourth wife, Mary, settled happily in the Venetian winter on the island of Torcello and later in Cortina. He shot duck and partridge; he tried to write. "He needed, though he did not yet know it, the rejuvenating spark of a relationship with a surrogate daughter—autumnal, deciduous, minimally tinged with the erotic, painfully delicious," wrote Anthony Burgess.

What is it about Venice that makes it the ideal place to fall in love? He found this surrogate daughter in an eighteen-year-old girl named Adriana Ivancich, soft-spoken, Catholic, devout, feminine, with the kind of femininity that was rapidly disappearing from America. He saw his attitude toward her as completely paternal, but turned her into the heroine of a novel, *Across the River and Into the Trees*, a dreadful novel, it has to be said, with a transparent plot: the story of an old soldier who knows he's going to die. He dies in Venice. The picture on the cover—not a very good one—was drawn by Adriana. When I went to see her last year, she explained that she'd burned all of Hemingway's letters because she was in love with a young man, who thought it a scandal that she had any kind of relationship with the old writer. "A young *innamorato*," she told me, "who threatened not to marry me if I didn't burn the letters. I've regretted destroying them so many times! And the worst of it is, do you know what? The young man ended up not marrying me."

Two years after the failure of the novel about the old soldier dying in Venice, Adriana also drew the picture—nothing special—for the cover of *The Old Man and the Sea*, and this time the young Italian brought Hemingway more luck, as the novel revived his reputation as a writer worldwide and contributed to his being awarded the Nobel Prize. Mary, Hemingway's fourth and last wife, always tolerated her husband's amorous adventures because she realized that he needed a young muse to go on. He won the Nobel Prize, but again felt washed up. When he was alone thinking of life and literature, he knew he was finished—with life and with novels—perhaps because Venice was behind him. He started to suffer a general physical and nervous deterioration. In 1960 he started work on a book of recollections called *A Moveable Feast*. He shut himself up in a very gloomy house, in an appalling house he owned in Ketchum, Idaho. You could see it was a house to die in.

When, after his suicide, *A Moveable Feast* was published, the book emerged as a kind of autobiography of his years of bohemia and literary education. In this book he says of Paris—and now this, unlike the abrupt end to his life, seems ironic—that there is never any end to it and "the memory of each person who has lived in it differs from that of any other. We always returned to it no matter who we were or how it was changed or with what difficulties, or ease, it could be reached. Paris was always worth it and you received a return for whatever you brought to it. But this is how Paris was in the early days when we were very poor and very happy."

Burgess regards the prose in this book as pure Hemingway, simple and very evocative, life-accepting, yet, as always in his work, touched by melancholy. It is a prose that speaks always of stoic endurance in the face of adversity. Although this endurance would end up shattered by a shot to the head, his melancholy melody is youthful. And his book about Paris blows like a hurricane-force wind into the minds of young men and women just starting to write. It is a book for future writers.

"That *brutto* shot!" Adriana Ivancich said last year when I went to see her, "I would have liked to have done something for him, but distance and indecision, you know what I mean, prevented me. And to think that young suitor, my *innamorato*, didn't even marry me, the fool."

Not knowing how to end my visit to Adriana—the conversation with her felt like Paris, there was never any end to it, and I knew I had to leave before it was too late—I told her I didn't know if she'd ever thought of it, but even the worst of Hemingway's writing reminds us that to commit oneself to literature one has first to commit oneself to life. I thought this might make her cry, but to tell the truth she didn't, among other things because she didn't understand a word of what I'd said. I decided to leave as soon as I could. And then she said something with the intention of making *me* cry. "Now I'm as old as my father, who's dead." I decided not to delay my departure any further. I kissed her hand ceremoniously and left.

I remembered a phrase I'd heard my mother say many times: "One has to know how to swim just well enough to avoid having to save anyone else."

46

I wasn't prepared for failure or, to put it a better way, I knew that, when failure arrived, I wouldn't be able to endure it. Perhaps because of this I did everything I could not to finish *The Lettered Assassin* and thus delay the arrival of the beginning of the end, the arrival of a foreseeable disaster. Though I was writing, I was afraid to write (especially afraid of finishing my book), I suspected this would lead me straight to failure. Similiarly, though I slept with women, in general I was afraid of doing so, afraid they'd find me sexually timid, disappointing. I was afraid of writing and of women. Irony would have helped me but, since I was scarcely acquainted with it, there was nothing it could do for me. Irony would have been perfect for de-dramatizing it all and letting me laugh at myself, reducing the intensity of my fear of writing and women. I'm sure that irony would have increased my self-confidence. But I scarcely knew what it was. Nevertheless, I was given an unexpected hand by some transvestite friends, who were able to point me in the direction of irony as well as to lessen my fear of women.

I remember very well the somewhat contemptible way my mind worked in those days: I became convinced that, as incredible as it might seem, there were beings in the world even more fragile than my feeble self, there were some people who needed my help and attention, and these people were none other than the neighborhood transvestites. It was that simple, and that strange. That's what brought me close to Marie-France, Vicky Vaporú, Amapola, and Jeanne Boutade. I will never forget them; they were a great help to me unbeknownst to them. This contemptible but useful feeling of believing myself necessary to them—attributable to the moral poverty of youth—ended up giving me self-confidence. I used to go over to my transvestite friends' houses and, if they had a problem, I would advise them what to do. In exchange they advised me, too, and helped me take a step forward, to know how to be less scared around women. After all, they thought of themselves as more womanly than women.

For a few months—the time it took to film *Tam Tam*, Adolfo Arrieta's underground film, the film with the most transvestites per square foot in the history of cinema—most of my social interaction was with transvestites. The filming contributed to an increase not only in my confidence with women, but also in my writing, since day after day Arrieta's aesthetic facilitated all kinds of happy discoveries for me, the lively cinematographic raw material that ended up being useful for creating my literary world, for creating *The Lettered Assassin*: mirror games, changes of appearance (applied even to the text itself), the erotics of transformation and, above all, my poetic prose viewed as a celebration. In fact, Arrieta's whole film was a party. It begins with a few scenes in New York in which the camera of the legendary filmmaker Jonas Mekas focuses on the small *journal* of a young writer (Javier Grandes) who is expected at a party in Paris. The party lasts as long as the film does. *Tam Tam* is the story of this continuous, boundless party, which takes place without interruption in Paris, by way of the south of Spain (Marbella), in an apartment of all apartments: that house in Paris where everyone is waiting for Grandes, who, being in New York, doesn't show up, but is thoughtful enough to send his twin brother.

When it premiered, the film was seen, perhaps somewhat rashly, as a *cinéma-verité* feature on the world of the new generation of bohemian artists of Saint-Germain-des-Prés. "The audience," declared Arrieta, "thinks everything in the film is real and say it's a snob's film as do the critics. However, those very *chic* ladies who walk around among young millionaires are mostly transvestites. After filming with me, they go and perform in the show at the Carrousel cabaret."

What Arrieta was actually making was punk cinema in the French style, and with its apparent excess of realism he was years ahead even of his compatriot Almodóvar. "An excess of realism. In the transvestite there is an enhanced femininity (women imitate *them*), but Arrieta just directs them as actresses, without insisting on excessive cosmetics or the easily flamboyant aspects of the situation," Severo Sarduy wrote about the film.

The central nucleus, festive Paris, was filmed in several Parisian houses that pretended to be just one, so that the shooting of *Tam Tam* was in some ways a huge traveling *fiesta* and the film could easily have been given the title of Hemingway's book, *A Moveable Feast*. In this film not even the lighthearted plot was what it seemed to be. Being involved as an actor helped me lose some of my fear of writing and of women, and so my terror of failure gradually decreased, you could say my fear of failure in the aspects of life I considered most important gradually decreased the intensity of my fear of total failure. Although failure hadn't yet arrived, why should I kid myself, I knew that sooner or later it would. All I had to do was finish the novel.

47

The memory of Bouvier the bohemian surfaces clearly today from my dark past as an apprentice lover and novice writer. It's a clear, sunny morning, it must be March 1974, not long since I arrived in the city; it's cold. Barthes hasn't gone to China yet. I feel like going for a walk. I put on my raincoat and my checked scarf and go down the stairs of my building three steps at a time and land in the street and there come face to face with an elderly man with noble features and a white beard. "A fog has descended over me," the old man says. I think he must be crazy, and he seems to read my thoughts: "I'm not crazy, I'm a former resident of this building, that's all. Many years ago I lived up there," he points more or less to where I live, "and there I came to a halt as an artist." I try to leave him behind, but he follows me. "Allow me to introduce myself," he says, "I am Bouvier the bohemian, up there I tried and failed to be an artist." He looks at me as if with pity, as if he knows I live high up there where he was unhappy. "Up there I came to a halt," he repeats. "All right, now I know," I tell him, and again try to escape. "What I mean is that this building has a strange atmosphere, a weird vibe, one's fuses get blown in there, one fails, I've ended up as Bouvier the bohemian because of this house," he tells me. Over time, I have retained above all the phrase about it being a place where one's fuses get blown, and in fact it turned out to be a premonition of what was going to happen. When he said it though, I thought the phrase was something that didn't concern me, just the words of a madman. But madmen do often predict the truth.

48

I went one Sunday to Neauphle-le-Château, invited by Duras to her country house, and I remember that after lunch, an hour before she told me the plot of *The Afternoon of Monsieur Andesmas*, we went up to the third-floor loft where, scattered across the floor, were the translations of her books, she had too many and didn't know who to give them to, but she didn't want to throw them out; she hadn't found any better place for them than this loft. Marguerite began to give me copies of the Spanish translations and to ask me my opinion on Carlos Barral, her publisher in Barcelona. I knew hardly anything about Barral, and so I simply resisted this question she pressed, repeating it over and over again, up there in the loft, while I began to imagine that in a large chest, in this place, I found, stained with damp, the manuscript of *The Lettered Assassin*, happily already finished and translated into several languages, actually written by Duras but published under my name (that was one more way of trying to overcome my fear of publishing), which, when the book came out, would bring me a certain renown as a *succès d'estime*.

This pretentious daydream with its mixture of laziness, terror and a certain idea of success, couldn't have been more wretched—it certainly is wretched to want someone to write your book for you—but curiously, despite its detestable character, the dream managed to push me towards serious reflection. I suddenly began to fear that the damp stains on the manuscript in the chest might erase the words that were to lead to my success. Suddenly, thanks to my literal belief in those stains and in that dream and, therefore, in my imagination, I began to reflect—an activity I didn't engage in excessively back then—and I remember as if it were happening now, coming down the central staircase of the house in Neauphle-le-Château, in marked contrast to the picaresque dream of the loft—as if arising precisely from that immense contrast—I thought I perceived the full power of the written word, and this led me, by way of a rather involved shortcut, to sense its importance as a means of acquiring a certain distance from what people called reality, which is—as it has always been for such a great number of young people—actually a very disappointing thing. I thought I suddenly perceived, coming down those stairs, the need I had for words and also the need for these to be useful to me so I could distance myself from the real world. On those stairs, I definitely began to turn into a real writer. But as I still had no access to irony, words could do little for me that day, although I didn't know it then, precisely because of my lack of a sense of irony. I was like the serpent that bites its own tail. Being young is certainly rather complicated, though this doesn't mean one should go around in despair, far from it. Of course maturity isn't so great either. When you're mature, true, you understand irony. But you're not young any more and the only possibility of remaining so lies in resisting, with the passage of time, not relinquishing that damp chest I imagined so vividly in Neauphle-le-Château. You can resist, and not be like those who—as the intensity of their youthful imagination gradually diminishes—accommodate to reality and worry for the rest of their lives. You can only try and be one of the stubbornest, keeping faith in imagination for longer than other people. To mature with obstinacy and resistance: to mature, for example, by giving a three-day lecture on the irony of not having been aware of irony as a young man. And then to grow old, very old, and tell irony to go to hell, but cling pathetically to it so as not to end up with nothing, and be the horrifying target of the irony of others.


### 49


A couple of lines from Gil de Biedma: "Now, let me tell you / how I too was in Paris, and I was happy. / It was in the heyday of my youth …" It seems it's always been generally assumed that young artists who go to Paris live an interesting bohemian existence, they go through hardships but ultimately come out on top thanks to the city itself, which is hospitable, free, and marvelous. But there are very tragic cases that contradict this idea. There is the Uruguayan short story writer Horacio Quiroga, for example, who went to Paris and instead of looking at his future with hope, plunged into the deepest despair. Luckily, I never found out about his case while I was living in Paris. Luckily, since it could have been catastrophic, as I would have felt even more encouraged in my fictitious despair.

There never being any end to Paris must have been for Quiroga, unlike for Hemingway, a real nightmare. Look at what the unfortunate Quiroga wrote in his diary: "What great anguish! There are moments when I almost weep. And for this to happen to me in Paris, without a single person to talk to! Each day that passes, instead of bringing more hope, is darker." He wrote this in his diary, where later on we find some sentences that are the exact opposite of Hemingway's notion that the memory of Paris is a feast that follows us around. Quiroga writes that the only thing capable of quieting his thoughts of suicide is an idea producing a new emotion, one which in theory should distance him from the memory of his time in Paris, yet not only doesn't distance him, but, he also senses, won't allow him to lose sight of it, even with the final pistol shot, since "even then, I tell you, I will have the horror or the memory of Paris."

50

More on despair. One day, Raúl Escari and I were sitting in the dangerous Café Blaise, at the top of the Eiffel tower. It was aperitif time, if I remember correctly. I decided to read him something Perec said in his book *Species of Spaces*: "There is something frightening in the very idea of a city; you have the impression you can fasten only onto tragic or despairing images." I asked Raúl what he thought of the sentence and he shrugged his shoulders. Then it occurred to me to say, "I hope things will get better soon." There was despair in my words, but also a certain degree of histrionics. Raúl smiled. "This means you believe there's hope," he said. "And isn't there?" I asked him. "Well of course there is, but not for us," he replied.

I reminded him of this brief dialogue when he called me this August in Paris after a mutual friend gave him the number of my hotel. As always he called from Montevideo, from Quiroga's country, as it happens. He called from the usual place, from the phone booth near the house where Lautréamont was born. He remembered absolutely nothing of this conversation about hope. "I'm calling from the phone booth—not from hope," he said, trying, I suppose, to let me know with this sentence (absurd, incomplete, but well suited to his purposes) that he wasn't interested in this topic of hope and, what's more, that a lot of time had passed since we'd spoken about it. "You know, I'm trying to remember and write down the conversations we had in Paris?" I told him. Silence. "Are you still in the phone booth?" I asked. "And what are you doing that for?" he suddenly answered. So then I told him I was preparing a three-day lecture in which I was ironically reviewing the years I spent in Paris. "And you talk about me the whole time?" he said, "Well, yeah," I replied, "but mainly about irony, about Paris, about Hemingway, about Marguerite Duras, and about how I wrote my first book." Another silence. "So, it's a lecture that's something like an auto-biography of bohemia and your years of literary apprenticeship in Paris," he said all of a sudden. "Well, yeah," I answered, "though I didn't really learn that much." "It sounds good," he said. "Among the many fictions possible, an autobiography can also be a fiction." Another silence followed. "But try," he added, "to be as truthful as you can, so you can be seen as you *really* are. And, if possible, por-tray me as I'm really not."

51

Sometimes at dusk, if I'd gone for a walk in the relaxing Jardin du Luxembourg, I made a detour before going back to my neighbor-hood to walk past the house where Gertrude Stein had an apart-ment in the 1920s, to walk by number 27 Rue de Fleurus. I wasn't going there, as Hemingway did, "for the warmth and the great pic-tures and the conversation" he found in that house, but because I thought it could bring me luck, since after all Miss Stein, in her role as patron, had been for Hemingway what Marguerite Duras—I as-sumed—was for me. As the more or less ambitious young man that I was, I aspired to have not a single but double patronage, and so I saw a possible talisman during my ritual of occasionally walking past that house and stopping to read the plaque, which reminded people that the place had been one of the hubs of world literature, but neglected to inform them that the great geniuses who came vis-iting here sometimes had to hear "a rose is a rose is a rose," one of Miss Stein's favorite phrases and irrefutable proof that even in the world's literary hubs, people have always talked nonsense.

"A dreadful writer," those who erected the commemorative plaque could also have added. Because Gertrude Stein, American exile who attempted to purify the English language and administer aesthetic shocks through an excessive simplification of language (forcing the reader to look at the outside world as if for the first time), was a terrible writer though she did impart some interesting teaching to the young Hemingway. She is the one who advised him to dispense with every kind of embellishment in his prose and to compress, concentrate, in short, destroy the old rhetoric by means of parody. In fact, without realizing it, she'd advised her disciple Hemingway to do what James Joyce had just done in an exemplary way in *Ulysses*.

When Hemingway read Joyce's book, months after receiving this advice, he called it: "a goddamn wonderful book." It was the only time he'd be able to say this in that house, as Miss Stein told him straightaway that if he brought up Joyce a second time in that room, he would not be invited back. But in any case his praise of *Ulysses* came to the attention of Ezra Pound, a friend of Joyce's, who decided to read the young Hemingway and saw great talent in him and encouraged him and ended up receiving boxing lessons in exchange.

I walked past the commemorative plaque at 27 Rue de Fleurus at dusk, sometimes fearing the spirit of Miss Stein would discover that I, seeking to give my text *verisimilitude*, had shifted most of page seven of the Spanish edition of *Giacomo Joyce* (a personal notebook by the author of *Ulysses*) into *The Lettered Assassin*, where in the introduction to the central manuscript, I mentioned the assassin's illustrated notebook, saying that "numbers in brackets indicate the pages of the notebook, and the text and drawings correspond page for page to the original"—on page seven of *Giacomo Joyce* something very similar can be read.

Since I'd based my text on a real notebook, Joyce's, I thought it would appear more realistic. There was no doubt I still had a very shaky idea of what verisimilitude really was, something that makes real novelists sweat the darkest blood. However, seen from the perspective of the present, I guess it was better than nothing. I remember how satisfied I felt believing I'd resolved without too much difficulty one of the items of that brusque instruction list Duras had given me for writing a novel. Clearly (I said to myself) I've still got to tackle some of the hardest items on the list, such as unity and harmony, time, style, not to mention narrative technique, which must be frightful.

I walked past that house on Rue de Fleurus at dusk sometimes and wished that doing so would bring me luck. It never did, at least while I remained in Paris, and so this August, when I went back again to see the talismanic house, I looked at the commemorative plaque, thought of Gertrude Stein and of the luck she didn't bring me and of the fear I once had that her spirit would discover my modest connection to Joyce, and I also thought of, or rather remembered, the problems I had in those days with unity, harmony, let's not even mention style or time. And on this occasion I gave vent to my feelings, saying out loud, risking being taken for a madman: "Miss Stein, are you there, can you hear me? Look, look closely at me, I'm Hemingway. Can you see me? *Ulysses* is goddamn wonderful goddamn wonderful goddamn wonderful ... Can you hear me, Miss Stein?"

## 52

One morning, I saw Jean Seberg *in real life*. She had her hair cut very short (like a Hemingway heroine), and was wearing sunglasses and a white dress with black polka dots. I saw her walk quickly past in front of one of the neoclassical pediments in the Palais de Chaillot where, in gilded letters, some solemn phrases by Paul Valéry are inscribed, written especially for this place and that suddenly, next to the quick step of the beautiful Seberg, seemed to have found their true meaning: *It depends on those who pass whether I am tomb or treasure.*

53

I called my mother once a month, always from the phone booth—specially equipped for long-distance calls—in the basement of the Relais Odéon, a café on the Boulevard Saint-Germain. It was a quick call I made monthly seeking to assuage my conscience. I thought that going for more than a month without speaking to her, without showing signs of life, would be unnatural in a son, would be taking things too far. But in reality she didn't care if I called or not, and I knew this perfectly well. Unlike my father (who wanted me to come back to Barcelona), she was indifferent about what I tried to make of my life. What's more, she thought I was a dull, gray creature, and she'd never kept this to herself, but instead—as if it amused her—had told me so on many occasions, intending to humiliate me, I think. She'd told me so—always when my father wasn't there—in many different ways, with all kinds of variations, one day she even compared me to Paris: "Son, you're grayer than Paris."

She didn't care whether I was in that city or not. She was a woman whose mind was on other things. Such as, for example, adding up all the numbers she saw. Some people read everything they see, even newspaper pages blowing down the street. She added up numbers. For instance, there were some people she never called on the phone because their numbers added up to something unlucky. She refused hotel rooms for the same reason. She didn't like the sum of the year I'd been born and perhaps for that reason made an effort not to feel too much affection for me, she was always finding reasons for me not to matter to her at all.

I called her from Paris when I knew my father wasn't at home and we exchanged four or five words and the conversation was generally cold, above all very strange, and not because I was—though indeed I was—but because my mother—I think this is now clear—has always been very much so, has always been hugely eccentric. In case it's still not completely clear: she couldn't stand there to be three cigarette butts in the same ashtray, screamed if she saw a loose button, wouldn't travel on a plane if there were two nuns on board, and she couldn't start or finish anything on a Friday. As if that wasn't enough, she never turned off faucets all the way. This last thing, by the way, was frankly exasperating.

My mother couldn't care less that I was in Paris, but one day, during one of those monthly calls, her attitude changed. It only happened once and perhaps for that reason became engraved in my memory. Not until years later did I find out that her strange attitude was due to the fact that my father had come home early that day and she found herself suddenly obliged to play the role of worried mother on the phone and to tell me I must come home to Barcelona and give up my bohemian whims, this "ridiculous liter-ary promise." That day at the other end of the line, I couldn't have been more confused, and that call remained in my memory as the strangest of all those I made from Paris. It was a city she knew well, since in her early youth she'd spent a few brief spells there, which only served to turn her into a person who occasionally said strange things, things that, before she married, my grandmother had been obliged so many times to explain away good-humoredly to visitors: "The child, you see, has lived in Paris," my grandmother would say. "Oh, well, that's understandable. If she's lived in Paris ..." the visi-tors would say in a half teasing, half affectionate tone.

"You're like a broken record," I remember she said to me suddenly that day (coinciding, I later found out, with the arrival of my father in the house), "always boasting about Paris, Paris, but what exactly do you see in Paris?" I was surprised; I remember I was about to tell her that I walked through the streets of that city with my heart be-wildered by sadness, but I didn't dare say anything. "What a disgrace for me," continued my mother, "to see my son turned into a broken record." She fell suddenly silent. When this happened, it was a sign that she was about to come out with one of her eccentric phrases, one of those things she'd picked up in Paris and which were often touched by a strange genius. As happened that day when she said: "Always Paris, Paris, you're like a broken record in a city that's ... full of broken lines. Look at the Eiffel tower, it's nothing but broken lines. Broken lines on the French bigshots' pants, broken lines on the concierges' foreheads, lines and lines. And you're the biggest broken record of all. You need to reconsider the broken life you're leading."

My mother was a woman of curious intuitions and strange strokes of genius. What has impressed me for a long time about what she said that day about Paris and its broken lines is the strange similarity to something Kafka wrote that I discovered not long ago … and that my mother would certainly never have read, for one reason because she never read anything and I don't believe she even knew of the existence of Kafka, that fleeting twentieth-century stranger, a man who saw a Paris much like the one my mother saw and wrote in his diaries: "Paris is striped … the lined glass roof of the Grand Palais des Arts, the office windows divided by lines, the Eiffel tower, made of lines, the lined effect of the side and central panels of the French windows on opposite balconies, the little chairs and tables in front of the cafés, with lines for legs, the gold-tipped railings in the public parks."

Kafka's "striped" Paris. I'd be more inclined to agree with Walter Benjamin, who in *The Arcades Project* saw Paris as the city of mirrors: "The asphalt of its streets, smooth as a mirror, and above all the glass-walled terraces in front of each café. A profusion of mirrors in the cafés to brighten the interiors and lend an agreeable spaciousness to all the booths and all the tiny nooks of every Parisian establishment. Women look at themselves here more than elsewhere, and this is where the specific beauty of Parisian women comes from."

My mother. My loopy mother. A character and a genius. I loved her, but she didn't love me. In any case, it upset me when she died. She spent the last years of her life more neurotic than ever, trusting everything to some little Moorish charms she'd bought in Granada. On her deathbed, in front of me and my father and two of her brothers she hadn't seen for years, she said a few words of farewell, a few last words that, due to their premeditated strangeness, sounded to me like an epitaph, though we didn't dare put them on her tombstone. "I'll laugh at the bitter things I said," she said. Her two brothers looked dismayed. "It's because she lived in Paris," I told them.

54

"You've come here to Paris ready to forge your own style, isn't that right?" Marguerite Duras asked me one day, in a treacherous, sombre tone. At first I chose to think I'd heard wrong, that she'd spoken in her *superior* French and had actually said something else. But no, she'd said exactly that. She repeated it and I realized I'd understood perfectly. I remembered that *style* was one of the entries on her list. I remembered when we were already in my car, a Seat 127. I'd agreed to drive the vehicle for the first time in many months. I had it eternally parked in front of my house—maybe I should say in front of Marguerite's house—because one of the front headlights was missing and I didn't know where to get it fixed or how much it would cost, but that day I'd agreed to drive the car because I'd bumped into Marguerite in the street and to my surprise she'd asked me—in fact, almost ordered me—to go with her to the Bois de Boulogne to see if it was true there were prostitutes there at night wearing First Communion dresses. She'd just read as much in *L'Express* and thought it insulting, an intolerable disregard for feminine dignity. If it was true there were prostitutes dressed that way, she was going to write an article somewhere, it was unacceptable. I got into the driver's seat, absolutely resigned to my tough luck, since I imagined that, due to the absence of one headlight, I would immediately have trouble with the traffic police (although strangely I didn't).

Those words of Marguerite's about my style are still ringing in my ears today. "I have no style," I finally told her after holding back from replying for a good long while. By then we were already driving through the Bois de Boulogne. We spent a long time driving around and found nothing. After an hour, tired of this wild goose chase, I said very politely but on the verge of losing my grip: "We've combed the woods twenty times now, and there aren't any First Communion whores, that seems obvious."

"And why are you missing a headlight?" she asked me then. "Because I don't know how to fix it or how much it would cost," I replied. She suddenly saw a symbol in my missing headlight. "You could say that, like so many young men, you've got a one-headlight style," and she laughed, coughed, laughed again, then repeated that I had a one-headlight style. Though I'd understood her perfectly, I chose to believe she was speaking her *superior* French. I pretended to pay great attention to the steering wheel and the truth is I would have loved to find a prostitute at that moment, just one, dressed for First Communion and put an end to the annoying subject of my literary style once and for all. An hour and a half spent going back and forth and all around the Bois de Boulogne and we still hadn't found what we were looking for, so we ended up having a couple of glasses of port in the bar of La Coupole—whenever I went there this is what I drank. And there she asked me if I wanted to hear Queneau's advice. I was about to reply when she said she wasn't going to give it to me, since it wouldn't do me any good. And she went on to make an extremely complicated remark to do with the missing headlight, and from then on spent the rest of the night speaking to me in her *superior* French and I barely understood another word she said.

Style! For many years I saw *The Lettered Assassin* as the work of a writer who was a stranger to me, cold and barely connected to life: something, moreover, not all that strange if we take into consideration that all I was thinking of was the death of my readers. Now I think I know why my first book has always seemed cold to me. I think it's due to the total lack of style. In those days I had no idea that, as Gide said, the great secret of works with style—the great secret of Stendhal, for example—consists of writing *on the spot*. Gide says of Stendhal that his style, what we might call the malice of his style, consists in his stirring thought being so alive, so freshly colored, like a newly hatched butterfly (the collector is surprised to see it emerge from the chrysalis). From this comes Stendhal's vivid, spontaneous, unconventional touch, sudden and naked, that captivates us again and again.

I think that in my first foray into literature, in *The Lettered Assassin*, I dissociated form from content too much, and emotion from the expression of emotion and thought, and these should be inseparable. Emotion and thought should always be inseparable, the reader should witness *live* thoughts stirred by emotions in the creation of a text.

Rare are the moments in youth when one writes with a stirring thought.

## 55

As far as I know there's never been a novice writer worthy of the title who hasn't worried about style. The following night, after that outing with Marguerite, I was walking around agonizing over the subject of style when I ran into Raúl Escari outside the Pommeraye cinema. There was a long line of people trying to get in to see the film of the rock opera *Tommy*. I knew one thing for sure that night, and I knew it as surely as everyone else in Paris: it wouldn't be long before it rained. Style, on the other hand, was something that seemed confusing, although something else was also certain: in trivial matters, style, not sincerity is essential. And, in important matters, style is also essential. To sum up: it's always very important. But what exactly is style? Is it essentially the way one has of smoking a pipe, for example? When I asked Raúl his opinion, he looked at me in annoyance and quoted Wilde: "Sin should be solitary, and have no accomplices." I turned the phrase over and over. Perhaps he'd wanted to point out that those who seek their own style should know that seeking it is hardly a subtle way of achieving it, since to achieve it all they have to do is be themselves. I played dumb, to see if I could get more information out of Raúl. "Is style a sin?" I asked. More and more people were gathering outside the Pommeraye and we decided to leave, walking in the direction of Rue Mouffetard. "The writers of the future will be dry, not very eloquent, Great Style will seem like a stodgy Easter cake to them," said Raúl suddenly. And then, not long afterwards, he added somewhat enigmatically: "Being constipated is the future of style." When we got to Rue Mouffetard, we went into Café Robin. And then Raúl, seeing how I was as disconcerted as I was anxious to know more about the subject, added, almost pityingly: "Look, it's raining or maybe even snowing and you want to tell me that. How do you do it? Well, you say: it's raining, it's snowing. That's style. Right?" Not even he could imagine the harm he was doing me with his wit. And the fact is, as the French maxim goes, there is no one so intelligent they can know all the harm they do.

56

In the deafness of eternal sleep, we are not importuned by Glory.

— MARCEL PROUST

And immortality? Did immortality count for nothing? Marguerite hadn't included it in her list. Why not? Should one not write with maximum ambition, always aspiring to create a masterpiece, an immortal work? Why hadn't she advised ambition? Did she see me as incapable of reaching immortality? It must have been common sense that made her leave it out; in the same way, intuition, genius, wisdom, and sensitivity weren't on the list either.

When I managed to see this, I calmed down. How could she recommend immortality to me? But still I was left with a strange feeling, a bitter aftertaste. Whenever I saw her, I felt *mortal*. One day, I mentioned this to Raúl. He didn't seem surprised by what I'd said. He became thoughtful, and I waited to hear what he had to say. As a little time passed and he was still thinking, I asked him what he was thinking. "That the glow of our names ends on our tombstones," he said.

57

Character is formed on Sunday afternoons.              – RAMÓN EDER

On Sunday afternoons I always felt very lonely. The neighborhood, in contrast, changed a great deal and filled with strangers, visitors from the outskirts of the city or even from the provinces who looked bored as they window-shopped in legendary, albeit closed, Saint-Germain. There was no way I'd run into anyone I knew in the cafés, and every Sunday I was overcome by a feeling of great unhappiness, I spent them waiting for the next day when it would be Monday again and everything could return to some sort of normality. Many Sunday afternoons, I went to the bookstore in the basement of the Saint-Germain drugstore and looked at books. Occasionally, as if to justify the long hours I spent there killing time—*fazer horas*, as the Portuguese say—I ended up buying a paperback book that blew my weekly budget. I was bored and I knew it, I looked at the same books ten, twenty times.

"Life is short, and even so we get bored," said Jules Renard.

Some Sundays I had the impression I was *killing time* so I could go back to Barcelona and tell people I'd lived in Paris. One day, towards the end of a Sunday evening when it was clear it would snow before too long, I saw in that bookstore in the drugstore someone from Barcelona I knew, the psychiatrist Alicia Roig, watching me. I thought she'd discovered my boredom and most of all that she'd seen I was alone and didn't know what to do in Paris. I tried to hide, but I knew it was useless because she'd seen me. I saw her approaching and blushed. "You live in Paris, don't you?" she asked in a friendly tone. I was totally convinced she'd realized how lonely and bored I was. I blushed even more. "Someone's waiting for me, excuse me, I think I've got to go," I said in a brusque, sharp way. "You only think you do?" she asked, smiling. I bought a paperback and had them wrap it for me as if it were a present. I bought the first one I saw and she found it strange I should be interested in the work of Afanasi Golopupenko. I had no idea who that writer was. "I think it's going to snow," I told her and left.

That encounter cut me to the quick. Shortly afterwards, at night, in the garret, I went to pieces. I bent over the typed pages of *The Lettered Assassin* and burst into tears. I felt more lonely and vulnerable than ever. The moon, shining through the small window, was reflected in the room's mirror, doubtless hung there to give the false and very Parisian illusion that the room was bigger than it was. The moon, dazzling me, seemed to be trying to get me to look out the window and see if it was snowing. I stood up, left my nocturnal desk. I looked and saw that snow was falling over Paris. I spent a long time contemplating the serene, slow, silent spectacle. When the monotony of the snow started to seem unbearable, I remembered that someone once thought how monotonous snow would be if God hadn't created crows.

## 58

One winter's evening, in the garret, as I was writing, I felt as if Elena Villena, one of the characters in *The Lettered Assassin*, was standing behind me dictating what I should say about her. "I'm not a lesbian," I heard her say clearly. I turned around and didn't see her, but I had the impression she'd just vanished a split second before. "Well, now you're going to be a lesbian forever," I told her. There was no reply. I loved knowing I had enough authority to stop my characters from rebelling, knowing that what had happened to Unamuno in *Mist*, what we'd heard about so often in school couldn't or shouldn't happen to me. And the fact is what I liked most about being a writer was the freedom I experienced in the solitude of my garret. A freedom far removed from the patriarchal and authoritarian world of family and politics I'd left behind in Barcelona. I hadn't turned myself into a writer and a free man in Paris so that some little lady, invented by me after all, could come and ruin everything with her whims and orders.

So from the start I was sure—and that's strange in itself, because I was sure of almost nothing from the start—that writers, through a certain mental effort, had to walk, as it were, all over their characters, and not let their characters walk all over them. I told myself it was essentially a matter of discipline and also of good manners and above all something related to the confidence a reader might have in us. And I think I was right. Because tell me now, ladies and gentlemen, wouldn't you lose confidence in me and wouldn't you think it chaotic and bad-mannered and a remarkable nuisance if, for instance, all of a sudden Marguerite Duras came back from the other world and walked among us and complained about the things I make her say here, and demanded I fix my car's headlight once and for all and demanded all those months' rent, and if I apologized to her, fixed the headlight and paid my debt?

With my first book, then, I learned—more through instinct than anything else—not to let my characters control me; but most of all, if I really learned anything in Paris—I'm not trying to be ironic—it was how to type. Before the garret I hadn't really been trained in the constant and monotonous use of the keys. As for style, I carried on after my first book still without a style of my own, that's the truth. It was more or less the same as when I'd arrived in Paris. I still hadn't much style, despite all the effort I made with the pipe and despair. I suspected that by killing off my readers, I was never going to find anyone who would love me, but I never fully comprehended that it was unnecessary to kill readers *textually*. The thing is that style consists precisely in bringing them to life, instead of killing them off, in addressing new readers with the greatest clarity and simplicity possible, no matter how strange what you want to say might be.

It took me a long time to understand—if I really do understand—what Stendhal realized as he was writing *The Charterhouse of Parma*. He decided that to achieve the correct tone, no matter how strange what he wanted to say might be, so his readers would understand exactly what he was trying to say, he needed, every now and then, to read a few pages of the Civil Code. "If I am not clear," he wrote, "*my whole world* is annihilated."

59

Since the garret had a tiny, repulsive communal bathroom on the landing and no shower, I took a long ride on the metro once a week, with a towel, to wash in the public baths in Austerlitz station, precisely where all the trains from my city arrived, a fact that filled me with a rather huge fear of being discovered by friends or acquaintances from Barcelona just arriving in Paris. Few things terrified me more than the possibility of one of them catching sight of me, that someone might suddenly see me with my lowly bath towel and discover the non-idyllic conditions in which I was preparing to be a great artist like Hemingway. Of course, one day, what I most feared happened. I heard my name, looked around to see who'd called me, and it was Antonio Miró, now a famous fashion designer, and then the owner of Groc, the beloved clothing boutique, on the Rambla de Cataluña in Barcelona.

Luckily, he saw me after my shower, not before. "What are you doing here looking so neat and tidy?" he asked me. I took a few seconds to react and I think my answer was cunning. "I have a date," I said, winking. "Goodness. What a schemer. You've brought a towel and everything," he replied.

Those long trips on the metro to have a shower always belonged to the world of the absurd, above all the journeys back to the garret, so ridiculous after the useless wash, since, after traveling back on the metro, I returned home as dirty as I'd been when I'd left. And on top of that, always worried that someone would be waiting for me at the door and would see me show up with my miserable towel and dirty face.

And the fact is that friends from the neighborhood sometimes came up to the garret to say hello, others to pry, and some, those who'd come from Barcelona, to attempt—I didn't usually allow it—to stay the night. Young Petra was one of the latter. In her case, I made an exception and said she could stay. I wasn't exactly fighting off women and her visit was a gift from the heavens. I'd slept with her several times in Barcelona, in fact she was the last girlfriend I'd had before leaving the city (I kept this a secret, since she was unattractive, and working-class). I thought she was horrendous, but that was precisely what turned me on so much. That, and the fact that she was the daughter of factory workers from the furthest outskirts of Barcelona, which turned me on even more, among other things because, unlike the girls of my own social class, sleeping with her filled me with less fear of relative or total sexual failure. With her I felt less tense and more uninhibited in bed and was able to learn as a lover, always with the advantage that, if I didn't rise to the occasion, no one from my social circle would find out and I could happily carry on with my sexual insecurities.

Young Petra knocked at the door and a few seconds later was walking around naked in front of me, her body blocking the big photo of Virginia Woolf cut out from a French magazine I'd hung up as a poster. Sitting on the mattress on the floor where I slept, I spent a long time observing Petra. It felt like we were in a brothel, though I soon saw that wasn't true, since in the brothels I'd seen in films, a vast stretch of mirrored floor consigned a female nude to an almost sacred distance; whereas, in the garret, between the four walls of such a meager room, the proximity of the nude, the closeness of stark-naked Petra bordered on aggression, though this was interesting, and it really turned me on.

"You can stay here for both nights," I said. Petra only wanted to stay two nights, since, despite appearances—she told me—she hadn't left Barcelona for Paris to follow in my footsteps, she'd just found a job and that was all. In two days she'd have her own garret: she was going to give Spanish lessons to the daughter of a woman who lived at number 25 Boulevard Malesherbes, who'd hired her in exchange for room and board and a few francs. All this sounded a little fantastical, the part about the Spanish classes seemed a bit implausible, it was most likely they'd hired her as a maid, and for that precise reason she had her *chambre de bonne*, that is, her maid's room, a garret like mine.

Two days later, she left my garret. We arranged that I would visit her the following Friday in her brand new home. And that's what happened. One nasty wet Friday night I took an endless trip by metro, changing trains twice, to go and sleep with Petra in her *chambre de bonne* on Boulevard Malesherbes. But I was in a bad mood, because that very same Friday I had a more attractive invitation to a party with some of Paris' *beautiful people*, at Paloma Picasso's house, on the other side of the city.

I headed to Petra's garret first with the intention of going to both places. There was a postal strike in Spain and I'd already gone twenty days without a money order from my father. I didn't have a franc, and meeting up with Paloma Picasso and her friends interested me because I thought the least I'd get out of it would be invitations to other parties among her circle of friends, invitations that would help me to get by, as I could eat for free at the parties. The trip to Petra's *chambre de bonne* was a genuine irritation. I went there feeling divided, torn between the evening's two options and determined to make them compatible.

Petra and Picasso. An hour's journey on the metro separated the two very different houses. The thing I remember most about Petra's room is that it was hideous. There were curtains made of cheap blue gingham material and a matching bedspread with a teddy bear on the pillow. The thought that at that very moment I could be talking to Paloma Picasso or with Duras's entire circle of friends was enough to make me weep. I told Petra I had an important engagement and didn't have time to sleep with her, I'd only gone there because I needed her to lend me some money, since the postal strike in Spain had left me without a single franc. Petra was annoyed. And I was very surprised by what she said, I hadn't expected it. "I'm going to lend you this money," she said, "but you should go back to Barcelona, you're wasting your time here. I'm wasting mine too, but at least I've got a job." She gave me nearly all the francs she had. I suddenly felt like her pimp, and that felt good. "Now go," she said angrily, but tenderly. I looked at the money. "I'm going to become the best writer in the world, and that's why I'm in Paris," I explained to her. I looked at the money again. "I'll pay it back as soon as the postal strike ends and my father starts sending me my salary again," I said. "What salary?" she asked. I didn't respond. An hour later, after my long nocturnal journey on the metro, I was *triumphing*—this at least was my ridiculous impression—in Paloma Picasso's salon, talking about Audrey Hepburn and *Breakfast at Tiffany's* with the filmmaker Benoît Jacquot, Duras's assistant director on *India Song*, the film then dominating the Parisian film listings. Jacquot, in turn, had just released his first film, whose title was similar to that of my novel: *L'assassin musicien*. There were luxurious lamps and tables piled with caviar in those rooms. With Petra's francs in my pocket, I felt like the richest man in the world and was very proud of having been so clever, such a pimp, and getting hold of this money, which I believed had turned me into a big shot.

## 60

A month and half after that night, Petra turned up at my garret again and, to keep her from staying there, after paying her back the money, I invited her to the cinema; as luck would have it, the film I chose happened to illustrate, in a disturbing way, what had gone on between us that night in the garret with the teddy bear, that night a month and a half ago when she was my money order and my whore and I her fleeting visitor and pimp and big shot.

"How about we go see a film by Benoît Jacquot, a friend from the neighborhood," I said. It was true Jacquot lived a few steps from my house, but his being my friend was somewhat more dubious. I'd seen him for a few minutes at Paloma Picasso's party. And on one single other occasion, that time at Duras's house, where he'd come with his wife, Martine Simonet.

*L'assasin musicien* starred Anna Karina, Joël Bion and the inestimable veteran—always in secondary role—Howard Vernon, who worked with Arrieta and was a keen supporter of young or risky filmmakers. Jacquot's film had an austere style, influenced by the cinema of Bresson and Duras, a slow rhythm, with sober and, to tell the truth, rather clumsy dialogue. Martine Simonet had a very small part, which seemed a glaring injustice to me.

The film was an adaptation of an unfinished story by Dostoyevsky that Jacquot set in Paris: the tale of a young violinist from the provinces who, convinced he has an exceptional talent for music, leaves the city of his birth to conquer the capital, where he doesn't get hired by any of the orchestras in which he tries to get a place. This leads him to declare he's not working because he's not interested in sharing his exceptional genius with the modest players of the world's orchestras, no matter how good they are. He considers himself the best violinist in the world and walks around the streets of Paris, staring with a strange mixture of conceit and envy at the billboards advertising concerts in the city and ends up with no option but to pimp out a poor servant girl (Anna Karina) who takes him in to her modest *chambre de bonne* because she's fallen in love with him—not with an arrogant, unemployed provincial musician, but with the poor, pathetic wretch she's found stumbling around the city saying he's the best violinist in the world.

61

On the 29th of April, 1974, I bought paper and an envelope and wrote the same letter that Arthur Rimbaud wrote on the 29th of April, 1870, to Théodore de Banville:

And if these lines could find a place in the *Parnasse contemporain*?
I am unknown; but what does it matter? Poets are brothers. These lines believe, they love, they hope: and that is all.
Dear Master: help me up a little. I am young. Hold out your hand to me …

I put the letter in the envelope and sent it to Monsieur Théodore de Banville, chez M. Alphonse Lemerre, éditeur. Passage Choiseul, Paris.

Seven days later, the post office returned Rimbaud's letter to the garret. The letter had arrived at Passage Choiseul (the scene, incidentally, of the writer Céline's adolescent hell), but they hadn't found any Monsieur Théodore de Banville there and they'd sent it back to Rue Saint-Benoît, where I waited for nightfall to open and read it. "I am young," I read out loud. And I waited the whole night for someone to come to my aid, knock at the door of my *chambre* and give me their hand. I spent that night waiting for Rimbaud.

62

I went to the cinema a lot.

*Johnny Guitar*, by Nicholas Ray, is the film I've seen the most times in my life. Whenever it was on in Paris in some late night showing, I was there in the nocturnal line, ready to watch the film for the umpteenth time. I was fascinated by the film's dialogues about love and I was captivated by the sense of security that emanated from the hero's strong personality. I thought that if I'd met him when I was young, my childhood would have been very different. I imagined myself sleeping in my child's bedroom, safe from all nocturnal terrors, in the knowledge that Johnny Guitar was guarding the house. I knew by heart everything the hero says in the film, above all the dialogues about love, like when Johnny (Sterling Hayden) asks Vienna (Joan Crawford) how many men she's forgotten and Vienna says as many women as he remembers.

One night in Paris, on the way back from a long night at Le Sept on Rue Sainte-Anne, a fashionable club and hangout for *beautiful people* (Ingrid Caven, for example, but also Yves Saint Laurent, Nureyev, Helmut Berger, Andy Warhol, and the *other* Josette Day, always gorgeous and accompanied by a monster), I walked with friends by the Seine, and Adolfo Arrieta suddenly pointed out the top floor of one of the imposing buildings by the river. "Up there, that big balcony you see lit up, is where Sterling Hayden lives," he told us.

I didn't know that Johnny Guitar lived in Paris. After Arrieta said these words, we walked on, almost all of us in respectful silence, as if we'd fallen under the spell of the hero's balcony above the river. After that day and that silence, there were other days, other silences. Alone or in company, I walked at night several more times along the banks of the Seine near Sterling Hayden's house. And I remember I always instinctively looked up toward the top floor of the building and searched for the balcony, and it was always lit. And I remember, too, how much it comforted me to walk past that place and look up and have the feeling that from this house by the Seine, from that sleepless balcony with the lights always on, the great Johnny Guitar was looking out for me, watching the sometimes pathetic drift of my steps by the river.

## 63

I went to the cinema a lot.

I felt genuine shock watching *Notre Dame de Paris,* the mediocre director Jean Delannoy's adaptation of Victor Hugo's novel. While the movie was dreadful, by any standards, the story of the hunchback Quasimodo and the beautiful Esmeralda touched me deeply. After the movie, I left the cinema and walked to the Hotel Esmeralda, next to Notre Dame—the famous *Esmegaldá,* indisputable center in those days of the bohemian heart of the city, a legendary space of liberty, where, rumor had it, the rooms had no keys and were all interconnected. Germán, a young Spaniard who worked in reception and was friends with Arrieta and Javier Grandes, told me that someone who came to the hotel a lot, and always caused some sort of scandal, was the transvestite who imitated Josette Day.

And who was the real Josette Day? Germán informed me that

she was the actress who'd starred in Cocteau's *Beauty and the Beast* and was famous above all because, after shooting this film, she'd married a Belgian who was one of the richest men in the world and she'd bankrupted him by getting carried away with her fascination for emeralds, or *esmeraldas*, as they're called in Spanish.

"And you tell me all this in the Esmeralda," was the only thing that occurred to me to say to Germán, who became absurdly annoyed at me for what he called the obviousness of my comment. I found his annoyance so unfair, and so disproportionate, that I left before long, not without first thanking him for telling me who the real Josette Day was. I walked out of the Esmeralda and decided to go up to the top of Notre Dame, where I'd never been, and see the legendary territory of Quasimodo. I went up with a group of tourists and, once at the top, was enormously bewildered by what I saw. The photographer Martine Barrat, a friend of some mutual friends, was immortalizing Raúl Escari with her camera, who at that precise moment was sharing a joint with William Burroughs, and it *was* Burroughs who was there with my friend, from the first moment I had no doubt about it, though my surprise and bewilderment at this discovery were huge. What was Raúl doing with that famous writer up there at the top of Notre Dame? Of course, if it was time for such questions, I should have asked myself what I was doing up there too.

I realized there were many things I didn't know about my good friend. I felt, moreover, so excluded from the scene that I didn't dare go up to them and say hello. Since they didn't see me, I preferred to say nothing, I saw myself as a poor wretch they would quickly have cast out into the world of strangers.

Over the next few days, whenever I saw Raúl I couldn't help constantly thinking he was hiding friendships and undoubtedly stories from me and that perhaps hell wasn't *other* people—as Sartre said— but in fact a few complete strangers no matter how well we thought we knew them. Until, one day, Raúl himself showed me Martine Barrat's photo. "I was with Burroughs the other day, did I tell you?"

he said with absolute simplicity and no mystery whatsoever. And if anybody was being mysterious and enigmatic it was me, especially when I said: "I was at the top of Notre Dame, but I didn't go over to you because you were with such a famous person, I didn't dare …"

Raúl looked at me as if I was the one who'd been smoking joints. In reality he looked at me as I'd looked at him up there next to Burroughs. But the most surprising thing of all is that shortly afterwards, demonstrating how well he knew me, he realized that, strange as it might seem, I was telling the truth and that I was speaking somewhat resentfully and prompted by jealousy. He believed me so much that he apologized, before saying that the next day, he'd arranged to play pinball with Serge Gainsbourg. Many times I've thought that our great friendship wasn't totally established until these two serious scenes of mystery, disturbance, and jealousy.

64

I went to the cinema a lot.

From my last days in Paris I have a strong memory of the afternoon I saw, by chance, on one of the small screens in the Quartier Latin, *3 American LPs*, a Wim Wenders short from 1969, where the soundtrack, the rock and roll music, is all important, much more so even than the images. I suddenly remembered the forgotten soundtrack to my life. "We have long forgotten," writes Walter Benjamin in *One-Way Street*, "the ritual by which the house of our life was erected. But when it is under assault and the enemy bombs are already taking their toll, what enervated, strange antiquities do they not lay bare in the foundations!"

That day, in that small cinema, a strange antiquity appeared that I had buried in the basement of the building of my life: the memory of the day in 1963 when I was walking down Calle Pelayo in Barcelona and heard the Beatles for the first time singing *Twist and Shout*, music that seemed different from all the rest and made me feel a strange happiness, unthinkable until then.

Discovering rock and roll saved my life, or at least gave me the impetus to look for it. Rock and roll was something my generation hadn't inherited from anyone and so there was no one to teach us how to like it. On the contrary, more than one person tried to convince us we should despise it. The Beatles' long hair, which now seems banal, was rather the complete opposite, I believe it was decisive for rock, because it created a sense of identity totally different to capitalism. In a way, it was a step toward revolution, as it was rock that gave many of us, for the first time, a sense of identity. And this was possible because more than anything, rock, in spite of our despair (fictitious or not), connected us to a strange happiness.

That day, in the Quartier Latin cinema, I recovered the strange memory buried in the foundations of the house of my life, the memory of *Twist and Shout* that had changed my perspective. *3 American LPs* begins with a car trip, and the camera spends a long time framing the landscape through the window as it moves along sideways. You see the city, shops, billboards, the outskirts, car cemeteries, and factories go past, as the music of Van Morrison plays. Off-screen, the voices of Wenders and Handke talk about the songs they're listening to on the car radio. The real hero of that film is rock and roll, which becomes the only vehicle of communication in a desolate, impenetrable universe. It doesn't matter what's outside— this isn't a road movie—but rather what's inside: the car radio, the soundtrack to the film, the rock.

Ever since that day, Van Morrison has been my favorite singer. I suppose it was an important day for me, since I discovered I needed to lose certain complexes and not consider rock music alien to what I might write. It was also the day I realized I didn't have to be intimidated by certain Spanish writers of my generation who claimed to be interested only in classical music and who, for instance, had felt sorry for me when it occurred to me to quote the Rolling Stones. It was the day I realized, not only should I not rule anything out when it came to creativity, but I shouldn't be influenced by the pitying looks of those pedants from my very backward country, haughty writers entrenched in a papier-mâché literature. It was the day I discovered that when it comes to writing I shouldn't rule anything out since, as Walter Benjamin said, the chronicler who narrates events without distinguishing between great and small ones is guided, as he does so, by this truth: of all that has happened, nothing should be considered lost to history. It was the day I discovered that there were writers and filmmakers abroad from the generation before mine—such as Wenders and Handke—who talked unashamedly about rock and roll, about the strange happiness a Van Morrison song can suddenly produce. I continued to live in despair, but with moments of strange happiness that now and then came to me—still come to me—from rock and roll.

## 65

I went to the cinema a lot and Edgardo Cozarinsky must have gone a lot too, as I often found him watching the same film as me. Cozarinsky, a late Borgesian according to Susan Sontag, was an Argentinian exile who seemed to have ended up feeling comfortable in the role of outsider. A writer and filmmaker, he lived between Paris and London, I don't know where he lives now, I think just in Paris. I remember I admired him because he knew how to combine two cities, two artistic allegiances—something I certainly couldn't do; until I arrived in Paris, it had never occurred to me that one could live in two cities at the same time, I found it hard enough just being in one—I also remember I saw one of his films, and read his book on Borges and film, and also his study about gossip as a narrative process and other texts, all of them always spellbinding. Ten years after I left Paris, I especially admired his book *Urban Voodoo*, an exile's book, a transnational book, employing a hybrid structure very innovative in those days that has since become more established in literature.

*Urban Voodoo* gave the impression Cozarinsky had written it after having taken very seriously what Godard said about making fictional films that might be documentaries and documentaries that were like fictional films. *Urban Voodoo*, a book that was ahead of its time in the way it mixed essay with fiction and advanced new and interesting tendencies in literature, seemed composed of stories that were like essays and essays that were like stories. It was also laden with quotes in the form of epigraphs, reminiscent of those films by Godard that are littered with quotes. Some of my books from the 1980s and '90s derive in part, though I suppose unconsciously, from the cinema of Godard. And I think also somewhat from the novelistic structure of Cozarinsky's *Urban Voodoo*, from that structure where the apparently capricious quotes or grafts lend a magnificent eloquence to the discourse: the quotes or cultural references are incorporated into the structure in a prodigious way; instead of placidly joining the rest of the text, they collide with it, elevated to an unpredictable power, becoming another chapter of the book.

I think the literary artifact *Urban Voodoo*, that book written by someone who struck me as feeling comfortable as an outsider, was particularly influential to my novel about portable plots, but I received this influence in the mid-eighties so it belongs to a period in my literary biography far removed from that covered in this three-day lecture, which speaks not of plots but rather, a plot to exorcise my youth by reviewing it ironically.


66


I went to the cinema a lot, to see *India Song*. For one reason or another I was always seeing *India Song*, Duras's best film. Someone hadn't seen it and I would go with him. I saw it many times when it first came out in 1975 and was playing in several Paris cinemas with remarkable success. I saw it many times and it always fascinated me and, what's more, it felt like it belonged to me, perhaps because I'd been there for so much of the filming, especially when they were shooting at the Rothschild palace in the Bois de Boulogne, a few steps away from where, two months before, Marguerite and I had spent a night looking for First Communion whores. Marguerite had discovered this palace on one of her long walks through the city, and from the first moment had been attracted to the place. Until the end of her days she was impressed by the space, and said that Goebbels had lived there, and some of the Rothschilds' servants had worked for the Resistance in some of the palace's secret rooms, behind the Germans' backs. After the war, the Rothschilds had decided never again to live in that palace. When Marguerite chose it as a location everything was in an extreme state of abandon, of collapse. It was a tremendously decadent house and ideal for the story Marguerite was trying to tell, which was simply a love story paralyzed at the height of its passion. Surrounding this love story is the outside world, India. And with it, horror, hunger, leprosy and the humidity of the monsoons. Horror appears fixed in a daily paroxysm. A few—faceless—voices are given the task of speaking and trying to reconstruct this love story that they vaguely recall, although they haven't forgotten the lover crying out in the middle of the reception at the French embassy, the cry of the vice-consul pronouncing the name of his beloved, the name of Anna Maria Stretter. The sound of boat sirens can be heard in the distance and the trilling of birds close by. The whole film is the echo of a great cry of love.

On some occasions with Raúl Escari, and others with Adolfo Arrieta, I went to the film set many times and witnessed how the Rothschilds' park was transformed into a colonial garden. An enormous quartz lamp attracted moths, which were scorched in their hundreds. The white light of the Parisian summer acquired the color of the monsoon. Marguerite loved it on the day of the preview, when people asked her in which region of India she had shot the film. I remember, at the end of the first showing, Robbe-Grillet approached her to say that, as with all her films, he had enjoyed this one very much. And I remember I was stunned and wondered if I'd heard correctly or if she'd gone back to her *superior* French when I heard her say to Robbe-Grillet that she was very sorry she couldn't say the same about his films. I think I had never in my life heard anyone speak with such frankness, and perhaps for this reason the words etched themselves deep in my memory. What's more, I have imitated this kind of frankness on a few occasions in my life, always with bad results, since in all cases those affected reacted badly and became enemies of mine and I've ended up, through a curious association of ideas, considering them to be enemies of the beauty of *India Song*, enemies of the crepuscular stretching out of the echo of a great cry of love in the Indian night: an association that with time I've come to realize was not as crazy as I thought, since it is exclusively my friends who like *India Song*.

### 67

I went to the cinema a lot and among my favorite films was always *The Conformist*, by Bernardo Bertolucci. I adored the contributions of Dominique Sanda, Stefania Sandrelli, and the ambiguous Pierre Clementi. And I also adored the extraordinary photography of Vittorio Storaro, but above all what most fascinated me about this film so different from all the rest was its highly unorthodox way of telling the story, a story that moves forward in leaps, as one moves when one is writing a novel and doesn't know what's going to happen if one is going to even reach the end. Bertolucci, just as Cortázar did in *Hopscotch*—a novel I read to feel more tied to Paris and admired in its day—turned the narration into a game. And I wondered when I would dare to start a novel in this playful spirit I'd encountered in Bertolucci and Cortázar, jumping from square to square with the primitive freedom the art of storytelling had in the beginning. Although not in the category of a perfect *hopscotch*, another Bertolucci film, *Last Tango in Paris*, also shook me quite a bit, especially the breathtaking beginning, with a disoriented and very desperate Marlon Brando—like me, I thought—lost on the streets of Paris. With a beginning like that, starting from such an extreme situation, anything seemed possible. This was a time when cinema was a mirror. A mirror even of my disorientation, I say disorientation because I was aware—and I suffered because of it—that, in the same way that cinema organized visual reality, good novels organized verbal reality. All this I knew, but, nevertheless, in spite of having discovered this narrative game, the jumps from square to square, an ideal pattern for telling a story, I didn't know how to organize my own reality. What's more, the shadow of an alarming question was hovering above my garret. What *was* my reality? If I didn't know, how could I expect to organize it?

I'll leap forward now and perhaps change the subject, but not the square. The rules of the game are there to be played with. I'm leaping to confess to all of you now that I feel lucky not to yearn for my years of writerly apprenticeship. Because if I could tell you that from those years I remember the intensity, those hours consumed writing in the garret, consumed all day long and then at night, bent over my desk while the world slept, without feeling tired, electrified, working till dawn, and even beyond ... If only I could tell you something like that, but the fact is I can't, there's not much nobility, beauty or intensity from these minutes of my youth spent writing. I know, it's deplorable. But this is my fate, I live without nostalgia. I don't yearn for my purity, or stimulating enthusiasm, or intensity. It's as if in Paris I skillfully postponed everything in order to truly feel the seduction of writing in these current years, those of my later life.

68

Legend has it that Hemingway, armed with a machine gun and accompanied by a group of French Resistance fighters, on August 25, 1944, after four long years of German occupation, went into Paris a few hours ahead of the allies and *liberated* the bar of the Ritz Hotel, the famous Petit Bar on Rue Cambon. More precisely the legend says that Hemingway *liberated* the hotel's wine cellars. Afterwards, he took a suite there and, in a near-permanent haze of champagne and cognac, he received friends or just visitors who came to congratulate him. Among those who showed up at the hotel was André Malraux, arrogant as they come. The French writer marched into the Ritz with a squad of soldiers under his command, transformed into quite the colonel with shiny cavalry boots. He hadn't gone to the Ritz to congratulate anybody, least of all Hemingway, who noticed him straightaway and immediately remembered that this proud colonel had abandoned the Spanish Civil War in 1937 to write *L'espoir*, a novel some simpletons had elevated to the category of a masterpiece. He soon saw that colonel Malraux was boasting about his squad of soldiers and laughing at the "worthless characters" under the command of Hemingway, liberator of the Ritz bar.

"What a pity," Hemingway said to Malraux "that we did not have the assistance of your force when we took this small town of Paris." And one of the staunch ragged men under Hemingway's command murmured in his leader's ear: *"Papa, on peut fusiller ce con?"* ("Papa, can we shoot this prick?")

On August 25 this past summer I went to the Petit Bar, the small bar that had its name changed twenty years ago and that the management of the Ritz now calls Bar Hemingway, though it's had lots of other famous customers: Marlene Dietrich, Scott Fitzgerald, Ingrid Bergman, Graham Greene, and Truman Capote, among others.

As I entered with my wife planning to celebrate the fifty-eighth anniversary of the liberation of the bar, I found the little place packed with a crowd of people who, in the midst of their terrible general drunkenness, gave the impression that they, too, were celebrating that date. Ugly, very inebriated people. What I saw there was a far cry from heaven. "When I dream of heaven," Hemingway said, "the action always takes place at the Paris Ritz." I felt immediately obliged to point out to my wife that this, contrary to what I'd hoped, was not heaven. "But it's preferable to heaven," said my wife, enigmatically. I was about to ask her what she meant when some of the people at the bar, seeing us looking for a table, exchanged words and some even laughed, I'll never know what about. "Have you seen how these clowns are laughing?" I said to my wife, who shrugged, since this didn't seem to affect her as much as it did me, as I've always taken things more seriously.

I remember, when I was young and living in Paris, I used to go to that bar, when it was still called the Petit Bar, and nobody laughed at me. On the contrary, there were people there who took me very seriously and gave me advice, lots of advice. I liked to sit on the raised alcove by the bar whenever there was a table free. One day, sitting at one of these tables with Vicky Vaporú, she deigned—this is what I call taking me seriously—to give me some advice I've never forgotten: "Whenever you feel like criticizing anyone, just remember that all the people in this world haven't had the advantages that you've had." Some days later I discovered the phrase was from *The Great Gatsby* and I asked Vicky for an explanation. She nearly cried when she saw she'd been found out, and right then I understood that her advice had been given in good faith, with very good intentions, and that no one in Paris took me as seriously as she did.

She nearly cried and apologized saying it'd been an homage to Scott Fitzgerald, who'd been a regular client of this bar and who'd written, moreover, a novella called *The Diamond as Big as the Ritz*, which was what she aspired to in life, to have a diamond of that colossal size. Vicky Vaporú, as well as being the best-looking transvestite in the Latin Quarter, was the one person who most resembled Holly Golightly from Truman Capote's *Breakfast at Tiffany's*.

On clear, cool Paris mornings, I would suddenly run into her in the neighborhood and she'd ask me questions that reminded me of Capote's heroine: "I thought writers were very old. Though, of course, Patrick Modiano isn't old. By the way, is Hemingway?" "He's dead," I felt obliged to reply.

On clear, cool Paris mornings I would suddenly run into her in the neighborhood buying bread and she would ask loud, very funny, or incredible questions for that time of day, especially given that we were waiting in line at the bakery. I remember one of these questions in particular: "Isn't it true that I'm not a sophisticated or counterfeit woman, but rather a genuine counterfeit?" Everyone waiting to buy bread turned to look at us, of course. In a way, that scene set a precedent for the feeling I had this August 25, when we walked into the old Petit Bar and everyone looked at us and some of them laughed at us. Is this what it means to grow up? When I was young (I thought), no one in this bar laughed at me, and what's more, they gave me advice and took me seriously.

One day, again at a table on the alcove, the actor Jean Marais, the star of Jean Cocteau's films, gave me a mysterious piece of advice I've been thinking over ever since. I'd gone along with a journalist friend who was interviewing him for a Spanish magazine. At the end of the meeting, Jean Marais found out I wanted to be a writer and, going off on a tangent before giving me advice, said that I must surely dream of being famous. "Isn't that true?" he asked. I didn't reply, I didn't really know what to say to him; more than fame what I really wanted was to triumph in Paris, but perhaps they were one and the same thing. "Fame," Marais said then, "is made of a thousand rumors and misunderstandings that usually bear little relation to the real person." I was only half listening to him and didn't really know what he was getting at, and foremost in my mind at that moment was how much he imitated Jean Cocteau, for he spoke like him, he'd soaked up the personality of his ex-lover and master, some of his gestures were exact copies of Cocteau's. When he announced he was about to give me some advice, I began to listen attentively.

"Make a double of yourself," said Marais, "to help you assert yourself and which can even come to take your place, to occupy the stage and leave you alone to work far from the noise." Some time afterwards, I found out—and it didn't surprise me in the least—that this advice was a famous phrase that Cocteau used a lot.

So, the bar at the Ritz was a place in which I'd heard all sorts of advice. I had not yet heard the piece my wife was about to give me when, this past August 25, at the sight of the panorama in the bar on the anniversary of Hemingway's heroic deed, I said to her that, if a party's being thrown, no matter what party, there's no reason at all for us to take part in it. I said this with the intention that we not stay there. Since she didn't say anything, I went on: "And anyway, we're not in the heaven Hemingway was talking about." At that point she gave me some advice that kept us in the bar until daybreak: "For that very reason I suggest we stay here awhile, let's take advantage of the fact this isn't heaven to have a bit of a laugh. They're not going to let us laugh in hell, much less in heaven, where it certainly won't do us any good."

This August 25, my wife and I liberated our most secret impulses, as if we were liberating the cellars of the Ritz, we liberated them perhaps a little too much. We began by ordering two daiquiris and, cheering up slightly, I told her about the military run-in there between Malraux and Hemingway. "I'm tired of you, Hemingway," said my wife suddenly, daughter and granddaughter of military men. And I should have remembered at that moment that bivouacking inside her —the most appropriate verb is precisely this military term, *to bivouac*—there was a personal, military sort of phobia, a solely nocturnal hatred, one fueled by alcohol—a hidden but serious antagonism toward me, and especially toward my obsession that someone will one day say to me, even if it's only a white lie, that I resemble Hemingway. But I didn't take that first outburst of aggression seriously enough. We ordered two more daiquiris and then another two and then ten more, and I began calling the daiquiris *Malraux cocktails*. It sounded good, I thought it sounded perfect:

*Malraux cocktails.* But everything had turned dangerous now, like a gigantic Molotov cocktail. Suddenly we realized it was past dawn and, to put it in Hemingwayesque terms, we were across the river and into the trees. We were laughing like completely happy clowns, the hours had flown by, and daylight was seeping into the bar. I was talking to some absolutely stupid Americans when suddenly my wife, in her extreme drunkenness, stopped laughing, because she thought that those "worthless characters"—she said this—were looking at her rudely. "What worthless characters?" I asked, taken aback. The worthless characters, according to her, were the stupid ones I was talking to, "your personal army," the last drunks in the bar. I looked at her and she reminded me of Colonel Malraux and I couldn't help it, I let it slip: "You aren't thinking I want to shoot you?" I should never have asked that question, never. I betrayed the fact that a secret phobia also "bivouacked" in me. There followed a "military skirmish," I in my role of *Papa* Hemingway and she in that of Malraux. There followed a terrible skirmish and I lost the war and two teeth, and I also lost trust in myself and trust in her. I could only hate my wife the next day when she told me I was more handsome. "With two missing teeth, you don't look so much like Hemingway anymore," she said ironically.

## 69

The first time Franco died—he died twice—I was quietly reading poetry in my garret. The dictator was on his death bed in a hospital in Madrid when a false rumor led Santiago Carrillo, the head of the Spanish Communist Party in exile, to announce on Radio Paris the dictator's death before the fact. My neighbor on the top floor—a mysterious black man who never spoke to me, except on this day—heard the news on his transistor radio and was kind enough to bang on my door; when I opened it, more scared than anything else—he was from Ivory Coast, six foot six and looked a bit like a cannibal—he said: "Morning, *tubab*. Franco from Spain *mort*, dead."Then he burst out laughing and showed me his pointed teeth, whether on purpose or not I don't know. The news made me very happy, although I kept my composure, I displayed a certain sang-froid, I suppose, trying to keep him from realizing he intimidated me. "What's that about *tubab*?" was all I said. He didn't answer, just went back to his room.

Naturally, I didn't carry on reading poetry. I went out to celebrate with the first friend I could find. In those days, aside from reading Borges (whom I'd just discovered) and the whole *noir pantheon of literature* (Roussel and Rimbaud first and foremost), I continued reading poetry by the Generation of '27, as I had in Barcelona, above all Luis Cernuda, Pedro Salinas, Juan Larrea, García Lorca and Jorge Guillén. I read a lot of poetry. That of the Generation of '27 had for a long time been influencing my let's call it literary education. In fact, in the period immediately before I moved to Paris, I'd done nothing but read poetry in Barcelona, and not only that of the Generation of '27 but also Juan Ramón Jiménez and Antonio Machado and some of the post-war poets such as Blas de Otero, and this had all been steadily influencing my apprenticeship before my life in the garret and gradually stirred me to write.

As for Spanish poetry, well, I never lost sight of it, I was loyal; after all, that was what had driven me, in my university years in Barcelona, to jot down a few naive early verses, which I still have, such as my poem "Youth Exposed to the Elements," which today I could ironically re-title "Despair in Black," since it was a very euphoric and optimistic poem, but at heart didn't hide my anguish and total bewilderment about life: "I had a world planned / filled with blackboards and old friars / who cried psalms / while they drank Latin / and spread dead geographies … but now I'm ready to radiate freedom / to feel at last I'm living the life / the old bastards never dreamed for me …"

Did I "radiate freedom" in Paris? Not much, though perhaps I radiated a risk of pneumonia. My electric heater broke once, and I spent several extremely cold days in the *chambre*. Without central heating, as in the house I'd grown up in, there was no true or, to put it a better way, complete freedom. Deep down I knew this, but I preferred to kid myself and believe that the cold and bohemia were sheer freedom. I was a frustrated poet who, having wanted to write great verses, had tempered my ambitions and accepted being merely (I already had my work cut out for me) a storyteller. But I carried with me the lost ideals of my wish to be a poet. Basically, what the criminal manuscript of *The Lettered Assassin* narrates is the death of the poet I'd wanted to be.

Anyway, when I found out about Franco's death, I was reading poetry. As soon as I heard the murderous general had died, I stopped reading and went out into the street to look for someone to celebrate with and found Javier Grandes, who knew nothing of the dictator's death and hugged me hard and we hugged each other a lot and jumped up and down so joyfully and so savagely that I ended up twisting my ankle. An hour later, my foot bandaged, I found out Franco hadn't died and started cursing Santiago Carrillo. Over the following few days, half immobilized by the accident, I returned to my poetry reading. And then, one day, Franco died again, my black neighbor's radio announced it again, and this time it was true, but now I couldn't jump for joy. Since I'd already celebrated and, besides, my ankle wouldn't cooperate. My neighbor knocked on my door again and again he called me *tubab*. For a minute I had the impression that every time Franco died, people called me *tubab*. The second death of the dictator found me reading poetry again. This time, reading "Song of Awakening," some lines by Claudio Rodríguez: "As if it had never been mine / give to the air my voice and in the air let it / belong to everyone and let everyone know it / just like a morning or an afternoon."

I opened the window in the garret. The dictator, the great murderer had died and, though one might not say, as Claudio Rodríguez did in his poem, that the wind or the light were mine, I said to myself that soon perhaps my voice would be in the air and would belong to everyone. At first, it occurred to me that Franco's death was a very important historical event, that it had something of Claudio Rodríguez's *song of awakening* about it. And I grew solemn. I said to myself that perhaps a new stage was beginning for me and for the wind and for the light. And suddenly …

It wouldn't be the last, but that was the first time in my life something like this happened to me. I was thinking that the circumstances at that moment were terrifyingly transcendent when all at once, without even realizing it, I wandered out of my solemn trance and ended up straightaway with a mere trifle, as a foreign word came into my head, a word that was nonsense, if you will, compared to the transcendence of the moment, but in the end I let myself relax, because my mood suddenly hinged on this trifle.

The foreign word was *Savannakhet.*

It was an eastern name that was obsessively repeated in *India Song.* It was an eastern name, a foreign word that sounded to me— because of the way it was pronounced by an Indian beggar woman in the film—more like a question than a proper name, a question in the form of a bloodcurdling cry, as if someone were crying out like the vice-consul and saying: And now what? It sounded just like Savannakhet. And now what. It sounded anguished. It was a cry, a question, it was a word as lost as the name of Venice in a deserted Calcutta.

It was a cry, a question, it was a word that later, in the film, turned into a song.

A song of Savannakhet.

And now what?

Franco had died and suddenly all I could think of was the trembling of monsoon light in a park by the Ganges. Franco had died and all I could think of was Savannakhet. It seemed frivolous. But then I said to myself: So what?

70

I came across a book that I decided had connections to my bohemian life: *The Time of the Assassins* by Henry Miller, a biography of
Rimbaud and at the same time an evocation of the years Miller was
poor and happy in Paris. In a preface written in Big Sur, California,
in 1955, referring to Rimbaud, he says that, in the symbolic language
of the soul, the French poet "described everything that is happening
now." According to Miller, there was a direct relation between Rimbaud and the great religious innovators. The French poet also proposed to re-invent life, to start over from zero. He is more alive than
ever, Miller wrote, "and the future is all his … even though there be
no future." I said to myself that, given how mediocre my present was,
it would be fantastic if the future belonged to me. I was prepared to
believe Miller when he said there was no future, I was prepared to
believe him in order to retain hope that in any case this future, even
without existing, could one day belong to me.

71

I went to Paris in August and traveled by metro to the absurd struc-
tures, erected by Mitterrand's megalomania, that house the Na-
tional Library of France. I went to this strange place as convinced
as W. G. Sebald was that there, "everything our civilization has pro-
duced is entombed," and convinced too that modern man, under the
hypnosis of progress and singular thought, does not miss what lies
in this pantheon—the traces of those who are gone— lost as he is
seeking the mirage of a future beyond his reach.

In the 1970s, too, when I was in Paris—as far as I was concerned
back then, Mitterrand was just a friend of Duras's who in 1943, at
the height of the Resistance, had hidden for two nights in my garret—back then, the future was certainly a mirage, but I refused to
accept this. Being young, I felt it was my obligation to believe I had

a future, even if I couldn't see it very clearly. On the other hand, feigning so much despair led me to spend days on end truly desperate, seeing everything as dark, the future very black. My youth was starting to look like what I called earlier, despair in black. This despair—at times feigned and at others genuinely endured—was my most loyal and constant companion throughout the two years I lived in Paris. Often, a sudden lucidity that seemed to arise from my least feigned despair told me I was burying my youth in the garret. Youth is extraordinary, I thought, and I'm suffocating it by living a bohemian life that's not leading anywhere.

One day, through Cozarinsky's book on Borges and cinema, I discovered the author of *The Aleph*. I bought his stories at the Spanish Bookstore, and reading them was a total revelation for me. I was knocked out, especially by the idea—found in one of his stories— that perhaps the future did not exist. The same idea I'd come across in Miller's book on Rimbaud. Once more I was perplexed by this negation, or refutation, of time, in this case, in a piece of writing about Orbis Tertius, the most important axiom of the philosophical schools. According to this axiom, the future has no reality other than as a fuction of our present fears and hopes, and the past has no reality other than merely as that of memory.

The past is always a collection of memories, very precarious memories, because they are never real. On this subject I heard Borges himself say something very beautiful and moving. I heard him say it at a secret lecture he gave at Zékian, a clandestine bookstore located on the second floor of a house on Rue Littré. It was Cozarinsky himself who put me onto the trail of this secret bookstore.

I went to Zékian with no future and I left without a past.

I heard Borges say he remembered one evening his father had told him something very sad about memory, he'd said: "I thought I could remember my childhood when I first arrived in Buenos Aires, but now I know I can't, because I think if I remember something, for example, if today I remember something from this morning, I get an image of what I saw this morning. But if tonight I remember that thing from this morning, then what I remember is not the first image I had of that thing, but the first remembered image. And so each time I remember something, I am not really remembering it, but rather I am remembering the last time I remembered it, I am remembering the last memory. So in reality I have absolutely no memories or images of my childhood, of my youth."

After recalling his father's words, Borges was silent for a few seconds that seemed endless to me, and then added: "I try not to think of things past because if I do, I know I am thinking about memories, not about the first images. And this makes me sad. It saddens me to think that we might not have real memories of our youth."

72

A few months after hearing Borges say we don't have any real memories of our youth, a girl who said her name was Sylvie stopped me in the street and, in a conspiratorial tone, explained that she'd seen me the day Borges was at the Zékian bookstore and wanted to let me know that next Tuesday, at six in the evening, there was to be a clandestine appearance by Georges Perec in that secret bookstore. "I'll wait for you there," she said, half shrouded in mystery, "don't be late because Perec will be very brief." Then she gave me the password to get in to the secret meeting and, turning the corner of Rue Saint-Benoît and Rue Jacob, disappeared forever. What I most remember about her is that she had the same hairstyle as Jane Birkin. And I say she disappeared forever because I didn't see her in the Zékian the following Tuesday when I went to the secret meeting, I didn't see her there and I've never seen her again in my life. A mystery.

I had a hard time making up my mind to go to the Zékian to see Perec. First because I had to go alone and my shyness made the prospect daunting, walking up those stairs again to the white painted door on the second floor of that building on Rue Littré where months before I'd heard Borges speak. And second because

I'd already seen Perec once, at the launch of a book by Philippe Sollers, and I'd already spied on him enough. All in all, there were many reasons I found it a real uphill struggle to go to the bookstore. But the fact is I ended up going. I said the password ("I am a man who sleeps") and went in, even more timidly than I would have in normal circumstances, since they made fun of me after I gave the password, saying, "Well, you don't look sleepy to me." There were some thirty people in the bookstore and I didn't know a single one of them. At six on the dot a man appeared who said he was Perec, but wasn't. More than that, he looked nothing like Perec. Among other things because he was a black guy and looked a lot like Tony Williams, the lead singer of The Platters. The false Perec's appearance was very brief and of the sort that a person, even if it is a memory from youth, doesn't forget.

This is what he said, more or less: "A long time ago, in New York, a few hundred yards from the rocks where the Atlantic's last waves come to break, a man succumbed to his death. He worked as a scrivener for a lawyer. Concealed behind a folding screen, he spent his time sitting at his desk and never moved from there. He lived on ginger nuts. Through the window he looked out at a wall of blackened bricks he could almost have touched with his hand. It was futile to ask him to do anything, to re-read a text or go to the post office. Neither threats nor pleas had any effect on him. In the end, he went almost blind. He had to be fired. He installed himself on the stairs of the building. So they locked him up, but he sat in the prison yard and refused to eat."

When he'd finished, he stared at the audience for a few seconds, then headed for the exit and left the bookstore, slamming the door hard. "Hitting rock bottom doesn't mean a thing," shouted the man sitting next to me. Everyone looked annoyed. And shortly afterwards the meeting broke up. I didn't understand a thing. I went out to Rue Littré and returned to the garret. I hadn't seen Sylvie, I hadn't seen Perec. And that slam?

How strange, I thought. Will I remember this in a few years? The following day, I transferred the phrase "hitting rock bottom doesn't mean a thing" to *The Lettered Assassin*, perhaps just so I'd remember this singer from The Platters in years to come.

73

In Paris, this August, each day on our way back to the hotel, we walked past the building on Rue Littré where there was once a secret bookstore called Zékian on the second floor. I couldn't make up my mind whether or not I should go inside this building to try to find out what was now in the apartment where long ago the Zékian bookstore was, and neither could my wife. Would the bookstore perhaps still be there and would it even still be clandestine? And why the hell, incidentally, was there once a clandestine bookstore in a free Paris and why did this seem almost normal to me?

I remembered perfectly and almost obsessively the spiral staircase leading to the second floor, where there was a white door on which, painted in black, above the spyhole, there was a minuscule but informative letter *Z*.

Though I constantly felt the temptation to reclaim the space in which I once saw the legendary Borges in person, I never made up my mind to take the first step. At the same time, this indecision, which I shared with my wife—she is also very indecisive—was in reality steadily heightening my curiosity to know what the enigmatic Zékian could have become. Was it perhaps now the residence of a nice, quiet, middle-class family unaware of its past and who would be quite alarmed to know that one day, in the dining room of their sweet home, Borges admitted he was saddened by the thought that perhaps we don't have real memories of our youth?

What could be behind the white door? The days went by, and we hadn't made up our minds to enter the building on Rue Littré and go up to the second floor to ring the bell on the white door—would it still be white?—where Zékian was. Until one afternoon, in Café de Flore, where we were taking shelter from the rain, we suddenly ran into our friend Sergio Pitol—we hadn't known he was in Paris and it was a nice surprise for us—who immediately became the leader of an expedition to the building on Rue Littré. He practically dragged us to the place. As soon as the rain eased off a little, he'd said, we'd find out everything we had to and we wouldn't leave the building on Rue Littré until we knew what was behind the white door, what kind of person or piece of furniture—he said this with a smile—occupied the exact place where Borges once said it was sad not to have real memories of our youth.

It surprised me, once we were in the building on Rue Littré, to see that on the second floor there were, facing each other, two residences with their respective doors, neither of which were painted white. Still there, just as I remembered it, was the spiral staircase, so we hadn't got the wrong building, but no doubt my memory had betrayed me. Surely there'd been a single door on the landing of the second floor. Suddenly, the whole investigation into the mystery of the Zékian started to revolve around which of the two was the white door of days gone by.

Despite my efforts, it was impossible to know which of the two doors was the one that I, almost thirty years ago, had gone through on two occasions. We decided to ring the bell of the one on the left, which was the one I thought more likely to be right. No one answered. We persisted, ringing several times. Nothing. "It's obvious this was the door to the bookstore since there's no one inside. The residents are so secretive, as you can see, that they've become invisible," said Pitol, making no effort to hide how amused he was by this investigation. Suddenly, it seemed to me he was acting as if he were inside one of his own stories. And I thought that his stories would be enclosed stories if they ended by revealing what they never reveal: the mystery that travels with each one of us. The style of Pitol the storyteller has always consisted in telling all, but not resolving the mystery.

Pitol was enjoying himself so much he ended up hammering

on the door, laughing his head off. Then we heard the sound of someone, behind the other door, opening the spyhole and peering at us. We rang the bell of this door a moment later. A woman of advanced years, an old lady, cautiously opened it a crack, leaving the chain on. "Are you looking for someone?" she asked. And then Pitol thought of a witty solution and asked in his impeccable French: "Monsieur Jorge Luis Borges? Does he live across the hall?" After a short silence, the woman told us: "They live there, but they're not in, they're never in."

Pitol's face lit up. Now we knew where the Zékian bookstore had been and could still be; the Borges family lived there, but they weren't in. We left the place laughing, having the impression we'd done all we could to resolve the enigma of the secret bookstore and of the world. We left there with the impression of having been closer than ever to the invisible truth.

## 74

I used to go to lots of gatherings of Argentinians with Raúl Escari and it must have been around July 1974 when, at a party held in the studio of the painter Antonio Seguí, I met Gilberta Lobo, an Uruguayan lady who was nearly eighty years old and at first sight seemed like a great personality, a very interesting woman, though she sometimes conveyed a certain anguish, since she seemed to be assailed from time to time by brief but intense bouts of unease. She knew everything about Spain, although she'd never set foot on Spanish soil. But this country was her only passion in life, as she told me. Men, on the other hand, had never been her great passion. She told me this and then boasted about having a similar name to Gilberte de Saint-Loup, a Proust character, and then started going on about men again; she appeared proud of never having married one. "They all end up being a real pain," she said, and asked me point blank if I'd like to go out for lunch the next day, just the two of us. "If you don't think you'd be compromising yourself going out for a meal alone with a young man," I said, trying to be clever, but with evident awkwardness. Seeing everyone laughing all around me, I added in time: "Or rather, alone with an old man." I realized at that very moment that the first phrase of mine, the one that had made Seguí's guests laugh so much, was exactly the kind of thing my mother might have said when talking about me (I was always a child to her: a gray child, it has to be said).

The following day I had lunch in a private dining room at a hotel on the Champs Élysées with Señora Lobo and felt, for a long while, like a child in the company of the kind of mother I would have liked to have had. "And does Marguerite Duras treat you well?" was one of her questions, as if competing with my landlady in the maternal feelings stakes. I felt really good throughout almost the entire meal. Protected. With a mother. Something I hadn't felt for a while. Perhaps, I thought, I'd never felt protected by a mother until this day. A mother, moreover, who didn't think of me as gray, but rather as someone with immense artistic potential—as she put it—which inspired me to feel creative and tell her the plot of *The Lettered Assassin*, although I told her a completely altered version.

A contributing factor—and not an insignificant one—in my transforming the entire plot of my novel must have been the three bottles of Bordeaux we'd drunk. The fact is I said that *The Lettered Assassin* told the story of a very attractive elderly lady with murderous tendencies, a woman who devoted herself to courting young Spanish men with whom she ended up making love until she killed them.

"So you see me as a man-eater?" she suddenly asked. I didn't know what to say. "What do you think I am? A praying mantis?" I didn't really know what she was talking about. "You think I'm one of those who eat the male after mating?" After saying this, she threw herself on me and I'll always remember this as one of the shortest but also most significant episodes of what might be called—placing a lot of emphasis on the issue—my sexual education in Paris.

She stuck her hand down my pants and I seized up in fright. "You don't seem very Spanish to me, more like a polar icecap," she said, quite annoyed when I kept almost entirely still, colder than a glacier. I was going to ask her if she was criticizing me, but the effects of the Bordeaux led me down another complicated path.

"Is your mother well?" I said.

No doubt a polite question, but absurd at that moment no matter how you looked at it, and absurd, moreover, for a woman of her age. Nevertheless, I was surprised to find out that, as incredible as it might seem, Gilberta Lobo's mother was alive.

"My mother is still admirably well," she said, and went on to explain why: through the use of her physical faculties, such as walking to Mass or numbly enduring funerals, her mother, at ninety-five years of age, had gradually acquired an extraordinary moral beauty.

"And your mother's mother?" I asked timidly and not the least bit sarcastically.

"Still dead," she replied.

I saw that this time she was really annoyed with me; she reminded me of my mother when she got seriously angry after one of my pranks. So anyway. I should tell you something, ladies and gentlemen, without the slightest touch of irony: never in my life have I had the impression of having so many mothers as on that day.

## 75

I've been told your name's Clara. Is that right? No? Well, I'm no mind-reader. The truth is nobody told me that was your name. I just wanted to briefly make contact with a member of the audience, step back a little from my papers, from the manuscript of this lecture. Get back to improvising again, to tell you and the audience in general that I'm not going back on something I've already said: I do like New York better than Paris. And I'm not going to deny that I would've loved to have swaggered down Broadway in Manhattan, in an honorary second lieutenant's uniform, just as Hemingway did in May of 1918. And to march as he did down Fifth Avenue. And I'm not going to deny that I like nurses who wear their hair *à la garçon* either and that nurses like me, of course they do. You're a nurse, I don't think I'm wrong there. Your name's not Clara, but you are a nurse.

I like nurses because they have a great capacity for sacrifice and resistance. Hemingway knew this very well, and often fell in love with them. In Italy, during the First World War, he was shot in the left leg by an Austrian machine gun and taken to the American Red Cross hospital, on Via Manzoni in Milan. There were eighteen nurses there for only four patients. And so Hemingway fell in love with Agnes Hannah von Kurowsky, the head nurse, an American of German origin who inspired the heroine of *A Farewell to Arms* and who led the ironical Scott Fitzgerald to say that Hemingway needed a new woman for each novel he wrote. Of course, you, Madam, you're not called Clara, but you're the new woman for this lecture, of that I haven't the slightest doubt, just as I have no doubt that there's never any end to Paris. That's fine, leave, nobody's stopping you. Just so you know, I didn't mean to annoy you. I'm just a tired man. Leave, go on. It's not important. Anyway, I was about to finish for today. Tomorrow I'll tell you whether I really wanted to triumph in Paris.

## 76

We were walking down Boulevard Saint-Germain when, as we neared the Relais Odéon, it occurred to me to suggest to Amapola (an Andalusian with a bit of a truck driver look about her) that we stop for a minute to play a game of pinball. Basically, it was a strategy to try to see Martine Simonet, who used to go and play on that machine as well. It was a gray autumn day and I was feeling deeply nostalgic and desolate and felt I'd only cheer up if I saw the beautiful Martine.

Amapola, possibly jealous because she'd guessed what I was up to, acted just the opposite to Martine and easily managed, with her unforgettable, whisky-soaked voice, to put me straight into a bad mood. "Listen," she said, "you're too old to play on that machine. We're not going into the Relais. You're looking more like a spilled deck of cards every day." I was intrigued by the image of the scattered cards. "What do you mean?" I asked. "Well, my boy, you're the perfect image of confusion and errant ways. Because, let's see now, what do you plan to do with your life?" I thought it disproportionate to attack me like that simply because she didn't want to stop and play pinball. "And where, might I ask, is it that we're going in such a hurry?" I replied. She stopped for a moment in the street and, coming out with one of her customary extravagant remarks, said in her strong Andalusian accent: "To kill ourselves in a fit of passion."

When we got to the Relais, I could see from outside that the machine was occupied by Javier Grandes. "At least let me go inside and say hi to him," I said to Amapola. We went in, she reluctantly. "What are you two up to?" asked Javier without taking his eyes off the machine. "Arguing," she said. "What about?" asked Javier. "Nothing," I said. "What do you mean nothing?" Amapola scolded me again. "We were talking about you and your confusion and errant ways." "And how did that come up?" asked Javier laughing. "He still doesn't know what he's going to be in life," she explained.

Javier, without stopping his pinball game, burst into his characteristic laugh and then, practically at the top of his voice, said to Amapola: "But he does know what he's going to be. A writer. The fact he's a little slow off the mark is another matter." Another joyous guffaw from Javier, I thought he'd clearly smoked a rather considerable joint. "Slow?" I protested. Javier stopped playing for a few moments, put his hand on my shoulder, and with his unmistakable accent from Fuencarral, the Madrid neighborhood where he'd been born, said: "What I mean is you're slow compared to Boris Vian. At your age he was already nearly dead, but he'd written about five hundred songs, three hundred poems, I don't know how many novels, fifty stage plays, eight operas, one and a half thousand music reviews. And that's not all, he used and abused the trumpet. And he was a great nighthawk, who used to flit from the Bar Vert to La Rhumerie Martiniquaise, from Tabou to Petit Saint-Benoît, from Trois Canettes to Vieux Colombier daily. Two marriages, I don't know how many kids, an engineering degree, thousands of conversations with the waiters at the Balzar, a thousand transgressions, he wore out the needles on the record players at the local rich kids' bashes, and, well anyway, I don't need to tell you."

I hung my head, practically destroyed, as if I'd lost a thousand games of pinball. "Oh great," said Amapola, "all we needed was for you to get depressed."

## 77

Did I really want to triumph in Paris? I try to delve deep into my rather shallow thinking of those years and I can't find the exact answer to this question. I do remember that I thought I should already be a well-known writer, but it was a shame that I lacked a certain essential element: having completed a book. But even if I did finish the book I was working on, my fear of publishing was enormous; I can still remember the awful fear I felt at the thought of publishing. I also lacked a wife who was beautiful and intelligent and loved me. I didn't have this either. I had nothing, really. And I said to myself: How unfair, maybe if I finish the novel and publish, I'll triumph, but I'm so scared. Though, who knows, maybe I'll get over my fear and publish it and triumph precisely because a beautiful and intelligent woman reads it, maybe a nurse, who'll love me straightaway when she reads my book. But then the terrible suspicion arose that I was unlikely to find a reader to love me considering I planned to kill my readers. There could never have been a more ill-fated prospect for a literary debut, because I was cutting off my own murderous lettered nose to spite my face, and on top of that I'd have to wait till I'd finished my book to start the next one which would really give me the chance to triumph, to find the woman of my dreams. And how was I going to triumph if I wasn't sure it was worth my while? How was I going to publish if I didn't want to finish the book precisely because I was scared of publishing? And if I found the woman of my dreams and didn't triumph? Ideally, I told myself many nights as I switched off the light in the sinister garret, I'd meet a beautiful and intelligent woman who'd help me triumph, who'd make good the saying that behind every great man there is a great woman. But how could I aspire to find such a woman if deep down I knew perfectly well I wasn't a great man? Would I become one some day? I told myself this is what my second novel could be about, the one I'd write when I got the damned lettered assassin off my back. I told this to myself and went to sleep. And then I imagined in my dreams it was Paris—not I— that had a great future and, moreover, it had streetcars.

## 78

I met a guy called Alfonso, a Spanish political exile and compulsive reader of everything he came across. He was without doubt an intelligent guy, but forced by circumstances to deal hashish in order to survive in Paris. Whenever I saw him, he was always dressed in boxing sweatpants with a shirt on top and a blue French sailor's sweater over the shirt, that is, he was dressed just as Hemingway very often dressed in his youth in that city. As for the rest of him, he looked quite a bit like the writer when he was young, above all like a photo I'd seen of him when he was Red Cross lieutenant. I always noticed how much he looked like Hemingway, but never mentioned it to him, I bought his merchandise (which was for Vicky Vaporú, who gave me a commission and so gave my fragile budget a little respite), put up with his envy or resentment that came from reading excessively about the class struggle, put up with his jokes about me and about my garret, and walked away. I didn't see the use in remarking on his resemblance to Hemingway, since he wore the sweatpants because he boxed in his spare time. But it was true that his blue French sailor's sweater was the oldest I'd ever seen, which made it possible—not very, but possible—that this sweater could be the same one that had once belonged to Hemingway. But I didn't say anything. What for? Until one evening he went too far with his jokes and started to laugh so cruelly at my garret that I couldn't take it any more and I asked him if he hadn't realized he dressed just like Hemingway when he was young and living in Paris. He reacted faster than I'd expected and managed to surprise me when he said: "That's because I am Hemingway. I thought you'd realized that."

When people ask me if I have my texts organized in my head before I write them or if they develop as they go surprising even me, I always reply that infinite surprises occur in the writing. And that it's lucky it's like that, because surprise, the sudden change of direction, the phrase that appears at a precise moment without one knowing where it comes from, are the unexpected dividends, the fantastic little push that keeps the writer on his toes. This is what "the boxer" Alfonso managed to do that day with his surprising reply, he managed to keep me alert and really on my toes, ducking and weaving more than acceptably. I realized I'd do well to carry on down the path he'd begun when he told me he was Hemingway. Because if it was true, if he was Hemingway (and he wasn't, of course), I had a unique opportunity to interview him. And, if he wasn't, it didn't matter: fiction has always been fiction and one has to believe in it gracefully when it appears. When it does, one must be aware that one is dealing with an exquisite fiction and, knowing this, believe in it. One mustn't be fussy when faced with situations of this sort. If Alfonso said he was Hemingway, the most practical thing I could do was to accept his claim and interrogate him to see how he defended himself being who he claimed to be.

"The rich are different from you and me," I said to him. This, as everyone knows, is what Scott Fitzgerald said on a certain occasion to Hemingway, who answered ironically: "Yes, they have more money." Instead, Alfonso replied with: "The curse of the rich is that they have to live with the rich." Although an ingenious reply, it wasn't altogether the most pertinent. Or was that how Hemingway spoke? Of course it wasn't, Hemingway didn't speak as if he were Oscar Wilde or G. K. Chesterton. I decided the best thing would be to give up on the interview, but first I asked him one last question, a question that concerned me directly: "Mr. Hemingway, what do you think is the best training for the novice writer?" Again when I was least expecting it, his reply surprised me. The unexpected jab came back, and I was able to go on interviewing him enthusiastically. "Let's say," he replied, and this sounded very like Hemingway, "that a novice writer should hang himself because he discovers that writing well is intolerably difficult. Then someone saves him mercilessly, and his own ego forces him to write as well as he can for the rest of his life. At least that way he'll have the story of the hanging for a start."

I couldn't have felt more excited, and asked him: "Mr. Hemingway, does the subject or the plot or a character change as one writes?" "Sometimes one knows the story," he said, covering his face as if he was boxing, "and other times one invents the story as one writes and hasn't the slightest idea how things are going to go. Everything changes as it goes along. This is what produces the movement of the story. Sometimes the movement is so slow it doesn't seem to be moving. But there is always change, there is always movement."

I grew even more excited. "Mr. Hemingway, when you write, do you ever discover you're influenced by what you're reading at that moment?" He concentrated for a few seconds then finally said: "Nothing I read influences me now, but there was a time when Joyce was important. This caused serious problems with my friend Gertrude Stein when it occurred to me to say that *Ulysses* was a goddamn wonderful book, and she said if I brought up Joyce twice in her house, I would not be invited back." "So what did you do?" I asked. "What could I do, my friend? I restrained myself. I never mentioned his name in her house again."

I spent quite a while interviewing him and I had the feeling I'd learned a lot, since in truth I listened carefully to some of his advice. "It's odd," he said toward the end of the interview, "that you're paying attention to my advice. Normally nobody listens or accepts it. It's strange that almost nobody accepts advice while they all accept money, it must be that money's worth more."

This sounded nothing like Hemingway to me. And what he went on to say, even less so: "I've tried to get out of poverty using what I've taught myself, but it's done me no good at all. I struggle to get by selling *shit*. When I was a child, we barely had enough to eat. I had a disabled mother and a drunken father. But of course, we had to keep up appearances. We were poor, but clean. I still don't understand how I acquired a social conscience, because I didn't have one, I was resigned."

It was only when he said this, which sounded nothing like Hemingway either, that I brought the interview to a close. A worldwide exclusive, I thought, some day I'll write it up. "Anything else you'd like to add?" I asked. "Put that I'm very fond of snow and winter and taking my little girls to piano class," he said. And in the face of the ferocious look I gave him—as if asking him to please stick to the script—he added: "What's the matter? I don't usually tell all, I'm governed by the principle of the iceberg. You'll have to make up the secret story of this encounter out of the unsaid, I'm not going to do all the work. A drunken father and a disabled mother. Remember that and put all your skill into telling the inscrutable story of my sadness."

Did I have a worldwide exclusive interview or a short story? It was dark by then and I had to go back to my neighborhood, where Vicky Vaporú was waiting for me to give her the hash. He, meanwhile, had a painter waiting for him. "I've arranged to meet Joan Miró at the gym where I box," he said. And I don't know ... The word "box" sounded very forceful, like a jab at the interviewer, or the storyteller.

79

And now that we're talking about Spanish exiles in Paris, I think the case of the crazy, young orphan Tomás Moll, who ended up becoming a real institution at the Café de Flore, might deserve our attention. Having inherited a large fortune in his native Majorca, young Moll, who watched with satisfaction how overnight an accident left him without a relative in the world, moved immediately to Paris—went into exile, he said—the city of his dreams.

He moved, or exiled himself, to Paris, seeking to forget the ragged, scruffy dead people he was leaving behind him (his Majorcan family was very decadent, but this isn't always a guarantee of elegance, far from it), and to lead the life of a dandy or a *flâneur*, two ways of life that were impracticable in his cramped home city of Palma de Mallorca. He soon gave up the second ambition, being a *flâneur*, and became sedentary in the Flore. He was fascinated and trapped by the terrace of this café to the point where, accompanied by a Venezuelan secretary he'd hired in Paris, he began to spend whole days there, devoted, with as much dandyism as possible, to preparing the appropriate material for an extravagant book he planned to call *How to be the Least Like Baroja Even Though You're in Exile in Paris*.

On one occasion, shortly after the young millionaire Moll had arrived in Paris, he'd attended, out of simple curiosity, the philosopher García Calvo's Spanish *tertulia* in the Café La Boule d'Or on Place Saint-Michel where, just as he'd guessed would happen, he was horrified by the bad-tempered atmosphere and the participants' scant elegance. The *tertulia* reminded him of the dirty, decadent family he'd left behind. Appalled at the filth—in his view—of a misunderstood dignity, he couldn't even bring himself to approach García Calvo and ask his opinion on Baroja's life during his first exile in Paris.

In any case, this brief incursion into La Boule d'Or turned out to be very advantageous for him, as he told me the day I spoke to him.

The incursion made him immune to any more follies or attempts to find better cafés than the Flore. He wasn't happy, he confessed to me that day, the only time I spoke to him. He wasn't happy because he noticed that all the people who approached him did so out of self-interest, because of his money. His secretary, at least, he'd sought out himself so as not to go through the irritating stage of suspicion and mistrust.

"So you must be suspicious of me, then?" I said that day when we exchanged a few words in the Flore. "Very," he replied. I'd approached him because I was intrigued to know how one wrote a novel with a secretary. Marguerite Duras hadn't mentioned anything about a possible need for an assistant on her instruction list. And even though I was practically certain it wasn't necessary to have a secretary in order to write, I didn't want to rule anything out in advance, since I wasn't exactly overrun with resources to keep my fragile condition of novice writer on track. This led me to ask young Moll what the intellectual contribution of his Venezuelan companion was or if he'd hired him purely because having a secretary looked very elegant. "Everything can be elegant, apart from being like Pío Baroja when he was living in Paris," he replied. And that was how I began to learn about the subject of the book he was working on.

Through the collection of data on Baroja's life around 1912 during his first exile in Paris—a meticulous study, on which several hired students were working, co-coordinated by the secretary, who informed Moll of their results conscientiously each day in the Flore—Moll was preparing a book that proposed a model of life for writers in exile or who would be in the future: an impeccable model, based on a shameless search for happiness, although diametrically opposed to the not at all exemplary life that, according to Moll, Baroja had led in Paris when, in his foul room in the awful Hotel Bretonne on Rue Vaugirard at a disgusting table covered with a tablecloth, he'd written *The Tree of Knowledge*.

"Just a stone's throw from there," young Moll told me that day in the Flore, "also on Rue Vaugirard, revealing the stark contrast between Spanish and American literature, in a splendid apartment at number 58 and surrounded by glamour, lived Scott and Zelda Fitzgerald. Baroja, in contrast, lived in a sordid room with a hide-away bed built into the wall. Spanish literature will never amount to anything if it doesn't get away from tablecloths and hide-away beds."

He told me, looking horrified—I suppose wanting me to share his horror—that Baroja only left his hotel room in Paris to *inflict dinner* on visiting friends, as Ramón Gómez de la Serna recounted in a portrait of Baroja, meals he insisted on blighting with long sermons on the importance of science and the biologist Metchnicov, in fashion back then because he'd recently judged that the long lifespan of some Bulgarian citizens was due to fermented dairy products. "So there," Baroja repeated over and over at these dinners, "what one should be is a Metchnicofff," (and he added three *f*s instead of the last *v*).

It didn't take a genius to see that the young orphan and millionaire's book was the delusion of a nutcase, who was being swindled out of his money by a good number of fake students, all friends of the Venezuelan secretary. But in any case, it was beyond doubt that the Flore, with its record of exiles, was the most suitable place to prepare a book about someone's exile, so I congratulated him on having chosen a setting as appropriate as that café. Anyway, I only spoke with young Moll that one time, but that doesn't mean I didn't follow, at a prudent distance, the laborious production of a book that, as the students hired by the secretary scandalously increased in number, grew longer and longer until one day, apparently, many years after I'd left Paris, the book became interminable for the young millionaire, it became literally infinite: something, I was told, that Moll himself verified without it mattering to him at all, rather just the opposite, since by then he'd discovered that the true charm of the book and true dandyism lay in the generosity of giving work to fake students. And so, despite it having proved infinite, he decided to continue with the preparations for a book that he should have cut short some time ago, especially when he began to read Baroja and discovered he adored him and had been unforgivably frivolous in wanting to trash him for details such as his missing a button on his shirt. If he didn't stop the preparations at that point, he was hardly going to do so now just because the book had become infinite. Why stop when the book was never going to appear anyway and prolonging these preparations would allow him to carry on helping, with all the dandyism in the world, a good number of young people in need of work, in this case, work that was— Moll knew it, the secretary knew, and in the end I'm told everyone knew—pure farce, simply the need to distribute the inheritance of an unpleasant Majorcan family?

Moll ended up becoming an institution on the terrace of the Flore, and even the Japanese sought him out in the 1980s to photograph him next to his secretary. He died of a sudden illness in February 1992. There's a brilliant photo from the end of the eighties, I think it's the winter of '89, in the doorway of the Café de Flore, where you can see the Majorcan millionaire and his Venezuelan secretary surrounded by smiling fake students who you couldn't exactly say had approached Moll and his assistant (by then he was also a millionaire) out of financial self-interest, but rather, as the secretary himself happily said, they'd been sought out by the pair; all of those unemployed youngsters had literally been captured, embroiled by them, caught up in the adventure of a senseless and endless book, but which after all made a living for a lot of people and moreover allowed the now not-so-young Moll, this great nutcase and strange orphan, to justify himself before death with a deed well done, even if it was infinite and therefore unfinished: to justify himself before death, and to be, moreover, due to his principle of generosity (and not his aesthetic opposition to built-in hideaway beds), a true dandy. A silhouette of a dandy alive in the golden exile of the Café de Flore.

80

I find it impossible to recall the first sentence of *The Lettered Assassin*—written once I had the finished whole book—without a great deal of affection: "So merged and intertwined are the occasions for laughter and tears in my life that I find it impossible to recall without good humor the distressing incident that forced me to publish these pages."

This long first sentence not only seems to me a good opening but—together with those of the dangerous criminal manuscript at the center of the novel—it is also one of the few sentences I now recognize as my own. And the fact is almost all the others sound highly affected or distant or seem copied from other authors. Oddly, I initially resisted including this long first sentence with which I now identify so strongly because I told myself I couldn't start my book with something so little in keeping with my actual life, since nothing like that had ever happened to me, never had my tears and laughter been intertwined.

But I soon realized that this sentence could end up being one of the few that over time I would end up recognizing as genuinely mine. I saw this thanks to Vicky Vaporú, who told me that life often ends up imitating art and I might eventually have the experience of seeing how with time I would feel absolutely responsible for that first sentence, and on the other hand not feel like the author of many of the others in my criminal book.

And, well, that's what's happened. It's true, quite a few years have had to pass—I see them as having been well spent—for something as uncertain as that first sentence of my first book to become certain. The fact is that as time has passed the occasions for laughter and tears have become intertwined in my life and now, for instance, I find it impossible not to recall with a sense of humor the mental state in which I wrote my most recent novels, that strange mental state that would lead me to weep at my own humor and laugh my head off when my characters die. And the thing is, life's like that, and so is art. In the long run, if you're patient, you discover that, just like laughter and tears, life and art have a tendency to end up merging and intertwining to form a single figure, at once comic and tragic, a figure as singular as that formed by the bull and the bull-fighter in those great performances we never forget.

81

A few days after the filming of *India Song* finished, Marguerite Duras felt very disoriented, I found out many years later; back then I didn't worry about how Marguerite was feeling, it never occured to me to wonder what her state of mind might be. I now know that the end of the summer of 1974 was awful for her; the end of that summer was hot and anguished, and lonely too. After the filming, everyone had gone back to their everyday lives, and Marguerite felt lonely. Empty, in a state of weightlessness, according to Laure Adler's biography of Duras. She went to Neauphle-le-Château, precisely where I went to visit her one day, at the end of that dreadful summer, unaware of this whole drama.

There, in Neauphle, she began hearing the same voices she'd been listening to throughout the days when she'd written the film's screenplay. "I'm not functioning at all," she told a friend, "I can't get back to reality." She started to think about a sequel to *India Song*. One night, she had a strange dream: she dreamed she was being burgled, that the apartment she had in Trouville was being emptied and, worst of all, even her sea views were being stolen. They took her papers, her money, her purse. She cried, but no one cared about her, she was all alone and without her sea views. When she woke up, she fell into a deep depression, and over the following days the dream returned again and again.

Her last two books hadn't worked at all, she seemed to be finished as a writer. She felt isolated, despised, frightened. "The failure of my last two books fills me with shock and fear," she wrote to Claude Gallimard, her editor. And then, talking about some praise she'd just received in an article, she told him: "You haven't had time to read it, I understand perfectly: but this article said about me (rightly or wrongly, that's not the point) that I'm a brilliant dramatic author ... You are overloaded with work. And I have to live. My political position is very awkward.... *I have to live, I am on my own* and I'm not young any more and *I don't want to end up in poverty* (the emphasis is hers). If I have to go back to suffering the poverty I knew as a child, I'll shoot myself. You can't turn the clock back, I want to defend myself, I'm no saint. No one is. The suffering of Bataille's last years (he was always a few francs short) doesn't seem normal to me ... If I don't sell here anymore, I'll go abroad."

I now know that, when *India Song* became a cult film in June 1975, this good reception surprised her and at the same time cheered her up a great deal, brought her out of the bad time she was going through. The film was shown at several multiscreen cinemas generally sharing the bill with the very commercial *Tommy*, the rock opera by The Who. These days, knowing the crisis she'd been going through, I understand perfectly why Marguerite was so excited— I remember being very struck by this—when she saw the lines of people outside the cinemas, the lines she thought were for *India Song,* when in fact they were generally for the other film, the rock film, which didn't mean her film wasn't a success, it just didn't have the mass appeal she thought, or dreamed, it had.

Raúl and I had laughed fondly at this delusion, this conspicuous longing or obsession with success of Marguerite's. It's odd, I tell myself now. It's odd, but of the entire story of fear and success, of laughter and tears, what has most taken hold in my soul is, primarily, that violent disappearance of the sea views in Marguerite's dreams, perhaps because I remember one of the last sentences she wrote, a sentence from *C'est tout*, her literary testament, where she said she didn't know when asked if death frightened her: "I don't know anything anymore since I've reached the sea." Or perhaps because what most terrifies me about the idea of eternal death is to never be able to see the sea again, the waves breaking in winter on deserted beaches.

But, above all, what most takes hold of my soul is this surprising sentence, which says a lot about her style that is so frequently bold, provocative and brilliant: "If I don't sell here anymore, I'll go abroad." What a fantastic threat! I can see her saying it now: with a childish smile, almost in jest. But what she said is terrible, we all know it. At the same time it's poetic. Terrible and poetic: Abroad.

## 82

A few days after the second death of Franco, I happened to see a photo in a magazine of an OuLiPo (Ouvroir de Littérature Potentielle) meeting in the garden of François Le Lionnais's house. Belonging to this workshop of potential literature were, among others, Georges Perec, Marcel Bénabou, Italo Calvino, and Raymond Queneau. I was puzzled by this. What could a workshop of potential literature be? I wanted to be a writer precisely so I wouldn't have to go to work in an office, much less in a workshop. But surely it was a different kind of workshop, a literary workshop, just as the abbreviation *Li* indicated in the acronym OuLiPo. But I was back to where I'd started. What could a literary workshop be? It didn't sound good. Could it be something to do with that weirdo Perec?

"Wanted:" it said under the photo, "successors to Raymond Roussel, precursor of this movement, by writing method as much as by his particular conception of literature." I was fascinated by Roussel and also felt I was, in some ways, his successor. Could I be an *Oulipian* without knowing it? Seventeen members of the group appeared in the photo and on the table was a portrait of André Blavier, the workshop's foreign correspondent, based in Belgium. I took particular note of this surname, Blavier, and that he wore his hair exactly the same as I did. Not to mention his pipe, which looked like mine. OuLiPo has stolen my pipe, I suddenly thought. The next day, I made inquiries about this Blavier. "He's a librarian and a *pataphysicist*," was all I could find out. The *pataphysicists* again!

*Oulipians, pataphysicists, situationists* ... I thought the most prudent thing would be to carry on being a *situationist*, though not a practicing one. I wasn't in the mood for too many new adventures. But I had to admit that Paris was so full of surprises that there was never any end to them. I thought if I decided to take a little trip to Barcelona I'd get some attention when friends or acquaintances asked me how things were going in Paris. "Well, it's the same as here, except up there I'm an *oulipian*, a *pataphysicist* and a *situationist*. And this, as I'm sure you'll understand, changes things a bit," I'd say to them with my hair cut *à la* Blavier, smoking my pipe. I'm sure I'd enjoy seeing their surprise or watching them go green with envy. It was about time I got a bit more recognition in my city.

83

A few days after the second death of Franco, I took a little trip to Barcelona, I don't know why, perhaps so my parents could see my bandaged ankle. The fact is one night at the beginning of December I went to the Bocaccio nightclub on Calle Muntaner and there I met the novelist Juan Marsé, who'd lived in Paris for a few years and whom mutual friends had told of my aspirations to be a writer. At first I thought of asking his advice on what a person should do to make the most of their time in Paris, but it seemed stupid to ask something when I couldn't care less what the answer might be. Then it occurred to me to ask him for some literary advice, just like that, advice related to the art of making novels. As soon as I'd asked, I regretted it, since I thought he might easily give me a list like Duras's, a list of instructions. I thought if he gave me a list or something similar, I'd immediately show him the piece of paper with Duras's strict instructions—I always carried it in my back pocket—and tell him thanks anyway but I already had more than enough written recommendations. But Marsé was no list of instructions man. "That's strange, kid, young people don't usually ask for advice," he said. And then he took the trouble to explain— and I will always remember this—that one of the hardest aspects of the writer's trade was having to throw away fragments of the novel we're writing, passages we really like but are no use to the project in general because they don't fit in with the plot or the structure. "It's irritating sometimes to have to get rid of pages we like," he said, and shortly afterwards he went off after a blonde everyone called Teresa.

The next night, still mulling over what Marsé had told me, I went back to the Bocaccio and didn't see Marsé this time, the only thing I saw as I walked into the club was that I didn't know anyone or, rather, at the far end of the bar, somewhat secretly, the writer Juan Benet was talking to the novice Eduardo Mendoza, who in those days had just published his first novel. I went discreetly over to where they were and heard one sentence, only one (because they immediately moved away from the bar, perhaps alerted to my spying), I got just close enough to hear the sentence Benet said to Mendoza and I heard it perfectly and have never forgotten; it was spoken—I remember it was raining heavily outside, a stormy night—as if by an actor in a whodunnit: "Today I wrote the first page of a novel, and I don't know what it's about, but I know I've got a year of obsession ahead of me."

Benet's system didn't seem at all bad to me, I made a note of it, and I think I remember that it sounded like a magnificent and timely piece of unsolicited advice. Soon after this some people I knew came into the club. Among them, Beatriz de Moura, who would end up publishing *The Lettered Assassin*, although that night I couldn't have known this, that night I didn't even talk about my book with her, we talked about another book, one by Julio Ramón Ribeyro, a Peruvian writer I'd never heard of. Beatriz asked me if, when I returned to Paris, I could put the galleys of this book into the writer's hands; she didn't tell me what the title was, just that it was going to be published as soon as the proofs had been corrected by Ribeyro himself. I wasn't planning on going back to Paris im-mediately, but this sped things up somewhat, since I was too shy to tell her I didn't know when I'd be able to get there to give Ribeyro the proofs.

Three days later, I was back in Paris. And shortly after I'd gone back to my garret on Rue Saint-Benoît I took a subway train that, if memory serves, left me very close to Place Falguière, where it took me a very long time—I got quite nervous—to find the building Ri-beyro lived in. It took me a while, but eventually I found it and then I remember I walked up a steep staircase with the immense, private satisfaction of someone preparing to carry out a mission he's been entrusted with. I now tell myself it's quite likely the proofs I was carrying were those of *Stateless Prose*, which over time has become one of my favorite books. I remember this assignment made me happy, since I felt as if I were finally responsible for something and I'd even found a respectable reason for my decision to move to Paris.

It was December 9, 1975, and that same day, after dropping my suitcase off in the garret, I carried out Beatriz's assignment straight-away. I went up the steep staircase, rang the bell, and Ribeyro, who was playing with his son in the front hallway, opened the door in-stantly. I was very shy. But, by the look of it, so was Ribeyro. "I've brought you this," I told him. I've since learned from his journal that for him there was a parallel between his son's activity and his own, between play and writing: "The state of mind that draws him to his toys is similar to that which puts me in front of my typewriter: dissatisfaction, boredom, the desire to call upon others, or the oth-ers we have inside of us, to speak ..."

Ribeyro took the proofs and looked at me in silence. He was tall and lean, he seemed to have an ambiguous fragility. "On behalf of Beatriz," I added quite nervously. In the seconds that followed I waited for him to say something. When it seemed like he was about to speak, I ran away, and I did so because of the panic my timidity and his own had induced in me. I sped down the stairs and when I got to the ground floor and felt like I was about to reach the fresh and liberating air of the street, I suddenly heard the writer's voice, muffled by his son's happy laughter, coming from high up in the gloomy stairwell.

"Calm down," I heard him say.

It's paradoxical, but time has passed, and now I remember this timid, fleeting, cold encounter as very warm. I don't know where it comes from, this warmth, which arrives from so far away and lingers so long afterwards.

## 84

Perhaps because my father had given me an ultimatum about money, the first night I spent back in Paris, I dreamed that André Blavier, the man whose haircut was exactly like mine, was trying to tell me something but didn't dare. Until eventually he told me: "Young people think money is everything, and when they grow up, they find out it's true."

## 85

Thinking over what Juan Marsé had said to me in Barcelona, I discovered that what he'd said about passages one sometimes has to throw away might be related to the enigmatic section *unity and harmony* that appeared on Duras's list. If I understood correctly, a novel needed to have a certain inner coherence and it was preferable for the story line to be consistent. Anything that breaks away from the plot, no matter how alluring what one might have written, should be eliminated. Wasn't this what Marsé had been telling me in the Bocaccio? Or perhaps he'd been trying to explain that as he wrote he came up with unexpected stories that grew uncontrollably off the central trunks of his plots and he had to give them up, often with some regret? Had he actually been talking about unity and harmony? Or had he been talking about something quite different? Could I accept as an unbendable rule that novels needed to have unity? Perhaps the best thing to do was what I'd been doing in *The Lettered Assassin*, where I'd never strayed from the backbone of the story. But it wasn't clear this was for the best either, since paradoxically, as I wrote the book, I'd been discovering it was highly debatable that a novel *must* have unity and harmony. For, what about digressions then? I knew, or rather sensed, that there were very good novels that were brilliant precisely because of their digressions. What's more, I said to myself, a book was like a conversation. Did a conversation have to deal with the same subject, take the same form or follow the same intention for hours?

I told Raúl Escari about my worries, and he told me that the subject of unity and harmony was a far more difficult question to resolve than I thought. "Why's that?" I asked in fright. We were at his house on Rue de Venise. I remember there was a Boris Vian record playing and we'd argued because—I suppose I was still traumatized by the figure of Vian—I'd wanted to listen to Harry Belafonte instead. He went off to his bookshelves and said he was going to look for an example of a writer's violent struggle for unity. And after a short time he came back with Flaubert's letters to Louise Colet: "In five months I have written seventy-five pages. Each paragraph is good on its own and there are pages that are perfect. I am sure of it. But, precisely for that reason, it's not working. It is a collection of well turned out and ordered paragraphs that are not connected to each other. I will have to undo them, loosen the joins, as one does to the spurs of a boat when one wants the sails to catch more wind ..."

"So," said Raúl, "it's not a question of unity or a degree of tolerance for digression. It's a more profound or complex matter than it appears to be. The paragraphs should be connected to each other. Nothing more and nothing less."

I didn't say anything, but I felt faint.

## 86

I was full of doubts, of course, not a particularly bad way to be, but I didn't know that. Doubting so much made me suffer, but I could have saved myself the anxiety and simply doubted, without any problem. I was unaware that to doubt is to write. Marguerite Duras would say so in 1995, toward the end of her days: "I can say what I like, but I shall never know why people write and how it is people don't write. In life, there comes a time, and I think it is total, that we cannot escape, where we doubt everything: that doubt is writing."

Allow me to improvise a little now, ladies and gentlemen, to stop reading for a few moments and tell you something I think will fit perfectly into the lecture at this time, when you now have an outstanding view of the "grayness" of my days in Paris. I think I should tell you that of all the sentences of Marguerite's that I've read, there's one I know by heart and which, as I understand it, speaks the truth about me and about the life I'm recounting in this lecture: "We writers lead a very poor life: I'm talking about people who write for real. I don't know anyone with less of a personal life than I have."

## 87

Jeanne Boutade looked a lot like Coco Chanel, but a more modern version. She was a sort of thin, immaculate sparrow, talkative and lively as a woodpecker. She talked a lot and often mixed up her facts, though sometimes she was surprisingly lucid; in general, she used to get into a huge muddle with the information picked up from the thousand books she claimed to have read in the last three years, specifically since she'd realized she was a grown-up now and, desperate to no longer be a girl, she had started to read novels and non-fiction to try and discover something about the world, to try and find out everything that, as a girl, hadn't interested her at all.

As for the writer, cartoonist, actor, and painter Copi, he'd been one of the previous tenants of my garret and had left a manuscript there and one day he decided to pick it up, and that's how we met. It turned out we had lots of mutual friends, for instance, we both had friends in what might be called the *Argentinian group* of Paris, a bunch of young people who often hung around Marguerite Duras and who I remember always seemed very comfortable in the company of her intelligent madness, very comfortable because, as well as being fun and conveying a feeling of liberty and euphoria, Marguerite took a lot of interest in all of them, she was always asking them indiscreet questions, she wanted to be up to date and know everything. As Copi said: "Marguerite is alone, but she feeds off others."

One day, Copi, Boutade, and I went to eat oysters in a brasserie in the neighborhood. I'll always remember that day, not just because it was the first time I ever ate oysters (Copi was paying), but also because I discovered there were people who could literally live off a secret, and also because the winter light was so beautiful, I'm sure I have never in my life seen another day with light like that. The three of us had happened to run into each other on Rue de Medicis, up by the Corti bookstore, and we'd started to walk together in the strong, clear wind, strolling along the wet gravel paths of the Jardin du Luxembourg. We hadn't yet decided to go and eat oysters when, on the other side of the Luxembourg, turning onto Rue Bonaparte, we almost bumped into the bohemian Bouvier who, pointing to the top of a building in that street, was telling a bewildered couple that as a young man he had spent his bohemian days up there. "I lived up there, and there, thanks to that building, I became blocked and I failed as an artist," he was telling them in a very singsong voice.

"Look, look at that old guy," said Copi. We'd all seen him before. Boutade had even spoken to him one night when she'd found him outside the doorway to her house and seeing him light a match without a cigarette in his hand, she'd asked him what he was doing and the old man had replied: "It's nighttime, right? I'm lighting a match so I won't see a thing."

He was mad, that much seemed obvious. But his obsession with blaming the buildings of the neighborhood—only those of our neighborhood—for his artistic failure was a constant enigma. The bohemian Bouvier was one of the topics of our conversation that day on the terrace of the brasserie, with braziers outside, where we stuffed ourselves with oysters, and Copi didn't stop behaving like a rat for a second. Copi had a huge tendency to identify with the roles he was playing and at the time he was performing his work *Loretta Strong* every night in a Paris theatre. This play told the story of a rat who'd been sent into space and who, after an accident caused the disappearance of the entire human race, is left all alone in the universe and holds forth like a madwoman.

It was his glorious rat-like conduct that lunch time that would open my eyes once and for all to the absence of any boundary between theatre and life and would also show me the immense capacity other people have for writing dangerously, that is, starting off, from the very first moment, from an extreme situation that forces the author not ever to lessen the tension with which he has begun the drama. Would I one day be able to write starting off from an extreme situation, just as my admired friend Copi always did? That's what I wondered that day as I ate oysters with the writer and with Boutade and, as I ate the oysters, I remembered Hemingway, on the one hand, who, whenever he had some money in Paris, used to eat them "with their strong taste of the sea and their faint metallic taste that the cold white wine washed away, leaving only the sea taste and the succulent texture," and on the other hand I kept thinking about how lucky I was to be able to eat these delicious oysters, to be able to eat them slowly drinking the cold liquid from each of the shells and washing away the taste shortly afterward with the clear taste of the dry white wine.

"Why does the bohemian Bouvier spend all his time accusing this neighborhood of having ruined his art?" asked Copi in the voice a rat would have if rats had voices and if, moreover, they were hoarse. Boutade thought for a while, all of a sudden she drank down a whole glass of wine and said: "Basically the old guy's quite funny. He doesn't realize what he's spared himself by not being a successful artist." And she then got into a muddle with various famous names and called the painter Miró Pablo.

"Think of Tolstoy or Hemingway, both triumphant. And remember what happened to them and to so many other famous artists when they grew old," said Copi.

"Sometimes, I used to eat at La Fragate and I would see Henry de Montherlant hidden there behind the piano, it was disgusting and at the same time you couldn't help but feel sorry for him, you could see he was about to commit suicide. There's not a single artist who, no matter how triumphant, doesn't end up a recluse, hiding away when he gets old," said Boutade.

"Maybe the bohemian Bouvier is an existentialist and Juliette Greco's boyfriend and that's why he's like that," I joked. I don't think Boutade even heard me. She'd been lost in thought for a few moments and didn't hear me. Suddenly she said, as if starting a litany of reflections: "They, the winners, kill themselves, or they go mad or turn into idiots, or they die of boredom, almost none of them endures old age gracefully. The bohemian Bouvier, on the other hand, thanks to his failure, has fantastic presence and dignity, don't you think so? Though he does take his obsession with the buildings of the neighborhood a bit too far."

"Sometimes I wonder if he didn't actually spend his bohemian days in my garret and my fate will be the same as his," I joked again. Boutade, who didn't hear me that time either, began to talk as if she'd suddenly had a flash of inspiration: "I'm sure the old man will never tell us why he's obsessed with the buildings of the neighborhood and he won't tell us because this secret is clearly very important, it's what keeps him alive, clearly it's all the bohemian Bouvier has left, the secret of why he acts like that. *He lives off that secret.*"

"That's not a bad idea," said Copi. But then he added ironically: "Though you could also say that the old man is one of those who knows that three people can keep a secret perfectly well provided two of them are dead."

This summer in Paris, walking through the neighborhood, I thought again of what Boutade said that day and it seemed to me it wasn't a bad idea at all and that perhaps the bohemian Bouvier really did live off his secret. I thought a lot this summer in Paris about that day with the unforgettable winter light when I went to eat oysters with Copi and Boutade. I thought so much I began to look the buildings up and down trying to hate them so I could blame them for my garret failure of those days, and at the same time verify at last what kind of secret it was that gave Bouvier so much life. But I didn't get anywhere in this respect. I ended up confirming that, just as Boutade and Copi had, and just as I would one day, the bohemian Bouvier, as everyone does, he'd taken his least communicable secret to the grave. Hemingway had already said as much with his idea about short stories, his famous iceberg theory: never tell what is most important.

## 88

"Having lived in Paris unfits you for living anywhere, including Paris." (John Ashbery)

## 89

One day I finally decided to replace the burnt-out headlight on my car. Since I still didn't know where to go to get it fixed, I decided to ask the man who ran a tire shop in an alley off Rue Saint-Benoît, across from my house. The mechanic's wife looked drunk and told me that to talk to her husband I needed to request an audience and invited me to sit down. I sat. A dog came over and tried to jump on top of me. The woman said: "These little dogs just love knees." And what I just loved was the phrase. I wrote it down in the notebook I carried to write down things I heard in the street that might be useful for my book. A few days earlier I'd started to enjoy taking notes aimed at what I was writing. I liked doing it, because I noticed it made me feel like a writer.

A little while later, waiting in Porte d'Orleans for a mechanic to fix my headlight, I thought again of what the other mechanic's wife had said and thought she must've been slightly drunk and this explained why she'd come out with such a lovely phrase. And I immediately realized there was a certain similarity between my brief episode in the garage and the famous passage in *A Moveable Feast* where Hemingway explains how Miss Stein had trouble with the old Model T Ford she drove, and a mechanic at the garage, a young man who'd served in the last year of the war, hadn't shown much interest in repairing it; he had been told off by the *patron*, who said to him: "You are all a *génération perdue*." Miss Stein, when she heard this, added: "That's what you are. That's what you all are. All of you young people who served in the war. You are a lost generation."

"Really?" Hemingway asked her. For Miss Stein none of these youngsters had any respect for anything, they drank themselves to death. Hemingway tried to make her see that wasn't the case and that it was probably the boy's *patron* who was drunk by eleven o'clock in the morning and that was why he came out with such lovely phrases. "Don't argue with me, Hemingway," said Miss Stein. "It does no good at all. You're all a lost generation, exactly as the garage keeper said."

That same day, that is, the day I got my headlight fixed, in the evening, with the light now working, I went past the place they fixed tires again. With the excuse of thanking her for telling me where to get my headlight repaired, I went over to the garage to see if the mechanic's wife was still saying lovely phrases or if by now her drunkenness had taken her beyond that, perhaps to a dimension of hideous phrases. She wasn't there. Her husband was there, however, playing with the little dog. "What can I do or not do for you?" he asked. He was very drunk. Maybe he'll say a lovely phrase too, I thought. "Nothing," I said timidly, although with a certain amount of audacity as well, which I suppose came from the timidity itself. "What d'you mean, nothing?" said the mechanic, putting the little dog on his knees. "Nothing," I said, "I've just come to say thank you because I finally have two working headlights, and I didn't want to leave it till tomorrow." He stared at me strangely, then said slowly in Spanish, "Leave it till tomorrow? Tomorrow is today." The stalker of notable phrases inside me that day was so happy to have heard *Tomorrow is today.* I wrote down the phrase and, faced with the possible angry reaction of the man, walked out of there with the speed some people employ when walking out of garages after having to pay a fortune for a tiny repair. I still had time to hear the mechanic, possibly annoyed now, say, *"Bonjour lunettes, adieu fillettes."* But this phrase didn't interest me in the slightest. A little while later, back in my garret, with the happiness of someone returning satisfied from a day devoted to phrase-hunting, I decided first and foremost to incorporate *Tomorrow is today* into my novel. *Tomorrow is Today,* and not what I'd had in mind (*Cloud of Now*), would be the title I'd give to a novel supposedly written by a character named Juan Herrera. As for "Those little dogs just love knees," I'd put this phrase in the mouth of Ana Cañizal, the most likeable of my female characters. "It's been a fertile day," I thought, giving myself airs. As if my vocation as a writer had been confirmed that day.

90

I remember very well a very cold November day (or was it December?) in 1974, when I finally decided to make an incursion into the Place de la Contrescarpe, so linked to the memory of Hemingway's days in Paris. Sitting on the terrace of a bar that was called the Café des Amateurs in the twenties ("It was a sad, evilly run café where the drunkards of the quarter crowded together and I kept away from it because of the smell of dirty bodies and the sour smell of drunkenness," it says in *A Moveable Feast*), in less than an hour, I saw some five or six stalkers of Hemingway's life go by, day trippers who climbed the steep Rue Mouffetard and once in the square went looking for the old Café des Amateurs, took photos and then, as if they were hardened mountain climbers, carried on up to stop in front of number 74, Rue du Cardinal Lemoine, where Hemingway lived in the early twenties. They must have looked at and photographed the commemorative plaque that recorded the writer's interlude in the place, said a prayer for their hero and discovered that the famous *bal-musette*, the popular dance hall on the ground floor whose accordions wouldn't let Hemingway write, had become a humble discotheque.

I remember very well that, sitting there on the terrace of the café, I suddenly recalled a scene from "The Snows of Kilimanjaro" where the protagonist, who's dying, thinks of all the stories he's never going to write: "He knew at least twenty good stories from out there and he had never written one. Why?"

Did I know twenty good stories too? I immediately wondered that day. The truth was I didn't, I hadn't lived much, I had very few experiences and, if I was honest with myself, I had to acknowledge that I didn't have twenty, I didn't even have one story aside from *The Lettered Assassin*, a book I'd better keep on writing, and after that the muses would have their say. It's not really that serious, I remember telling myself. After all, it's a matter of patience, some day I'll be a good writer. But I also remember, then I set off a chain of questions in my head: Why the hell am I not already this good writer I'll be one day? What am I missing? Experience in life and reading? Is that what I'm missing? And what if I never get to be a good writer? What'll I be then? Will I spend my whole life being an inexperienced, unlettered young man, incapable of writing well? Will I be able to cope? I thought again of *The Lettered Assassin* and this time thought I should finish it right away and try and embark on a new project, a new, better book. But how was I going to improve on it when I spent so many hours sniffing around in all the books I had in the garret in search of ideas and never found a thing, and this made me live out every hour to the rhythm of my black despair?

If I were really a writer, I said to myself, I wouldn't have such atrocious problems. But would I have to wait until I was older not to have them? Did one ever get to be a real writer?

If I were really a writer, I said to myself, Africa would be mine. And why Africa? Because I'd know the melancholy of returning to where I'd never been. Because I'd go to places where I'd already been before ever having gone there, cities I'd already been to before ever having gone.

If I were really a writer, I'd try like Rimbaud to *create* all the celebrations, all the triumphs, all the dramas. I would try to invent new flowers, new stars, new flesh, new languages.

If I were really a writer, I would be absolutely modern. And when dawn came, armed with a burning patience, I would enter splendid cities. If I were really a writer, my days would go by in a very different way. If I were really a writer …

## 91

One night, I was jolted awake by a torrential storm raging over Paris. I shut the little garret window, threw a shawl over my shoulders, listened with some pleasure to the thunder and pretended to be frightened of the lightning. I remembered what I'd overheard Juan Benet say a few days ago in Barcelona, a sentence spoken on another stormy night. And I suddenly felt an enormous desire to start another novel, to leave, for other days and other nights, the final pages of *The Lettered Assassin*. I went to my desk and remembered that, after all, I was Mediterranean and, despite detesting the vulgarity of sunbathers' summers, I still adored the sun and the sea. In the midst of that storm, I bent over my desk and triumphantly wrote the first sentence of my new novel: "I love the sun, sand, and salt water." I filled a whole page talking about my fascination for the

Mediterranean, and never managed to move on to a second page. "Today I wrote the first page of a novel, and I don't know what it's about, but I know I've got a year of obsession ahead of me," I'd heard Benet say. I too had written the first page and I didn't know what my novel was about. So far, everything was perfect, everything the same—but from then on, everything was different. I spent hours waiting for my year of obsession to begin, which it never did. What would a year of obsession be like anyway? Not as simple as I'd thought at first. And, besides, what exactly might that obsession be? The following day, the storm over, I returned, downcast and humiliated, to *The Lettered Assassin*. I wrote for a few hours in the morning and then went out to buy a Spanish sports paper and eat in a very cheap Chinese restaurant on Rue du Bac, and on my way there I ran into Martine Simonet. I would have given anything for her to come and have lunch with me. Instead, walking quickly, she gestured from her side of the street to mine as if to say that the storm last night had been very heavy. Then she disappeared around a corner. She didn't even give me a chance to tell her I loved the sun, sand, and salt water. Perhaps it was better that way, because that day, if I'd been able to tell her that, I might also have said something more. "For the last year you've been my obsession," I might have said, for example.

## 92

At the end of 1950, when *Across the River and Into the Trees* appeared, the critics shook their heads. No and no. They were unanimous. Hemingway was done. But, not exactly one to give up without a fight, he wasn't going to let his arm be twisted so easily. He was someone who was in his element when faced with adversity. Life and literature were just that for him: a stage for the exaltation of man's most winning and heroic virtues. When the critics shook their heads, Hemingway came out with his usual sarcastic snarls, threatened to crack a few of their heads open, but none of this went beyond bluster, and he went back to work hard in an effort to prove he was very far from done. And then he wrote *The Old Man and the Sea.*

This book, about the courage of a man faced with failure, told the story of the tough and solitary struggle of an old Cuban fisherman. "He was an old man who fished alone in a skiff in the Gulf Stream and he had gone eighty-four days now without taking a fish." The book told of the old man's solitary struggle against a marlin that he vanquishes the way a matador kills a beloved bull. *The Old Man and the Sea* restored his international prestige as a writer, it moved ordinary readers to tears and surely contributed to his being considered for the Nobel Prize, an award he received with both great annoyance and secret satisfaction. He thought it awful to be given the same stupid prize they'd given to the mediocre Sinclair Lewis or the indescribable William Faulkner, whom he now saw as "a bourbon-soaked verbalizer." In any case, the Nobel made him more successful than ever: preachers based sermons on his novels; people kissed him, weeping, in the streets; his Italian translator was so moved to tears by *The Old Man and the Sea* he could hardly make any progress on its translation.

I read one of the lines from *The Old Man and the Sea* over and over again in the garret: "Man is not made for defeat. A man can be destroyed but not defeated." I read this over and over again especially toward the end of my days in Paris, when a certain sensation of absurdity mixed with failure began to overcome me, and I had to keep telling myself that I hadn't been defeated at all, simply because I hadn't engaged in any sort of battle. But this wasn't sufficient consolation because the feeling of absurdity remained, something we might also call a sensation of "why."

Why life, why write about an assassin, why Adjani's eyes, why my parents, why Hemingway, why Paris, why everything, my God, why? I remember walking quickly through the neighborhood on many occasions pretending I was going somewhere when really there was no place in the world where anyone was waiting for me. And one day, wandering more aimlessly than ever and very depressed, I met someone even more depressed than I was. It was near the end of October 1975, the very day they buried the great French boxer Georges Carpentier. I was wandering around with nowhere to go and sad as sad can be, when I saw, to my surprise, Alfonso sitting on the terrace of the Himes Bar. It was odd to see him there because he never left his neighborhood. In any case, there he was, his head bowed, the very image of a person in the depths of depression. I approached him. Since he liked boxing so much, I thought naively that he'd been to the former world champion's funeral and that his despondency had something to do with that death. I said hello and asked him if Carpentier's death had upset him, and he gave me a look of hatred I don't think I can ever forget. I wasn't expecting that. I never found out what it was that had so upset him, but the fact is that in a matter of seconds, I still don't really know how, we ended up in an absurd argument and he started to tell me, with unusual insistence, how much the young artists of that neighborhood got on his nerves. "Those whose lives have no plan or meaning," he said, "those who smoke pipes and go from café to café thinking they have to drink absinthe all the time and that it's a heroic feat to cheat their landlady out of her rent and that this makes them more of an artist." After these words, I felt perfectly depressed. My life had no plan or meaning. The great truth about me could not have been better expressed.

A few minutes later, returning to the garret, the sound of the door closing—hermetically as usual—seemed to me that day identical to that of a cold tombstone as it closes forever over a dead man. Was this even a place to fall down dead? If I died that night, it would take a very long time for anyone to notice my disappearance, look for me, find my corpse. I'd surely rot there inside the garret for a few days, until I started to reek and they kicked the door down.

Thinking all this made me instinctively clutch my head in my hands all of a sudden. The loneliness, the anxious searching, the familiarity with the absurd, all this was part of my world but none of it helped me write, it just worried me. I knew or had heard of other writers who'd put their anguish to good use. But I had no idea how to get anything out of my anxiety. I stayed with my hands over my face until deciding to lie down on the horrible mattress on the floor and not think any more, make my mind blank, I set myself the aim of not trying to comprehend, not analyze anything. I thought perhaps that was what wisdom consisted of. But the mere fact of having thought something, even if it was thinking that I didn't want to think, brought back the feelings of bitterness, anxiety, that anguish I still hadn't learned to translate into my literature.

However, as compensation for so much anguish, thinking about it led me to suspect that all those writers who knew how to translate their problems into their books and who had an *already made* vision of the world were actually ridiculous, since if literature was possible it was because the world wasn't *made*. Or was it just my world that wasn't? I decided to go outside again and smash Alfonso's face in. I realized straightaway, luckily, that this would simply be suicidal, since Alfonso, among other things, was an expert boxer. Besides, it wasn't exactly him I should be angry with, since he'd had the decency to tell me the truth. I decided to get out of there in a hurry anyway, leave the garret that was feeling like my tomb, and go to Rue Jacob, I left and even tried not to think I was going, tried to think of nothing, to analyze nothing, to be nothing (to be exactly what I was: nothing); depressed, I went to Rue Jacob to buy myself a piece of cheesecake, a sad little nothing piece of cake.

93

Jeanne Boutade—pseudonym of Estela Carriego—would often repeat this phrase: "No man knows who he is, no man is anyone." She claimed it was an old French saying. But one day, reading Borges, I discovered the famous phrase came from Macedonio Fernández.

Boutade had most likely heard one of her Argentinian friends say it and then forgotten where it had really come from. Did she know who Macedonio was? His name probably rang a bell. I was in a similar position. About Borges, however, we both knew more every day, especially me, who had discovered him very late but now couldn't stop reading him and finding ideas in his texts. The astonishing creative parasitism of Pierre Menard, for instance, with his exact yet distinct replica of the Quixote, which could be summed up as follows: if I write something that you've already written, it's the same, but it's no longer the same. Funes the memorious, the skilful forgeries of works of art, the *being in others* (as Pessoa would say), the belief that "perhaps we all know deep down that we are immortal," the *aleph* and the suspicion that poetry might be the elusive name of the world. If up till then I'd seen photographs of people or places I occasionally ended up seeing *in real life*, now this story of Borges's *aleph* represented a real step forward in my vision of the world. I saw that not only could one see certain people or places *in real life*, but, also, there existed the possibility—let's call it the wonder—of *seeing more*.

In a review Borges wrote of *Citizen Kane*, I found some lines that helped me discover a new weak spot of Hemingway's. Borges said that Welles's film had at least two plots and one of these was so stupid it was almost banal, chronicling the life of a millionaire who accumulated statues, gardens, palaces, swimming pools, vehicles, libraries, men and women, and ended up discovering that all his collections were vanity of vanities and, finding himself at death's door, yearned for one object alone in the universe: the humble sled he'd played with when he was a poor and happy child.

Since I'd started reading the world by Borges's standards, I found it impossible not to feel a certain compassion for Hemingway, who'd had a thrilling life, won the Nobel Prize and been adored or envied by half of humanity and, nevertheless, at the end of his days, with the same, almost banal, stupidity as citizen Kane, he wrote in *A Moveable Feast* that he felt nostalgic for the days of his youth in

Paris, for the time when he was poor and happy. All he needed to say then was that he dreamed of a sled.

I kept finding ideas in Borges's writing—and also in writing about his work, for example, I read once that he was referring to a tradition, because the modern world appeared as a place of loss and decline; at the same time he was referring to the notion of literary change, because literature affirms the value of the new. Borges rewrote the old, this is something I, as a novice, understood straightaway. With the help of some texts Boutade lent me, I seemed to sense that Borges had invented the possibility that we modern writers could, in rare proximity to the genuinely literary, practice the art as well, that is, we could keep writing, no less.

In those days, since I kept finding ideas in Borges, it wasn't long before I associated him with Orson Welles again, the night Jeanne Boutade and I went to see *F for Fake*, which, through interviews with the painter and forger Elmyr de Hory and Clifford Irving (author of an apocryphal biography of Howard Hughes), played with the notions of truth and lies in art. The film's subjects were Borgesian: falsification and the slippery border between reality and fiction, for example. *F for Fake* reminded me of Vicky Vaporú in line at the bakery, asking me if it wasn't true that she was a genuine counterfeit. The film, though it never mentioned Borges, revealed plots, frauds, labyrinths I could write about if I still wanted to become a real writer. To do so I'd have to welcome the invention of the real, in the same way as I'd have to invent myself if I really wanted to be a writer. *F for Fake* increased my passion for apocryphal books, for reviews of fake books, for the world of the great impostors, of men who pass themselves off as someone else, of men who are someone, and those who are no one.

The influence, the shadow of that film was to be a long one, and would change the direction of my apprenticeship. It began to influence me the very moment I left the cinema and my friend Boutade commented enthusiastically: "I told you. No man knows who he is, no man is anyone. Not even Epimenides knew." I asked if Epimenides was her new boyfriend. She laughed, shook her head. "He's an ancient sage," she said, and then quoted his words that had gone down in history: "The next sentence is false. The previous sentence is true."

I went back to the garret that night transformed into a man who didn't know who he was. And shortly afterwards, after reading a story by Borges about knife-fighters, I imitated the forgers and fakers in Welles's film in *The Lettered Assassin* and, quoting Borges without quotes, I wrote of "a knife-fighter who gradually leaves his strength in his weapon and in the end the weapon has a life of its own (as Krespel's diabolical violin did for Hoffman) and it is the weapon that kills, not the arm that wields it." It was the first time that, with a steely resolve, without acknowledging him, I quoted a man named Borges, *I was in another*, I quoted a man who was someone, and I was a man who was no one.

## 94

One night in the garret I read that in the thirteenth century Kubla Khan dreamed of a palace and built it according to the vision he'd had. Then I read that in the eighteenth century, the English poet Coleridge, who knew nothing of this Mongolian emperor's dream, took a narcotic one day so he could sleep and dreamed a poem about the palace and woke with the certainty that he'd composed or *received* a three-hundred-line poem that he remembered with singular clarity, fifty of which he was able to transcribe—a fragment survives in his oeuvre under the title "Kubla Khan," fifty lines, because the rest was lost due to the arrival of an unexpected visitor.

I fell asleep after reading the story of the dictated poem and I dreamed my mother was my sister, that she was a very young older sister with whom I had incestuous experiences. When I woke up, I felt I could remember with singular clarity the sexual episode I'd just dreamed and leapt to my desk to transcribe it in its entirety.

But, as soon as I sat down at the table, I forgot a large part of what a supposedly inspired voice had dictated to me. Using the remains of the dream, that is, the only image I more or less retained, and adding elements of my own, I composed page three of the central manuscript of *The Lettered Assassin*, a page I'm proud of, since for the first time—despite the fact it wasn't a real event but a dream—I managed to reconstruct and distort something I'd previously lived through, because a dream should be considered something lived, in the same way that dreams infiltrate our daily reality and even help us know how to manipulate it through writing: "And then he remembered an episode from his life: as a child he went into his sister's room one day without knocking and surprised her naked in front of the mirror. Ariadna, who was twice his age, flew into a rage and harshly inflicted a cruel punishment. She tied his hands and feet and whipped him as hard as she could until blood ran down his little body. She then agreed to untie him on the express condition that, on bended knee before her, he kiss her feet and thank her for the punishment he'd received. He did so and it was then, beneath the whip and kneeling before his sister's remarkable beauty, that a sensation of enjoyment and pleasure was aroused in him for the first time, intimately linked to his discovery of the female form. He always thought this episode would gradually fade from his memory but he was wrong. Because he had no other desire than to find his dead sister again and find himself back between those long-lost walls once more, to hear Ariadna still calling him in the tone of voice that had been so familiar ever since the long fevers of his childhood."

## 95

Of all my memories of youthful tedium, I don't know why, the same moment of profound boredom always surfaces, just one, from an afternoon in Paris that seems to be unforgettable. I can easily place myself back in the precise moment of boredom that day: I'm in my garret looking out through the miniscule window toward the belfry of the church of Saint-Germain-des-Prés. I'm telling myself, one more time, that I live at the center of the world, and suddenly I realize I've said this to myself a thousand times now and I'm repeating myself, which is a clear sign of boredom. I remember then that someone once said the center of the world is the place where a great artist has worked, and not Delphi. Am I a great artist to think I'm at the center of the world? And do I really believe that Saint-Germain-des-Prés is the center of something? It seems like naivety on my part. But it's not good for me to be so lucid, so I push these questions away. And go back to being bored.

How awful. Don't I know how to be with myself anymore? At school I was told that, according to Erasmus, one who knows the art of coexisting with oneself is never bored. It seems I've forgotten this art. I'm not at the center of the world and, what's more, I'm bored. Isn't intelligence for escaping boredom? This is the only thing that can help me. I clear my mind, make a game of finding a way out of my moment of boredom. I tell myself suddenly that to be bored is a waste of time. I write down this sentence on a blank page earmarked for *The Lettered Assassin*, the famous blank page that's supposed to scare writers so much. I wrote it down with the pencil I found a year ago, when I first arrived in the garret, in the top drawer of the little dresser, beneath the window where a few seconds ago I felt bored. This stub of a pencil must have belonged to one of the former tenants of the garret. Did it belong to Copi? Or to Javier Grandes? Or to the friend of the magus Jodorowsky, who lived there before Copi? Or to the Bulgarian theatre actress? Or did my black neighbor leave it here when he slept with the Bulgarian actress? Or did the pencil belong to the cineaste Milosevic, another former tenant? Or to Amapola, the transvestite who'd spent five months here? Or to Mitterrand, and since then generations of tenants have preserved the pencil from destruction in homage to the most illustrious of the former occupants of this small bohemian space?

I'm almost not bored anymore! Focused on this mental exercise, I imagine what *Comrade Morand*—that is, Monsieur Mitterrand—did for the two days he was shut up between these four melancholy walls. He must have had a pistol to defend himself. And a pencil, the pencil that's still here and could be in a museum of artefacts of the French Resistance. I imagine Mitterrand facing this same mirror. He's got the pencil behind his ear and he's smiling. He writes down something Comrade René Char said not long before that delighted him: "The downfall of the believer is finding his Church."

Afterwards, he stows the heroic pencil in the drawer so it can be found and preserved like a relic by the unfortunate bohemians who will pass through the garret over the years to come. He laughs again, turns back to the mirror, draws his pistol—now I'm not bored at all—he likes himself in this pose. (As for me, I discover that this uncontrolled or unconscious flow of the tide of my imagination in the mirror is like the practice of literature, with the invention of characters, for example.) Mitterrand looks at himself, laughs, plays with his pistol, *pow pow*, and says out loud: "People with no imagination think that everyone else's life is mediocre too."

## 96

I heard Romain Gary say in a lecture that for the writer, characters must always have a real presence. Were any of *The Lettered Assassin*'s real to me? None of them, actually; they almost all bore my initials the right or wrong way around, and were like extensions of my personality. Maybe my narrator assassin, having Adjani's eyes, was slightly real to me. And perhaps my mother, whom I presented as my sister. And perhaps also poor Ana Cañizal, who unlike the others didn't have my initials and moreover had a certain life of her own because at least I'd been able to imagine her, or rather, locate her in a reproduction of a Balthus painting I'd seen in Vicky Vaporú's house.

The mysterious atmosphere of that painting—a female dwarf

drawing open a curtain, and the light coming in through the window reveals a beautiful murdered woman—was what I wanted to achieve in my novel. Was it atmosphere Duras was referring to in her list of instructions with the enigmatic *setting(s)* section? It wasn't entirely clear to me. And what about the *dialogue* section? It was the least enigmatic of all, although still, just like the rest of them, highly problematic, at least for a novice like myself. Because dialogue generally demanded the reproduction of trivialities and this seemed difficult to combine with good literature. Apparently it was the easiest to solve of the items on Duras's list, it seemed easy to reproduce dialogue, and, nevertheless, it could end up being the most difficult of all. This is what I thought, while wondering, besides, whether it was justifiable to use dashes for dialogue and thereby fill up the pages quickly. Or should one use a pen and not a typewriter, employing quotation marks, in order to get dense, full pages, like great stains of writing, where the ink occupies every space, with the least white space possible on a page of compact handwriting, and no obvious gaps?

I was young, I opted for the first, for dashes. The other system, using quotes, filling the entire page as if it were a battlefield, I quite logically found terrifying. But then one day I read in the magazine *Tel Quel* that including dialogue in novels was the most antiquated and reactionary thing in existence, no matter whether with dashes or quotes, it was retrograde. I read this while drinking a cup of tea with milk in the Café Bonaparte, near my house. I thought this went even further than I'd anticipated on the matter of dialogue. My bewilderment was such that I took Duras's crumpled list of instructions, which I always had with me, out of my back pocket. Beside the word *dialogue* I wrote: "reactionary." Then, not wanting to totally disorient myself, I went in search of some sort of certainty and thought of Hemingway, master of the art of dialogue in stories. Then, I looked around me and confirmed that there were people at every table in the Bonaparte engaged in dialogue. However, this second certainty didn't change things that much. All these people

engaged in dialogue surely voted for the right-wing politician Gis-
card d'Estaing and, what's more, there was obviously nothing poetic
about them, they were overwhelmingly vulgar, and what they were
saying probably was as well. I tried to keep calm before making a
radical decision with respect to dialogue in my novel. I paid for my
tea and went back to the garret and, after some nervous reflection,
I cut out all the dialogue I'd written up till then, apart from three I
considered essential; I'd pay a little price for being reactionary, but
I wasn't prepared to change my entire novel.

97

I needed to have the odd secret and be wicked sometimes, feel per-
verse, perceive myself to be quite different on the inside to the *situationist* I was on the outside, have a bit of Jekyll and Hyde about me.
Or, I should say, to be Hyde every once in a while, not to be such an
innocent, radical leftist, a good guy. I believe I was perfectly correct
to think specifically of Hyde for my transgressive plans, since over
time I've discovered that in reality the fundamental theme of Ste-
venson's novel—back then in Paris, I hadn't read it, but, like everyone, I *knew* the story—is the envious fascination the conventionally
good person feels for his *wasted* opportunities for evil.

Perhaps this also explains why, for example, on one particular
occasion, one day when I cashed my father's money order in the
morning, I pretended to be rich and rotten and capitalist to the core
and went deliberately to Café La Rotonde to drink champagne and
there, without anyone noticing, naturally, I devoted myself to inwardly letting off steam and flirting with the idea of transforming
my mind into something monstrous in an attempt—now I see this
very clearly—not to *waste* all the opportunities to be the great son
of a bitch I thought I could be if I wanted.

However, deep down I was so good, so innocent and stupid that
every time I attempted this I ended up feeling ashamed of my-

self, which is, without going into too many details, what happened that day. I went to La Rotonde and on my seventh glass of champagne decided to free my mind of all moral and political ties, and summoned up the figure of a former customer of that café, the artist Domergue—a painter of elongated women, star of what we might call *calendar art*. I then evoked the figure of his domestic servant—"my housemaid," Domergue called him—a little man with a bulging forehead and a black goatee, who sometimes sat with Domergue's painter friends in the café and had a drink with them, though he never said a word.

I devoted myself to laughing inwardly at this little man—I'd gone to La Rotonde exclusively for this—I laughed away like a son of a bitch at that poor "housemaid." I spat on the little man's memory, but then I remembered an anecdote about him and grew ashamed of my spitting, regretting the excessive irreverence with which I'd treated the little man who never spoke in La Rotonde; or rather, he spoke once when Domergue's painter friends asked him if he cleaned any other bathrooms, to which the little man replied that he didn't. And when Domergue's friends asked him what, in that case, he spent the rest of his time doing, he said, looking at painters and overthrowing the Russian government. They all laughed at the doubly witty remark. "That's what we do, too," they said. What they didn't know was that this man was Lenin.

98

For quite a while I took the word *experience* on Duras's list as a humorous touch she'd included so as not to completely overwhelm me, but one day I began to suspect that perhaps *experience* was also meant to be serious, there was no reason to believe otherwise. If this were true, it was really annoying. The word *experience* always sounds dreadful, but when you're young it sounds even worse. I'd once heard someone say: "Experience is like a comb for a bald man." I couldn't agree more. I was sure experience was absolutely useless.

What I didn't yet know was that you needed to have experience to know why it was absolutely useless. Besides, did I really know I didn't have any? I neither knew nor didn't know it, I simply didn't want to think about it, since I found the subject hugely annoying, typical of the no less annoying adult world.

But one day I ran smack into *experience,* and it was an unrepeatable experience. I went to Studio des Ursulines to watch a documentary on American writers in Paris, on the *lost generation,* and heard Hemingway talk about his *iceberg principle.* I'd read about this principle, but had never heard it spoken about live, in Hemingway's very own voice. Though he was no longer my absolute idol, I was impressed by his presence on the screen and by his words. "I try to write," I heard him say, "on the principle of the iceberg. What we see of the iceberg is only a tenth of it, the rest is under water. The story that isn't there in the story, the part under water, is constructed out of the unsaid, out of implication and allusion."

And later something else: "*The Old Man and the Sea* could have been over a thousand pages long, but this wasn't what I wanted to do. First I have tried to eliminate everything unnecessary to conveying the experience to the reader, in spite of the fact that experience at sea, for example, was something I had a lot of. But this experience does not explicitly appear, though of course *it is there,* but it can't be seen. This is very hard to do and I've worked at it very hard. For example, I've seen the marlin mate and know about that. So I leave that out. I've seen a school (or pod) of more than fifty sperm whales, and once harpooned one nearly sixty feet long and lost him. So I left all that out. But the knowledge is what makes the underwater part of the iceberg."

As I left Studio des Ursulines, I had the impression I'd just learned more about *experience* than at any time up till then. But having this impression didn't make me exactly jump for joy. I walked out with this question ringing in my head: What sort of personal experience of mine, when it comes time to write, can I leave in the submerged part of the iceberg? To be honest, I had to acknowledge that if experience were a class, the grade I'd earned the hard way was an *F*. Just what sort of experience did I think I was gaining with my farcical garret life?

To spare myself some anguish, so I could carry on writing *The Lettered Assassin*, I set about convincing myself that all this stuff about experience was entirely debatable and surely one could write without it, there was no shortage of examples. All one had to do was exchange Hemingway's Kilimanjaro for that of Raymond Roussel, author of *Impressions of Africa* and an extremely cerebral writer who never exploited his personal experiences, but instead devoted himself, thanks to a method of phonetic combinations he'd invented, to telling stories that emerged from the prose itself, a kind of chilly poetic narrative directly connected to his strange way of traveling, the polar opposite of Hemingway's.

The author of *Impressions of Africa* didn't travel in order to have experiences he would then use in his books or leave quietly in the invisible part of the iceberg. Roussel traveled not to discover anything new, but rather to see up close the exotic universes that had filled his childhood in the form of stories and novels—not to have stories to tell or to hide while he told parts of them, but just to verify that what he'd read about as a child really existed. These marvelous words are his: "It seems apt that I should mention here a rather curious fact. I have traveled a great deal. Notably in 1920-1921 I traveled around the world by way of India, Australia, New Zealand, the Pacific archipelagos, China, Japan, and America. I already knew the principal countries of Europe, Egypt and all of North Africa, and later I visited Constantinople, Asia Minor, and Persia. Now, from all these travels I never took anything for my books. It seems to me that this is worth mentioning, since it clearly shows just how much imagination accounts for everything in my work."

Agonizing over the matter of the creative imagination and whether or not experience is necessary to writing, I went to consult Raúl Escari about my doubts. "You ask me everything," said Raúl, "have you noticed that?" I ignored the affectionately impertinent remark and set about telling him that, due to my lack of experience and to keep this from harming me when I came to write, I was starting to feel inclined to align myself with Raymond Roussel and his concept of literature, and therefore practice a cold and very cerebral kind of writing in clear opposition to the fireworks of the classic expert-in-everything, bon vivant Hemingway.

Since Raúl remained silent and everything appeared to indicate he didn't really approve of my plan to tell stories that emerged from the prose itself, I asked him if he thought I was being unfair to Hemingway. Then, with an expression I'll never forget, he resolved the matter like this: "Look, it's quite simple. If Hemingway had really been a scrawny little weed who spent his life fantasizing or inventing the stories in his books he said he'd experienced or that were behind what he described, this wouldn't change things one bit, he'd still be the great writer he was. But he wasn't a weed, and he wasn't scrawny.

## 99

There are passages in Paris in which the closed atmosphere seems to presage the end of something. Of our world, for example. Of our time in Paris, as happened to me. Those *passages* Walter Benjamin studied at length—covered galleries, which might sometimes seem very beautiful to us, but their asphyxiating atmosphere can also remind us of our soul when reality hits us in melancholy moments and tells us the truth, announcing that the end is nigh. Louis-Ferdinand Céline said in *Death on the Installment Plan* that the sinister Passage Choiseul—the passage itself—had ended up becoming aware of its filthy asphyxia. And he also said that with its stink of urine and leaking gas and other subtleties, this alley, where his mother sold lace and where he'd spent half his life, was fouler than the inside of a prison, and, moreover, a bad omen. One day, when I was least expecting it and in the last place I would have expected, the Passage des Panoramas, I bumped into Petra, whom

I hadn't seen for months. As soon as I saw her, I don't know how, but I immediately smelled urine and gas leaks, and sensed the asphyxiation of that covered passage, as if not wanting to contradict Céline. Petra, so ugly and so belittled by me, was arm in arm with a burly pimp, a real pimp, not one like I'd thought myself when I was with her.

As if she'd immediately seen all the worry in the world on my face and, perhaps prompted by an urge for revenge, Petra said something she'd said to me once before and, though it had then had little impact on me, this time it shattered my fragile morale: "You should go back to Barcelona, you're wasting your time here. I'm wasting mine too, but at least I've got a boyfriend and a job." The worst thing was that I didn't answer her, I didn't reply because pathetically I feared a violent reaction from the pimp. Despite not being aware of it at that time, I now think that this cruel and depressing incident was a little like an omen that something was going to end for me, it was surely the beginning of the end of my time in Paris.

## 100

On October 29, 1965, Ben Barka, the leader of the Moroccan opposition to King Hassan II, had arranged to have lunch with a journalist and a filmmaker in the Brasserie Lipp on Boulevard Saint-Germain, across the street from the Flore. As he was on his way into the restaurant, two policemen from the *brigade mondaine*—Inspector Souchon and his subordinate Voitot—identified themselves and politely invited him to get into the car where Antoine Lopez, agent of the French counterespionage services, awaited him, and said he had orders to put him in contact with a high-ranking official. It is known that they headed for a villa in Fontenay-le-Vicomte, where all trace of the Moroccan politician was lost forever.

Ten years later, at the end of October 1975, I went to have lunch, as I often did, at the café-restaurant in the Drugstore Saint-Germain, which was right next to the Lipp, and also across from the Flore. I always used to eat there alone, sheltering behind the Spanish sports papers *Marca* and *Dicen*, which I'd read from cover to cover. That day, I'd just finished my first course and was waiting for the waitress to bring me the second when two tall, burly men approached me, two remarkably broad-chested gorillas who identified themselves as secret police and discreetly invited me to follow them to the restroom, where, noticeably nervous, they pinned me up against the wall, frisked me and asked why *I* was so nervous. "And you," I asked them, "why are you both so nervous?" They had their reasons to be nervous, since they thought I was the Venezuelan terrorist Carlos, the same man who not long before had planted a bomb that left a trail of death and destruction in this very establishment; the same man who, according to the waitresses' statements, had been seen before the attack having lunch several times in the restaurant, reading newspapers in Spanish.

The two policemen, who soon realized they must have made a mistake, finally asked me to take them to my garret on Rue Saint-Benoît (which I, trying to let them know I had connections, had told them I rented from Marguerite Duras), they wanted to verify that I wasn't in fact manufacturing bombs there and was only, as I'd said, the innocent writer of a first novel entitled *The Lettered Assassin*.

This incident also had something of the beginning of the end of my time in Paris about it. This is what I sensed when, escorted by the two immense gorillas, I was about to cross Boulevard Saint-Germain on the way to the garret. A touch of humor now punctuates the memory of what at the time felt like a difficult moment. Luckily I had no idea that exactly ten years before, in similar circumstances and also across the street from the Flore, two policemen had made a man on his way to have lunch at the Lipp disappear forever. I think if I'd been aware of the precedent of Ben Barka's disappearance I would have died of fright. As it is, the memory of that day is punctuated by a touch of humor—as we passed the

Flore, a friend of Arrieta's—a gay painter who tried his utmost to look like Andy Warhol—not realizing my two escorts were policemen, shouted as I passed: "Well, aren't we in good company today!"

Did they have evil intentions, like Souchon and Voitot, those policemen who frisked me in the restroom of the drugstore and then came up to my garret and, after a quick look around, stayed for a few minutes reading the opening pages of the manuscript of *The Lettered Assassin*, perhaps thinking my as yet unfinished book might be a collection of secret documents on international terrorism? I don't think so; once the business was over, they seemed quite inoffensive to me. In any case I'll never know, just as I'll never know if they were the two policemen killed a few weeks later by the terrorist Carlos as they tried to arrest him in a Paris apartment.

The two gorillas searched the garret, saw that no one was making bombs there, took a long look at *The Assassin*, and finally the tall gorilla asked me if I'd read any Simenon. I didn't know what would be the best thing to say and decided to tell the truth, I said I hadn't. "Well," said the short gorilla, "we'll be leaving now." They seemed to be in a good mood all of a sudden, as if they'd managed to get out of an awkward situation. And, although they didn't apologize to the innocent young man whose lunch they'd interrupted, the short guy did something quite thoughtful once they'd left the garret and were out on the landing on their way to the stairwell. He turned around suddenly and with all the ironic kindness a policeman is capable of, said: "Living alone in a dive like this is not such a good idea." And the other policeman added: "It's not good to live in the dense solitude of criminals." This last came as quite a surprise. It was a strange sentence to hear spoken by a policeman, or by anybody for that matter. Anyway, did he think because I was writing about a lettered assassin I was potentially a solitary criminal? Many years later someone told me that "the dense solitude of criminals" was an expression Simenon often used.

## 101

One winter morning, walking with Arrieta through the Jardin du
Luxembourg, down a tree-lined side avenue we spied a solitary, almost motionless, black bird reading the newspaper. It was Samuel
Beckett. Dressed in black from head to toe, there he was on a bench,
very still, looking desperate; it was scary. And it almost seemed
like a lie that it was him, that it was Beckett. I'd never imagined
I might run into him. I knew he wasn't one of the dead legends,
rather someone who lived in Paris; but I'd always imagined him as
a dark presence flying over the city, never as someone you might
come across reading the newspaper in despair in a cold, lonely, old
park. From time to time he turned a page, seemingly with such
anger and intense energy that if the entire Jardin du Luxembourg
had shuddered we wouldn't have been at all surprised. When he got
to the last page, he sat there both engrossed and distracted. It was
even scarier than before. "He's the only one brave enough to show
that our despair is so great we don't even have words to express it,"
said Arrieta.

## 102

In *Vita nuova*, Dante tells us that he once listed the names of sixty
women in an epistle just so he could secretly slip in Beatrice's name.
Borges thinks Dante repeated this melancholy game in the *Comedia*;
he suspects that he constructed the best book literature has managed to achieve just to be able to insert a few encounters with the
long-lost Beatrice. And I have the impression that—admitting the
all too unmissable disparities—I unconsciously played this melancholy game in *The Lettered Assassin*, I have the impression I wrote the
whole book just to be able to insert a poem into it, a single poem, the
last one I ever wrote and only one I've ever published. Seen from this

angle, all of *The Lettered Assassin* would be an excuse for me to be able to bid farewell to poetry through these lines: "Exile, you'll walk with neither tears nor tomb / and sail close to time past and from there, / further away and into the distance, / eyes towards the Never Seen, / heading for Circe, dead beauty, / where, silently passing / the sunless cities, you will find me. / I'll be the wrecked ship that lands / on the beach of my friend, / who is celebrated in vain."

These days I see *The Lettered Assassin* basically as my farewell to poetry. The hidden plot of the book would be the quiet tragedy of a youth who's bidding farewell to poetry to succumb to the vulgarity of narrative. While Hemingway hadn't worried even the slightest about this shift from poetry to prose ("the lyric facility of boyhood that was as perishable and as deceptive as youth was"), I on the other hand was seriously affected. *The Lettered Assassin*, with its tormented description of the death of a poet, bears full witness to this fact, it speaks not only of my personal drama but also of the drama of many young writers who, at the start of their creative process, if they are imaginative, tend to construct poetic worlds of their own, shaped to a large extent by their reading; but later on, as the intensity of their imagination gradually diminishes, they fall into everyday prose and feel they've betrayed their early poetic principles. Some, the most intelligent and stubborn of them, resist giving in so easily and keep faith with poetry for some years more, but what they don't know is that, no matter what they do, poetry already abandoned them a long time ago. No one can escape this devastating law of poetic life, no one. Although, the vast majority of humanity escapes it, all these people battered and crushed by the tyranny of reality who've had the debatable luck of never having even distinguished between poetry and prose.

## 103

*"M. D., qui a beaucoup lu, aujourd'hui lit très peu"* ("M. D., who has read a lot, today reads very little"), begins Benoît Jacquot's essay in a book the French publisher Albatros had just published on Marguerite Duras, and which I bought to catch up on my landlady's creative world. Lacan and Maurice Blanchot, among others, contributed to this volume. I remember Raúl Escari got unusually excited by this first sentence of Jacquot's essay, and for several days he went around repeating it to everybody, including Duras. And I also remember in the book there was a kind of collective celebration of the film *India Song*, which had just opened to acclaim in several Paris cinemas. Her second husband, Dyonis Mascolo, said, for example, that *India Song*, even with Dreyer as a precedent, represented the true birth of cinema, and heralded a great future for this young art. Duras had blazed a trail with this film. Maurice Blanchot wondered what *India Song* was. Could it be said to be a film or perhaps a book or not one thing or the other? After reading Blanchot's essay, I had the impression I knew less about Marguerite than I knew before starting to read the essay. Jacques Lacan, meanwhile, said he was left open-mouthed when he'd read *The Ravishing of Lol V. Stein.* And he also said other things I've forgotten or, rather, that I didn't understand, not that this worried me too much, since by then I was used to not understanding Lacan.

This anthology opened with some words from Duras herself where she confessed that she wrote in order to be busy with something. And she added: "If I had the courage to do nothing, I'd do nothing. It's because I don't have the courage to do nothing that I write. There is no other reason. It's the truest thing I can say on the matter." I was impressed by the sincerity of these words. A few days after reading the book, I ran into Marguerite on Rue Saint-Benoît and when our short conversation in the street drifted towards literary terrain, it occurred to me—already knowing what she'd reply—to ask her why she wrote. I thought that, as soon as she began to answer me with her predictable reply ("it's because I don't have the courage to do nothing ..."), I'd interrupt her with a broad smile on my lips to tell her I knew how the sentence went on, since I'd read it in the compilation of essays on her work I'd just bought, interested as I was in all books about her (and this way she'd see I was interested in her world).

But I was in for a big surprise, because I was expecting one answer and got another. "I write to keep from killing myself," she said laconically. Stunned, I mumbled a few semi-coherent words; I didn't know what to say or how to go on. Luckily, Duras practically ordered me out of her way, as she had to go to the Flore, she added: "It's awful, because I have to meet Peter Brook, who always brings me bad luck, the last time I saw him I was almost run over by a car in front of the Flore."

Did she write to keep busy or to keep from killing herself? Which was it? Was she entirely sincere, or was she practicing literature all the time? Do we have to wait until an author dies so a biographer can recount the life as it's been lived and not just as the writer claims it has been? I'd read, I don't know where, that André Gide used to say an artist shouldn't recount his life exactly as he's lived it, but rather live it exactly as he is going to recount it. And, in the middle of all this, what was I planning to do? Live my life as I planned on recounting it? And how did one manage something like that?

I walked along reflecting on all this, until I got to the garret and went up exhausted by so many questions. Later, with time, I've discovered that Duras was a great specialist in the negative, a professional of *pathos* or its precise simulation. Few sentences are as seductive, as hypnotizing as the one we find in her book *Écrire:* "Writing: writing arrives like the wind, it is naked, it is ink, it's the written word, and it passes like nothing in life passes, nothing except, of course, for life itself." It's a fascinating sentence. But should we believe it to the letter? Besides, what does it say? If it's saying anything at all, it's actually something very simple. It's something truly simple—simply that literature is the same as the wind. You have to admit that's particularly well put. Marguerite always liked to play with fire, I know this now, I didn't know it then. Marguerite, I now know, loved to lay bare the challenge of the incessant futility of words.

That day, exhausted by so many questions, I went up to the garret, looked again at the book on Duras and *India Song*, and suddenly experienced a few minutes of unexpected happiness when my attention alighted distractedly on the caption of a photo in the book: "Marguerite Duras, aged seventeen. Sadec (Cochinchina)." All my attention centered on the last word, the one naming a legendary country. I'd never until then been aware of it, but my landlady had been born in Saigon, a city linked to my maternal great-grandfather, who had participated in the Spanish punitive expedition that fought alongside the French in the mid-nineteenth century in that distant place and had entered Saigon, though the French raised their flag and kept the spoils and regarded the Spanish as auxiliary troops. But my great-grandfather was there in Saigon with Colonel Palanca, and there he stayed for some years.

As a child, my mother—like so many other Spanish mothers of the time—used to threaten to send me to Cochinchina if I misbehaved. But, unlike the others', my mother's threat was not entirely empty given the connection tying us to this remote country, a connection that all of a sudden seemed ongoing in my contact with Duras, the writer arrived from Cochinchina.

The discovery of this oriental connection gave rise to a long scene of deceptive happiness when in the following minutes, stretched out on the mattress on the floor—that horrible bed where I wasted away my days—I speculated on the mysterious contact linking my family to Cochinchina, and some strange, exotic, passionate stories came into my head. It was as if I were writing, but having much more fun than I did writing, since I didn't have to comply with the rigid rules of Duras's list. Suddenly, on the journeys of my imagination, I discovered for a few unforgettable minutes that my mental prose could sail over tranquil surfaces like a ship quickly gliding, with a favorable wind in its sails. The stories of my relatives and Cochinchina glided along, and wrote themselves in this wind, free and unfettered. I discovered the virtues of combining imaginary writing on wind with "the courage to do nothing," as Marguerite would say. I felt delighted with life and suddenly fell asleep, as if the joy of not writing had the power to send me to sleep.

Hours later, I woke up. I stayed in bed and kept very still, looked at the window, looked at my knees, remembered my happiness before falling asleep, listened to the sounds—as incomprehensible as ever—of the black man in the room next door. The happiness with which I'd fallen asleep soon switched to regret for not actually having written anything, only imaginary strokes in the wind. If I thought about it properly, it was appalling. I'd fallen asleep from happiness, that was true. But also from stupidity and sheer idleness. I thought if I was so lazy about writing, why didn't I travel to the far away foreign light of Cochinchina? Nobody there would force me to write, I could inscribe stories on the wind. Could I really inscribe them? Cochinchina's name had changed some time ago and it was now called Vietnam and it was hell and not a place for idlers. While it was true no one would force me to write there, what was certain was that they wouldn't let me drift off to sleep from happiness and, moreover, I'd be forced to work. I remembered when my mother, finding out I sympathized with left-wing ideas, said to me: "Very well, if you're a Communist go to Russia. You'll soon see how they make you work over there."

104

It felt like *The Lettered Assassin* was coming to an end; to boost my morale a little, I told myself that at least the *plot* of my book was original. But then suddenly, on January 12, 1976, I read in *Le Monde* that Agatha Christie had just died and I was filled with dismay to learn from a footnote that she'd written a detective novel, *The Mur-*

der of *Roger Ackroyd*, in which the reader discovers at the end that the narrator of the book was in fact the murderer. I hadn't expected something like this. Had I wasted the last two years of my life writing *The Lettered Assassin*? I believed my idea of killing the reader with a narrator who doesn't reveal she's the murderer until the very last line was highly original and unique. My heart sank when I saw this wasn't the case; I was really under the impression that if there was anything of interest to the book, it was the originality of this trap set for the reader.

What did I have to do? Start over again?

Everything's been invented, I told myself. Or did I perhaps believe that someone could still be original?* I spent a few downcast days, until one evening, all of a sudden, in a fit of good humor, I decided to swap the photo of Virginia Woolf (presiding as a poster over the garret, reminding me that I too had *a room of my own*) for a gigantic photo of Saint Agatha Christie, the true lettered assassin and the grand old lady of Crime. And I joked to myself that the next tenant of this garret would be a crime writer. Then I realized that in days gone by it would never have occurred to me to think about the next tenant of this *chambre*. It was as if, just like *The Assassin*, my time in Paris was coming to an end.*

---

* That day I told myself everything had been invented, but I had yet to find convincing evidence for this, supplied a few days later, by a short extract from Beckett's *Molloy*, which I opened at random at one of the bookstalls on the banks of the Seine: "You invent nothing, you think you are inventing, you think you are escaping, and all you do is stammer out your lesson, the remnants of a pensum one day got by heart and long forgotten, life without tears, as it is wept. To hell with it anyway."

## 105

Do we invent nothing? Was the narrator of *Molloy* telling the truth? What about learning? Do we learn nothing either? Are the *writer's years of apprenticeship*, for instance, so exalted and so hackneyed, merely a fallacy? Do we live without learning a thing and then simply, as Beckett said, go to hell? Is the fact that we invent nothing perhaps the only thing we can learn in this world? The *coup de grâce* came when Arrieta presented me with the novel *Jacob von Gunten*, by Robert Walser. I opened it to the first page, and began to read: "One learns very little here, there is a shortage of teachers, and none of us boys in the Benjamenta Institute will come to anything, that is to say, we shall all be something very small and subordinate later in life."

What an outlook.

I remember one rainy day, sitting on the terrace of the Café Rien de la Terre on Rue Sainte-Anne, toward the end of January 1976, agonizing over Walser's book and wondering if the famous *years of apprenticeship* might not actually be a false myth.

"I have learned one thing, I've learned how to type, that's for sure," I thought shortly before calling the waiter over, paying the bill, leaving the café and at the same time leaving behind my apprenticeship years. "And to hell with it," I remember thinking.

## 106

A few days later, I went to the theater for the opening night of a play called *Cairo*, written by two inseparable young friends, the Argentinians Javier Arroyuelo and Rafael López Sánchez. I went with Raúl Escari, who knew both of them very well, and with Julita Grau, a friend from Aiguafreda, a village in Catalonia where as a teenager I'd spent summer vacations with my parents. Julita, who'd always stood out as a precocious intellectual, had just arrived from Barcelona and came to see me in the garret. Although this worried me because I didn't know what she was after, I was very happy to see her and we recalled some parties and certain gardens of awful Aiguafreda. After inventing a thousand excuses in case she wanted to stay the night in the garret, I eventually invited her to come to the theater.

Paloma Picasso, who would soon marry López Sánchez (and years later divorce him, the division of property costing her a real fortune), collaborated in the staging of *Cairo*, designing the jewelry the actors wore and at the same time bringing glamour and an audience to the work of these two young Argentinians, who were part of the Paris theater counterculture and playwrights for the Theater TSE, which was run by another Argentinian, Alfredo Rodríguez Arias.

From the first moment, I realized I wasn't going to understand the play very well. Julita Grau contributed invaluably to my understanding absolutely nothing at all when, at the end of the first act, trying to help, she told me the play was very much part of the *psychoanalytical trend in its severest, most Lacanian aspect* and the very fact that the title in Spanish, *Cairo*, was missing the article *El* was a clue in itself. A clue to what? I didn't get an answer. When the performance was over, Raúl went backstage to congratulate the writers, and we went with him. And, I don't know how, we ended up in Paloma Picasso's grandiose Mercedes convertible smoking gigantic Havana cigars and driving along the freshly sprayed streets of Paris with her and Raúl and Julita and the authors of *Cairo* on our way to Le Sept nightclub, on Rue Sainte-Anne. Never in my life have I felt so grand. There, sitting in the back seat of the magnificent convertible, with Glenn Miller playing on the radio, I pretended to see myself as the king of the Parisian *dolce vita*, as if I'd just conquered the city and was, in every sense, Pablo Picasso's heir.

The triumphant Catalan Ricardo Bofill was a loser compared to me! There's never any end to Paris, I thought. And I took my time over the agreeable thought that I was king of Paris, a young god way above the vulgar folk, scourge of the idiots. And I remembered Jacques Prévert, who used to say he had one foot on the Rive Droite, the other on the Rive Gauche, and the third up the ass of all the imbeciles. And I also remembered Martine Simonet and thought how great it would be if she were walking the streets at this hour like a poor Cinderella and saw us go by and was impressed at how much my bohemian life had improved. And I also thought how perfect it would be if waiting to cross at a traffic light was my garret neighbor, the impertinent black man. "Goodbye, *tubab*, goodbye," I'd say to him, blowing Havana cigar smoke in his face.

I was thinking all this when Julita Grau asked me if I was writing anything at the moment and I told her I was just finishing a novel that would slay its readers. And when she asked what I was planning to write next, I took a long pull on my Havana and suddenly came up with the title of a play I would write called *South of the Eyelids*. And when she asked what this play was about, I made the most of a pause in the conversation between Paloma Picasso and the two Argentinian writers to look up at the starry sky of Paris and say with false modesty, though unable to disguise the haughty voice of one who believes himself to be light years ahead of his contemporaries: "Well, let's not talk it up just yet, but I have a feeling it's going to be an interesting piece, a psychoanalytical study of the gaze." Picasso and the playwrights looked strangely at me. I wasn't at all embarrassed, quite the contrary. "A psychoanalytical study of the gaze," I repeated, totally convinced I was a real big shot.

107

The following morning, Julita Grau came to the garret again. I immediately wondered: What does she want this time? I thought: I should have gone to bed with her last night. The fact is, I thought, women only want one thing, for men to want to go to bed with them. But if you go to bed with a woman, she can screw you over. And if you don't, she'll screw you over anyway for not wanting to.

I recalled an English novella I'd read not long before that described the iridescent feminine fantasy of sitting in a garden at the end of the afternoon, reading and waiting for the man who returns every day to her home and to her arms. Could that be what Julita wanted? I wondered. And if she admitted that's what she wants, should I believe her? And besides, did my fantasy involve coming home on a commuter train weighed down with a heavy briefcase to find an intellectual little woman who'd been lazing around all day reading Unamuno?

"What are you thinking about?" she asked. "Nothing. Have you come to say goodbye?" "No," she replied tersely. I got very nervous. "Tell me the truth, what do you see in me?" She didn't seem surprised. "Probably an improved version of yourself," she replied with great aplomb. "I don't understand." "I see you," she said, "as a complete person, and not the confused mess you see yourself."

She stayed seven days in the garret. From Saturday to the following Friday. On the morning of that Friday, I found out by chance that my father had hired her to get me to fall in love with her and convince me to go back to Barcelona. I found this out and was dumbfounded, mentally destroyed. She cried.

## 108

In January of the year he would kill himself, Hemingway, a frail old man, white-headed, pale, meagre-limbed, but apparently somewhat recovered from his latest crises, was allowed by his doctors to return to Ketchum. His friend Gary Cooper had recently said that a happy man is one who, busy with his work during the day, and tired at night, has no time to think of himself. But Hemingway did have time. He'd been asked to contribute a sentence to a presentation volume for the newly inaugurated president of the United States, John F. Kennedy.

He worked for a whole day and didn't come up with the sentence. "It just won't come anymore," he stammered to his friend George Saviers. And he wept. He never wrote again. When spring came, they say he saw nothing of it and didn't even realize it had come.

Always dressed in black, head bowed, he lived in a permanent state of despair. Some of the heroes of his books, with their stoic endurance in the face of adversity, with the extraordinary *elegance* of their suffering, would go down in history and live on, at least for a while, in humanity's memory. But he was in despair and his stoic endurance was foundering. And he couldn't do much about it. When one is in the midst of adversity it's too late to protect oneself. He took an old hunting rifle and two cartridges from the gun rack to stash in a closet. His wife caught him and called the doctor and the doctor asked Hemingway to put the rifle back in the gun room. He had to be readmitted to the hospital. Before getting into the car that would take him to the plane that would take him to the hospital, he made a dash to the gun rack and put a loaded gun to his throat. "Shanghaied," he said. Just a preview of what he would finally do in July.

### 109

I don't think it'll be long before I absent myself from here. I'll leave with my conscience, which for me has always been a growing irony, which as it became big and strong, tended at the same time, paradoxically, to disappear. It was something I gradually discovered as I've gone through life and it's grown ever larger, this conscience that would be nothing without irony. I'll leave here to dissolve, dissociate, disintegrate, smash to bits every little outbreak of personality or conscience, any nostalgia for Paris. After all, to be ironic is to absent oneself.

### 110

Hemingway came back from the hospital and withdrew even more into himself. As Jeanne Boutade said, there are many writers who, no matter how successful they've been, end up recluses, hiding away when they get old. But what exactly happened to Hemingway? "Possibly growing gloom," says Anthony Burgess, "at his failure to be his own myth; more possibly a sexual incapacity which, considering his prowess in other fields of virile action, deeply baffled him.... With fame, anyway, any kind of sense of recognized achievement, the incursion of a chronic melancholy may be expected, expressible as a death urge. Or, simpler, Hemingway saw himself as an exception to the Thoreauvian rule of, like all men, having to live a life of quiet desperation: he could not cope with the stress that most men endure gracefully; he was too godlike to be expected to have to cope."

"At the end of his life," says Borges of Hemingway, "he was beset by the inability to continue writing and by madness. It pained him to have dedicated his life to physical adventures and not to the single and pure exercise of his intelligence."

"Last week he tried to commit suicide," an old waiter says of a customer in Hemingway's story "A Clean, Well-Lighted Place". And when the young waiter asks why, he receives this reply: "He was in despair." "What about?" the young man asks again. "Nothing."

Hemingway exchanged the sun and cheerfulness of the clean, well-lighted cafés of Cuba for his desolate house in Ketchum, Idaho, the perfect house for suicide. On the morning of Sunday, July 2, 1961, he got up very early while his wife was still asleep, found the key to the storage room where the guns were kept, and loaded a double-barreled shotgun. In "A Clean, Well-Lighted Place" there is a prayer: "Our nada who art in nada, nada be thy name thy kingdom nada thy will be nada in nada as it is in nada." He put the twin barrels to his forehead and fired. And to hell with it.

III

Many years later, Marguerite Duras also withdrew into herself. This happened twenty years after I left my garret. My biography of those years shouldn't end the moment I left the city but rather twenty years later, when Marguerite withdrew into herself, she drifted away from the world and left off writing forever, left off her hand-to-hand combat with writing, left off seeing her friends. I received the news in Barcelona when Javier Grandes, now living in Majorca, told me that on a visit to Paris he'd called at her house to say hello and she'd told him she didn't know him, she didn't remember him, she'd returned to the savage state of childhood and no longer remembered anyone, she only remembered Saigon.

She said the same thing to many other people, and in her last days she spoke only of death and of the savage years of childhood and the sweetness of her native land. One night, she put her hands to her throat and spoke the name of one of her characters. "Anne-Marie Stretter," she said. It was only a preview of what would happen, a preview of the arrival of the mortal monsoon and the final deathbed scene, where they say she said that after death nothing remains. "Only the living who smile and support each other." And to hell with it.

112

When I started *The Lettered Assassin* I'd planned to write the book starting with the first chapter, then the second, and so on, but very quickly I let fate lead me, proceeding at times even in a zigzag so that, as I said before, the eight pages of the murderer's notebook (which come in the middle of the book) and the book's opening sentence ended up being written at the very end, something that will not surprise anyone who remembers Pascal's words: "The last thing one finds when writing a work is what must appear at the beginning."

The eighth and final page of the central notebook describes the death of that poet, who at heart, without my knowledge, was a likeness of myself, representing my tragic move to *criminal* prose after renouncing poetry. I wasn't sure this eighth page would be the last I'd write of the manuscript, but I guessed it, since after all I was narrating the death of a poet, any poet, which was the objective the previous pages had been leading up to. On this last page I wrote: "Wine trickled from his ears, and his legs thrashed the floor like two blind masts. It all ended at dawn ... I embraced him, spoke his name. Like his sister in days gone by, on the long winter nights, I called to him in a familiar tone of voice. But he could no longer hear me. Everything was calm, the first morning birds arrived. A shut-in smell of pipe tobacco and old silk and old parchments. I was (I now knew) embracing a corpse."

It was a very rainy day, I remember quite well, when I wrote these sentences of the murderer's manuscript; I wrote these sentences that spoke of the withdrawal of a writer grown old, I wrote them and understood that the novel had surely reached its end. It was January 30, I remember perfectly. Before going out for a walk and something to eat and to think about whether the central manuscript of my book was finished or not, I went to the Relais Odéon to see if I could find Martine Simonet and wish her a happy saint's day. It was January 30, 1976, Saint Martine's Day. It was raining hard and people hesitated before crossing the street, as if they were torrents rather than streets. The cars moved slowly, scared of skidding. I, for my part, was scared of having finished the novel, but then I told myself if that was the case I ought to face reality. I didn't find Martine and ended up going into a bistro on Rue de Seine I'd never been to before. It must have been a bad restaurant, because it was half empty. The set menu was written in chalk on a large blackboard, the tablecloths were made of paper, the tables very small, and the serving girls wore black and white uniforms. As I ate a steak with potatoes, I thought I might be mistaken for the terrorist Carlos again. But it didn't take me long to realize how ridiculous it was to think a thing like that. I ordered another *pichet* of *rouge*. The pitcher made a stain with glints of ruby on the white paper tablecloth, and this reminded me of what I'd just written on the eighth manuscript page: "Wine trickled from his ears, and his legs thrashed the floor like two blind masts ..." I realized that in a way as simple as it was unexpected, some hidden Muse had given me a sign that I shouldn't agonize over the matter any further: the novel was finished.

Should I see that moment as the most extraordinary in my life? I'd just completed my first novel (I didn't yet know I lacked one more sentence, the one that came first in the book). I must have started to become aware of finding myself at one of the crucial stages of my existence. Or not? I thought hard and saw that, for the sake of truth, I had to admit, nothing seemed important about the moment, since no matter how hard I tried to see it that way, it was all happening without any solemnity or emotion whatsoever. I brought the wine to my lips and caught the young waitresses exchanging glances. There were so few customers they must have been bored and noticed how strange I was and were laughing. I thought: Oh, if only you knew I've just finished a novel. I drew myself up. I thought, many years later, *The Lettered Assassin* will be translated into French and someone will write: "Paradoxically, this attempt at killing the reader marked the birth of a writer."

When I left the restaurant, it had stopped raining, the wind had died down, the sky was clearing. I started walking back to the garret. But when I got to Rue Saint-Benoît I felt I no longer had anything to do up there, in my house. After all, the novel was finished. Did I have the famous feeling of emptiness they say seizes a writer upon completion of a book? No, I felt none of that. I did however feel a great desire to find Martine and wish her a happy saint's day. I headed back toward the Relais Odéon; I thought perhaps now the weather had changed she'd have finally decided to go out and I'd find her there. And I was heading back to the Relais, walking down Boulevard Saint-Germain, when driving past me like a force of evil, with the music at full blast, too close to the curb on purpose, went Paloma Picasso's Mercedes convertible and my pants were totally soaked. I didn't see who was driving, but Paloma was in the car and beside her, under spectacular hats, were the Argentinian playwrights. It all happened very fast. They splashed my pants deliberately and then drove away laughing hard, mocking the stupefied expression on my poor, humiliated, bohemian face.

113

A few days later, at dusk, I was in the garret calmly getting ready to clean my pipe when all the lights went out. At first, I even joked to myself that this was like saying goodbye to the lights of bohemia. But as the minutes went by and night began to fall, I gradually realized this was serious. My black neighbor reluctantly lent me a candle and I spent the night with the whole *chambre* in semidarkness, waiting for daybreak to go and see Marguerite and tell her what had happened. Should I be indignant? Not with her, of course. After all, I owed her seven or eight months' rent. What did I expect? Not to pay and have the lights of bohemia burning eternally in my garret?

About ten in the morning, I went down to the third floor and rang Marguerite's bell; she must have been right behind the door, because she opened it that very second. She was surprised to see me at that time of day. Unless I'm mistaken, I remember she asked me about my novel. "I've finished it," I said. She found this very amusing, as if she thought it incredible or improbable that books could end. She laughed in that unforgettable way, a malicious, childlike, mocking laugh, one that deep down tried to convey a certain feeling of friendship. However, soon after there was a jug of cold water. "And have you come just to tell me you finished your novel?" she asked. I didn't know how to broach the subject of the electricity. Besides, the expression on her face had changed, she wasn't laughing at all anymore, now she looked rather scary. "I'm not in for anyone, not even for myself," she said, confirming my fears. I could have died right there. "Come back later," she said, and shut the door.

About half past twelve, I tried again. My hand shook as I rang the bell. When I least expected it, the door opened. "What's the matter?" she asked me. A little scared, I told her the electricity meter wasn't working. I had to explain it to her, in my *inferior* French, about five times before she finally understood what had happened. She then stood still, looking at me. She stood there for quite a while, looking at me. Still. Suddenly, she said, "Wait a minute, I'll be right back." She soon returned with a leather document case, which contained a great many electricity bills and receipts. She handed me the document case and I didn't know what to do with it. With one of her typical energetic gestures, she snatched it out of my hands and said, "Fine, let's go to EdF."

A few minutes later, with the leather document case, we were at number 69, Rue de Rennes, outside the monstrous EdF building, Électricité de France. On the first floor we were received by an employee who spoke for a few minutes to Marguerite in a bureaucratic language impenetrable to me. They were shuffling a lot of papers back and forth with lots of figures on them and talking for a long time in more and more complicated terms until the woman practically ordered us—as if she suddenly felt offended by something Marguerite had said—up to the second floor, where we were received in an office by a very well-dressed man, I remember, above all, his strange obsession of constantly introducing the name of the actor Gérard Depardieu into the conversation. Every now and then, Marguerite raised her voice, annoyed at something. Everything was very confusing. "How long is it since you last paid?" she asked me suddenly. But I'm not sure this was exactly what she said to me, she'd started to speak in her *superior* French. She didn't wait for my reply. The well-dressed man took out more papers and launched into an impenetrable explanation that ended with the recommendation we go to an office on the first floor, where a very polite official directed us back to a window next to the window where the first employee had attended us when we arrived. At this new window, after a conversation I'd swear was basically about an umbrella store at number 73, Rue de Rennes, a man who looked like the actor Lino Ventura finally gave Marguerite a piece of paper, a single, simple piece of paper, though absolutely covered, it was true, with numbers and symbols in red.

After we left the building, in the middle of Rue de Rennes, she gave me the piece of paper and said something I didn't understand at all, it seemed as if she was deliberately speaking her *superior* French. I didn't understand what she said to me, but I did understand what was written on the piece of paper. I understood perfectly that I had to pay over forty years' worth of electricity bills, that is, not only was I responsible for paying for the lights of bohemia used by Copi, Javier Grandes, the transvestite Amapola, the filmmaker Milosevic, the Bulgarian theatre actress, and the friend of the magus Jodorowsky, but I also had to pay the outstanding electricity bill from the French Resistance, that of Comrade Mitterrand for the two days he spent in the garret.

Marguerite made some remarks to me in her *superior* French that I didn't understand at all, I only understood the last thing she said, I understood it clearly, it was the very same famous piece of advice that years before Raymond Queneau had given her, that criminal piece of advice—deep down I knew I more than deserved it for having written a criminal book—it was passed down as an inheritance that had tied her forever to a chair and a desk and condemned me to the same thing. "You must write," she said, "don't do anything but write."

I think it could be said I went to Paris solely to learn how to type, but also to receive Queneau's criminal advice.

But, of course, back then I didn't know that yet. I listened to Queneau's advice but, overwhelmed at the thought of having to pay for the lights of bohemia for at least three generations of artists, I was unable to thank Marguerite for it; I accompanied her to the doorway of the building on Rue Saint-Benoît and with a silent bow thanked her for her negotiations with Électricité de France. Though I wasn't to know it, it was the last time I'd see her. I bowed and then added humorously, timidly, remembering the bohemian Bouvier: "Tonight, in the garret, I'll light a match so I won't see a thing."

I slipped out of her life as I might have slipped out of a sentence.

Afterwards, I went and ate a *croque-monsieur* in the Flore, drank a blackberry liqueur and analyzed the situation. I spent six days analyzing it and on the seventh I returned to Barcelona. When my father asked why I'd come back, I told him it was because I'd fallen in love with Julita Grau and, besides, Paris was always rainy and cold and so dark and foggy. And so gray, added my mother, meaning me, I guess.